Praise for *Mary Clay's*
DAFFODILS Mysteries*

(*Divorced And Finally Free Of Deceitful, Insensitive, Licentious Scum)

"Witty and hilarious..."
Midwest Book Review

" ... a crisp pace with plenty of humor ..."
Romantic Times BookClub

"*The Ya Ya Sisterhood* meets *The First Wives Club*.
A cleverly done light mystery that's a rare find ..."
The Examiner (Beaumont, Texas)

"The Turtle Mound Murder is light and
accentuated with the familiar mannerisms
of Southern women. ... A fun book."
Southern Halifax Magazine

"Bike Week Blues is one of the funniest capers
this reviewer has had the privilege of reading."
Harriet Klausner, #1 Reviewer, Amazon.com

"Sometimes we just need something fun to
read. The DAFFODILS Mysteries fit the bill."
The DeLand-Deltona Beacon

Meet the DAFFODILS*

(*Divorced And Finally Free Of Deceitful, Insensitive, Licentious Scum)

Leigh Stratton, Ruthie Nichols and Penny Sue Parker are sassy, Southern sorority sisters with very unique views ...

On Each Other:

Penny Sue was an exasperating flake, but a person would be hard-pressed to find a better friend.

* * *

Ruthie hasn't been right since she drove off the bridge and cracked her head.

* * *

"Always thinking, that's why Leigh was president of the sorority," Ruthie said matter-of-factly.

"That's why she's always covered in spots," Penny Sue sniggered, pointing at a splotch on my blouse.

On Men:

"Even straight men act like a pack of dogs, sniffing each other and posturing. All that butt slapping and carrying on, it's in their genes, goes back to ancient Greece where they played sports in the nude."

On Psychologists:

Penny Sue threw back her head and laughed. "Of course, dear, he's a therapist. They're all weird. You teach what you need to learn."

On Fashion:

Penny Sue chose a black leather halter top with a Harley Davidson emblem in the center, below the boobs. She wanted to buy leather shorts to match, but Ruthie convinced her otherwise.

"One continuous yeast infection," Ruthie pronounced quietly.

Those four words eclipsed all my arguments about propriety and image.

A DAFFODILS* MYSTERY
**Divorced And Finally Free Of Deceitful,
Insensitive, Licentious Scum*

The
Turtle Mound
Murder

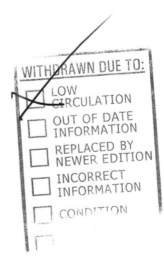

DAFFODILS Mysteries
written as
Mary Clay

The Turtle Mound Murder

Bike Week Blues

Murder is the Pits

New Age Fiction
written by
Linda Tuck-Jenkins aka Mary Clay

Starpeople: The Sirian Redemption

A DAFFODILS* MYSTERY
*Divorced And Finally Free Of Deceitful,
Insensitive, Licentious Scum

The
Turtle Mound
Murder

Mary Clay

An if Mystery
An Imprint of Inspirational Fiction
New Smyrna Beach, Florida

For C.J. and Bob
April 17 was a very good day

Published by Inspirational Fiction
P. O. Box 2509
New Smyrna Beach, FL 32170-2509
www.inspirationalfiction.com

Cover Design: Peri Poloni-Gabriel, www.knockoutbooks.com

This is a work of fiction. All places, names, characters and incidents are either invented or used fictitiously. The events described are purely imaginary.

Copyright © 2003 Linda Tuck-Jenkins
ISBN 0-9710429-5-0
EAN 978-0-9710429-5-7
Library of Congress Control Number: 2002115428

10 9 8 7 6 5

Printed in the United States of America

Chapter 1

*"**Damn, girl, you** look like hell!"*

I slid into the booth next to the window at the Admiral's Dinghy, a locals' hangout in the restored district of Roswell. Penelope Sue Parker, my long-time friend and sorority sister, was already finishing a glass of wine. From the gleam in Penny Sue's eye, it might have been her second.

"Thanks, that makes me feel real good," I said sarcastically.

Penny Sue studied me, sipping wine, sunlight bouncing off the two-carat diamond on her right hand. "You look like you haven't slept in a year. Heavens, you have dark circles under your eyes." She raised her glass, signaling the waiter. "What's wrong, honey? You still depressed?"

"I'm going to change my name," I said in a rush.

"I don't blame you. I'd get rid of that skunk Zack's name as soon as possible. I'm surprised you haven't done it sooner. As far as I'm concerned, you'll always be Becky Martin."

"Leigh," I corrected. The waiter arrived with two glasses of wine. I stared at the glass the waiter put in front of me. "What's this, Penny Sue? You know I shouldn't drink; I've been taking antidepressants off and on for months."

"Pooh, one little glass of wine won't kill you. It'll help you relax." Penny Sue pouted, fingering the substantial emerald hanging from her neck. "What's this stuff about Leigh?"

"My middle name. I'm sick of being Becky. Good old Becky; sweet, cute Becky; dumb shit, blind Becky."

"You were just too trusting," my friend assured me.

Stupid, trusting, the label made no difference; Zachary Stratton had played me for a fool. As soon as the kids were off to college, my loving husband took up woodworking. Each night when I went to bed, he'd retire to his shop in the garage for a couple of hours. A partner in Atlanta's most prestigious law firm, Zack claimed rubbing and sanding wood relieved the stress of his hectic day.

Wood, hell—it was silicon breasts!

While I snored blissfully, Zack sneaked out to meet a strip club dancer he'd set up in a house a few blocks away. The scam worked for over a year until Ann, our younger, was picked up for DUI late one night. I rushed to the garage to tell Zack. The tools were cold, and his car was gone.

A staunch believer in a person's right to privacy, I'd never intruded on Zack's domain. I made an exception that night. In a matter of minutes, I found a carton of wooden figurines identical to the ones he claimed to have made. In a sickening flash I realized the find's implications and gagged, recalling the times I'd ooed and awed over the silly statues. Rage suppressed the tears and gave me the strength to carry the box to the center of the garage. When Zack returned home, I was waiting, feet propped up on Exhibit A.

"I'm forty-six; Becky is a child's name." I took a drink of wine and glared. "Leigh, now there's a woman's name. Momma got it from *Gone With the Wind*. You know, Scarlett, Vivien Leigh. I deserve that name, don't you think?"

"Absolutely," Penny Sue said, raising her glass in salute, "Leigh it is. What in the world brought this on?"

"My therapist said it would help me release the past."

"Are you still seeing that squirrelly guy downtown?"

"No, I gave him up months ago. He was too strange."

Penny Sue threw back her head and laughed. "Of course, dear, he's a therapist. They're all weird. You teach what you need to learn." The New Age explanation for the purpose of life, the phrase was Penny Sue's pat answer to everything. "Why did you drop Dr. Nerd?"

I scanned the room to see who might be listening. "The jerk crossed the line when he suggested I attend a Sufi ceremony, saying a novel experience would help my depression. It was novel, all right. By the time I arrived, everyone was naked, lying in a pile. My therapist was on the bottom."

Penny Sue snorted with amusement. "Figures. I would have guessed as much. What about that other one? The attitude healer in Vinings? Did you ever try her?"

"Yes, lord, another dead end."

"What happened? Ruthie said she was good."

I sat back and folded my arms. "That's not saying much—Ruthie hasn't been right since she drove off the bridge and cracked her head. I signed up for the *Heal Your Mind, Heal Your Life* workshop, figuring it would give me a chance to see the therapist in action, before going for a private session. Am I glad I did; that lady's in dire need of analysis herself.

"Waltzes in the first meeting and announces she's a reincarnated priestess from ancient Egypt. Then, she starts in on visualizing the future we want." I waved expansively. "Nothing wrong with that; except we can't just imagine it, we've got to visualize her way. We have to cut out pictures from magazines and make paper dolls. She did it, too. All her pictures came from bridal magazines. Paper dolls? Bridal magazines? Does that tell you something? And I'm supposed to follow her advice? Yeah, right."

Penny Sue chuckled. "That explains why Ruthie liked her. Ruthie's always had a fetish for wedding gowns. Remember how she wore one to the Old South Ball at Kappa Alpha each year?"

"I'd forgotten about that. The gown wasn't so bad, it was the veil—"

"With sunglasses! Wasn't she a sight?"

"How's Ruthie doing anyway?" I asked.

"The same. Lives with her father; works on charities and an occasional political campaign. She's still into New Age stuff; you know, meditation and crystals. You should give her a call. She's always going to meetings and seances. I've been a few times, it's fun. Nothing else, it would get you out of the house."

I leaned forward. I could already feel the effects of the wine. "Maybe I will." Getting out with people was what I needed; I knew I'd become almost reclusive, dreading the thought of running into old friends and having to re-tell the story of The Big Split. Yet, the loneliness fed the depression, which made me more reclusive, and on and on until there was nothing except a dark emptiness. A great, gaping void in the center of my chest; a black hole which could not be filled by therapy or pills. "Does Ruthie ever date?"

Penny Sue said, "Heavens no, she'll never remarry, at least as long as her father's alive."

Ruthie's father was J.T. Edwards, a retired railroad executive who lived in a restored mansion in Buckhead. I blinked back tears. "Probably just as well."

"What's got you so down?"

I blotted my eyes with the back of my hand. "Zack moved out last week while I was visiting my folks."

"That's terrific news! Y'all living under the same roof while you fought over the property settlement was sick. I told Daddy so." Penny Sue's daddy was Judge Warren Parker, founder of Zachary's firm. "Daddy likes you and feels bad about the situation, but Zack's a valuable asset to the firm, because of his connections with the telephone people. They love him."

"Naturally," I said. "He takes them to strip joints whenever they come to town. That's how Zack met Ms. Thong."

"Who?"

"His little lap dancer. I found a picture of her in a silver thong bikini at the bottom of Zack's sock drawer."

Penny Sue shrugged. "Daddy promised to have a word with Zack, advise him to give you a fair shake. You know, fifty-fifty."

My cheeks flamed. "It worked," I said, trying hard to control my anger. "Mr. Fairness took half of everything in the house. Half of the pictures on the walls, half of each set of china, and half of the furniture, right down to one of Zack, Jr.'s twin beds."

"Half the Wedgwood?" Penny Sue asked. I nodded. "No wonder you're depressed."

"The Wedgwood's the least of my worries, he could have had it all. It was the spite that gets me. We're supposed to sign off on the property settlement tomorrow. I can't imagine what else he's got up his sleeve. A person who'd take half the sheets—I mean all the top sheets, no bottoms—is capable of anything."

"No doubt." Penny Sue drained her glass and clicked it down. "Girl, you need a vacation."

"Vacation? After tomorrow I may not be able to afford lunch. Besides, I have to sell the house."

"Hire a realtor; you need a change of scenery. New Smyrna Beach is beautiful in the fall, and Daddy hardly ever uses his condo anymore. Remember what a good time we had there in college? Come on, Beck—er, Leigh—it'll be relaxing, do you a world of good."

"I'll see how the settlement goes," I replied.

Thankfully, the waiter arrived to take our order, shutting Penny Sue down. I chose the Caesar salad, while she ordered quiche with a Dinghy Dong for dessert.

"A Dinghy Dong? Isn't that the extra large chocolate eclair?"

Penny Sue cut me a look. "So?"

"Comfort food? What's wrong, did you breakup with the Atlanta Falcon?"

Penny Sue raked a hand through her meticulously streaked hair. "Honey, I'm dating a Falcon *and* a Brave, now. But, a Dinghy Dong's something else; I always have room for one of them."

From Parker, Hanson, and Swindal's twenty-third floor conference room in downtown Atlanta, the people on the street looked like ants foraging for crumbs. I could sympathize, I had a bad feeling that's what I'd be doing at the end of the day.

I should never have quit my job, I thought ruefully. Until the fateful night when I found out about Zack, I'd been a part-time bookkeeper for a local car dealership. Money wasn't the issue, though I enjoyed having funds of my own. The job gave me a sense of purpose, something to think about other than bridge and local gossip. But I couldn't concentrate and started making mistakes after I discovered Zack's other life. Afraid I might do serious damage, like fouling up an IRS report, I decided to quit.

Although most of my sorority sisters were pampered Southern belles, my family was a hundred percent middle class. I was one of only two sorority pledges who had not "come out" at a debutante ball. That never bothered me, or them, for that matter. By my senior year I was president of the sorority and a regular at all the posh, hotsy-totsy balls.

Which was how I got hooked up with Zachary. A six-foot-one handsome blonde from a poor, farming family, Zack was in his last year of law school when we met. He'd dated Penny Sue initially, but was dumped for her first husband, Andy Walters, the amiable, if dumb, captain of the football team.

I see now what a shameless social climber Zack was. I suppose he figured that if he couldn't have Penny Sue, I was an acceptable second, since I traveled in all the same circles. Second indeed. Considering Zack's lackluster grades and dirt farming roots, Parker, Hanson, and Swindal would never have given him a glance if it hadn't been for my friendship with Penny Sue.

Which was an ironic twist—I set Zack up in the firm that was about to squash me like an ant. I turned my back to the window angrily. Well, this was one bug that wasn't going to roll over and die.

I sat at the end of the conference table and fished a thick file of documents from my briefcase. Where was my attorney? Max Bennett promised to come early. He knew I didn't want to face Zack alone, especially on his own turf. How could Max be so insensitive? *Easy, he's male and a lawyer*, I answered my own question.

I had really wanted a female attorney, but decided a woman would be powerless against Zack's firm and the Atlanta good-ol'-boy network. Bradford Davis was handling Zack's case, a PH&S senior partner whose great-great-grandfather was a Confederate General who defended Atlanta in the War of Northern Aggression. I figured I needed a legal heavyweight of my own. I chose Max because his ancestors on his mother's side went back to Colonial times, and he'd handled several high profile divorces with good results. In any event, he'd seemed nice enough the few times we'd chatted at charity events and cocktail parties.

Appearances can sure be deceiving. However the day turned out, I would be happy to be rid of Max Bennett. I'd had a bellyful of his red, sweaty face; off-color jokes and patronizing remarks— not to mention the fact that he hadn't done one thing right.

The process had dragged on for nearly two years because Max couldn't or wouldn't stand up to Bradford Davis. The present meeting had been postponed four times at Bradford's request, once to accommodate a state bar golf tournament. In fact, Max was so openly solicitous of Bradford, I'd wondered if the two had something going on the side. I voiced the theory to Penny Sue, figuring she might have some insight since her second husband had turned out to be bisexual.

"Who can tell?" Penny Sue said. "Even straight men act like a pack of dogs, sniffing each other and posturing. All that butt slapping and carrying on, it's in their genes, goes back to ancient Greece where they played sports in the nude."

The idea of Max and Bradford romping around buck-naked was too much. I laughed out loud at the very moment Max, Bradford and Zack arrived. Clearly thinking I was snickering at them, each instinctively checked his fly. Even they noticed that synchronicity, which made me laugh even harder.

Scowling, Bradford and Zack took seats at the head of the table in front of an ornately framed painting of Judge Parker. Max sat next to me at the opposite end. He nodded coldly as way of greeting.

"I believe we can dispose of this matter quickly," Max said, passing a three page document to me. "Mr. Stratton provided a list of your joint assets and their market value. He wants to be fair and proposes to divide your belongings right down the middle. Since a quick sale could depress the value of your property, Mr. Stratton has offered to buy-out your share by making monthly installments over a five year period. In that way, he can dispose of the property in an orderly fashion."

I flipped to the last page of the document. The total was $1.1 million, including $550,000 for the house. "This can't be everything."

Max cleared his throat. "Uh, no, it does not include household furnishings, which have already been divided, or personal items such as your cars."

The total was far too low. My rough calculation put our assets at well over two million. I scanned the list. All the values were ridiculously low, and a number of investments were missing altogether. Zack was trying to cheat me, just as I'd feared. "These estimates are wrong," I said loudly, staring defiantly at Zack.

Bradford smirked. "You must remember, Becky dear, that the markets have been off the last few years."

"Leigh," I corrected.

"As you wish, *Leigh*," Bradford replied, putting particular emphasis on my name as if it had a bad taste. Zack snorted with amusement. "Names aside," Bradford continued pompously, "the property was evaluated by Walker & Hill, the most reputable *independent* appraiser in Atlanta. Surely, you cannot find fault with that."

Independent, hell! Zack played golf with Taylor Hill at least twice a month. I gave Max a pleading look. He patted my hand and flashed a thin, sleazy smile. I wanted to backhand him in the mouth. Luckily, Judge Parker entered the room at that moment and stood by the door, listening. I was too angry to meet his eyes.

"In our experience, it is difficult to get full value from the disposal of community property," Bradford continued. "Buyers expect bargain basement prices in the case of a divorce. It's very difficult to overcome that mind set."

"I've found the same thing in my practice," Max chimed in.

I glared at him. *Who's side are you on?* I wanted to scream. Of course, I knew the answer: he was a good-ol'-boy, a member of the *club*, and they were all going to stick together. "What about the stocks and bonds?" I demanded through tight lips.

Bradford consulted another list. "The securities were liquidated last November to take care of family debts."

November? Zack went to the Caribbean on business in November. Could he have sold the stocks and deposited the money in an off-shore bank? "What debts?" I demanded hotly. "I want to see proof."

"General household expenses." Bradford looked to Max. "We provided all of this to your attorney. There were several credit cards—"

Credit cards? "I haven't seen any proof!" Could Zack have spent that much money on his stripper? Then, it dawned on me. Zack had opened a bunch of accounts, taken-out cash advances and deposited the money in tropical banks. What a sneaky jerk ... all our savings gone and I didn't have a prayer of finding it.

Bradford continued, "Your attorney has reviewed these documents. We've also filed a copy with Judge Nugent. Of course, the judge would like a property settlement before he grants the final decree."

I pushed the paper away. "This is not fair; Zack has hidden our assets. I won't sign it." I caught Judge Parker from the corner of my eye; he winked and canted his head. I wasn't sure what that meant, and Bradford gave me no time to think about it.

He slammed his folder shut. "That is your prerogative, Mrs. Stratton," Bradford intoned snobbishly. "However, I caution you that a court battle could be *very* long and expensive."

The emphasis on *very* was crystal clear. While Bradford was probably handling Zack's case for free, I had to pay my own legal fees. Max's tab already topped $30,000. Holding out for a trial might double or triple the bill. And, what did I stand to gain? Nothing. The good-ol'-boys would protect each other to the end. I glanced at the Judge who nodded slightly. Damn,

I hated giving in! But, the deck was stacked against me, it was time to throw-in my hand. My eyes stung with tears, from frustration more than anything. I blinked them back and raised my chin resolutely; I would not give those men the satisfaction of seeing me cry.

I jabbed Max with my elbow, hard. "Give me a pen," I spat the words. He rolled his chair back and handed me a Cross ballpoint. I signed the document with an angry flourish, pocketed the pen, and strode stiffly past Judge Parker and out of Zack's life.

* * *

I called my therapist as soon as I got home.

"How do you feel?"

"Angry, betrayed, hurt. Those men made me so mad." I tugged my scarf off and wrapped it around my fist, wishing it was Zack's throat.

"No one can make you feel anything. You choose your feelings. If you're mad, you've chosen to feel that way."

Chosen to feel that way? Those scuzz balls ganged up on me. "It's the injustice that angers me. No one—not even my own lawyer—did a thing to help me. Bradford, Max, and Zack walked in *together*. Don't you see, it was a done deal before anything was said. I was set up!"

"So, you feel like a victim?"

"Yes, I'd like to cut off their private parts and hang them from their ears." I unraveled the scarf and pulled it tight, like a rope.

"Violence doesn't solve anything, does it?"

"For godssakes, I wouldn't really do it. It's a fantasy; a delicious fantasy at this moment." I balled the scarf up into a tight ball.

"Lashing out is a common reaction to situations like this. Let's talk about it. I can work you in tomorrow morning at eleven."

"I'll get back to you." I slammed down the receiver. *Lashing out is a common reaction.* I hurled the scarf against the wall. Damn! Then, I drew the blinds and went to bed feeling more depressed than I'd ever felt in my life.

But, sleep did not save me. My head had hardly hit the pillow when I was awakened by the sound of a siren ... no, the doorbell. And shouting.

"LEIGH. BECK-KKY LEEE-EIGH. We know you're in there."

It was Penny Sue. I had on my slip and didn't bother to find a robe. I looked through the peephole at the optically-widened images of Penny Sue and Ruthie, who was holding a gigantic bouquet of flowers. I cracked the door; Penny Sue barged through.

"Get dressed, girl. We're going to celebrate."

"Celebrate what?"

"The divorce, of course. Free at last, free at last. Praise the Lord, free at last! Besides, you're now qualified to be in the DAFFODILS."

Ruthie thrust a vase of daffodils into my face as Penny Sue fastened a silver and gold brooch to my slip strap. Both women were wearing the same pin, a circular swirl of graceful leaves, stems and daffodils in full bloom. Penny Sue's brooch served as the clasp for a wispy Chanel scarf; Ruthie's accented the square neckline of her black silk chemise.

"The what?" I asked testily, eyeing the daffodils and brooch that hung limply from my slip strap.

Penny Sue replied, "DAFF-O-DILS: Divorced And Finally Free Of Deceitful, Insensitive, Licentious Scum."

Deceitful, Insensitive, Licentious Scum. A smile tugged at my lips. I was definitely qualified, and so were Penny Sue and Ruthie.

I figured Penny Sue had probably founded the club. Her second husband, Sydney, was a television producer who'd had an affair with his male assistant. As painful as Zack's infidelity was, at least I hadn't been thrown over for a man. The huge settlement the Judge got for Penny Sue (Daddy took Sydney's escapades very personally) undoubtedly helped. Her third husband, Winston, wasn't much better; he had an eye for young secretaries.

Ruthie had also endured her share of heartache. Harold, her ex, was a cardiologist in Raleigh, North Carolina. A heartless cardiologist at that. (Maybe Penny Sue was right about teaching what you need to learn.) Ruthie worked as a librarian to put him through medical school, only to be ditched for a nurse the week after Harold finished his residency. Not one to mope, Ruthie Jo had packed up Jo Ruth, their only child, and taken a train back to Atlanta, where she'd lived with her father ever since.

I studied the bouquet of flowers. The symbol of Spring and new beginnings, there was something intrinsically happy about a daffodil. "Where in the world did you find daffodils at this time of year?"

Penny Sue responded, "My florist in Buckhead stocks them for me."

"A lot of members in the club, huh?"

"No, I just like daffodils." Penny Sue quick-stepped a jig. "Perk up, girl, it's party time."

I ignored her antics and headed for the kitchen with the flowers, my friends following close behind. "I appreciate the offer, but it's been a terrible day. I don't feel like celebrating." I put the vase on the sideboard and filled a glass from the kitchen tap. "Want something to drink?" I asked, holding up the glass of water.

"You didn't take any pills, did ya?" Penny Sue asked, eyeing me like a mother hen.

I sat down and buried my head in my hands, the brooch clanking heavily on the tabletop. "No, nothing like that."

"Good, 'cuz we've got champagne!" Penny Sue pulled a bottle of Dom Perignon from her oversized Louis Vuitton bag as Ruthie searched the cabinets for stemmed glasses.

"What are you doing here?" I asked, accepting a glass of the fizzing liquid.

"Daddy called me," Penny Sue replied.

My spine straightened reflexively. "*Daddy?* Why didn't Daddy help me today?" I said through gritted teeth. "I was rolled, raped ... swindled. Swindled! Lord, I can't believe it took me so long to make the connection—Parker, Hanson, & SWINDAL. I never stood a chance!"

I was shouting now and it felt good. Hell with my therapist. At that moment, I chose to be mad—foot-stomping, dish-throwing mad. Mad, furious, LIVID. I gulped the sparkling wine.

"Daddy wanted to help, but he couldn't interfere overtly. He called Judge Nugent after the meeting—they go back a long way, you know. Anyhow, he asked Albert to go ahead and grant the divorce, but to take a close look at the property settlement."

"What does that mean?" I asked wearily.

"Monday: the marriage is history. Tuesday: Zack will have some explainin' to do."

"Glory, there is a God." I stood and raised my glass. "To the DAFF-O-DILS."

"DAFFODILS." We clinked our glasses.

"Now, get some clothes on. We're going to have a fancy dinner and plan our trip to the beach."

Chapter 2

New Smyrna Beach, Florida

"We're sisters cut from the same cloth," Penny Sue chirped as we sat at the light next to the Bert Fish Medical Center.

I studied the tan medical building to keep from laughing. If we were cut from the same cloth, it was a patchwork quilt.

Penny Sue was tall, pudgy, with streaked brown hair and decided kewpie doll tendencies in makeup and dress. Expensive, almost haute couture, yet kewpie doll, nonetheless. Ruthie was shorter, about five six, and disgustingly slim. A typical strawberry blonde (fair and freckled), she favored clothes with tailored, simple lines—the ones that were so plain and drab they shouted: mega-bucks.

I, on the other hand, was middle-of-the-road. I was Penny Sue's height, though a little slimmer, and my shoulder-length brown hair was darker than hers by a couple of shades. I bought my clothes at Dillards, favoring elastic waists and comfort whenever possible. When I did dress up, I opted for tailored suits and dresses which didn't shout anything. Rather, they spoke in a normal voice: I came from the career department.

"Who's Bert Fish?" I asked to change the subject. New Smyrna Beach had grown a lot since we were in college. I seemed to recall a brick medical center and a much smaller hospital in the olden days.

"I just saw that," Ruthie responded, consulting the tour book she'd been reading, much of it aloud, for the whole trip. "Here it is. Bert was a local lawyer, criminal judge, and a 32nd Degree Mason. He was the Florida campaign manager for Franklin Roosevelt ... paid back with Ambassadorships to Egypt, Saudi Arabia, and Portugal. Hmm-m, Portugal was not so good for Bert. He died there in 1943 under mysterious circumstances—his body was never found. In any event, he willed a big part of his estate—orange groves—to Volusia County."

"How nice," Penny Sue remarked with an edge of sarcasm, clearly bored by the pithy tidbits Ruthie'd peppered us with during the seven-hour trip. The light turned green, and we started up the hill to the South Causeway bridge. "We're going to have a great time, Leigh. A week from now, you'll be a new woman.

"Here we are," she enthused as we rounded the top of the tall bridge that spanned the Intracoastal Waterway. "Looks just like the French Riviera, don't you think?" Penny Sue rambled. "I feel like I'm in Europe every time I come here."

The view was spectacular. Stucco townhouses with red tile roofs lined the inland waterway to the left, virgin wetlands to the right, and the Atlantic Ocean directly ahead. A sailboat on the horizon completed the picture of tranquillity. Likening it to the French Riviera might be overstating things a tad, I thought, but the view was beautiful. I sank back contentedly, thinking the trip might be a good move. "I didn't know you'd been to France," I commented.

"I haven't," Penny Sue replied. "This is what I imagine it to be."

"I went with Harold. It doesn't look anything like this," Ruthie said from her minuscule spot in the backseat. Under normal circumstances the bright yellow Mercedes would hold five comfortably; however, traveling with Penny Sue was never normal.

Ruthie and I each brought one large suitcase; after all, we were only planning to stay a week or two. Penny Sue showed up with provisions for an expedition. She had three enormous Hartmann suitcases, a cooler, a boom box, and God-knew-what-all-else. The bottom line being the backseat was loaded to the ceiling, leaving only a sliver of room for one of us. Though Ruthie and I switched seats each time we stopped—which proved to be often—Ruthie's nerves were clearly beginning to fray.

"Details, details. You sure are getting crabby," Penny Sue called over her shoulder as the car rounded the corner to South Atlantic. The luggage in the backseat shifted, sending the boom box onto Ruthie's shoulder.

"Who wouldn't be crabby; you drive like a maniac. Besides, I've got to go to the bathroom."

"Again? Your hormones must be going."

"My hormones are fine."

"Have you had them checked? You're at the age when they start dropping. Peeing a lot is one of the first symptoms."

"I've had them checked. My hormones are fine."

"You'd better look into that bladder urgency pill. Having to pee all the time isn't normal."

"Don't start on that," Ruthie warned. "I wanted to fly, remember?"

"We wouldn't have gotten here any sooner, and this way we have my car."

Ruthie stared out the window peevishly. "Yeah, but airplanes have big seats and bathrooms."

"Hold on for a little while longer. There's the Food Lion." Penny Sue waved to the right. "The condo's only a couple more blocks." A few minutes later, she took a left onto a road marked

Sea Dunes. A small compound of duplexes—three two-story buildings overlooking two single-story beachfront units—the structures were carefully placed to grace each condo with an ocean view. The car bounced down the rutted sand lane which led to the Judge's unit in the single story building that over-looked the beach. Grunting and grimacing with each bump, Ruthie sighed with relief when Penny Sue finally brought the car to a stop between a van and pickup truck parked in front of the weathered, clapboard duplex.

The truck was a big red job—a true testosterone statement—with lots of chrome, spotlights mounted on the front, oversized tires, and a bumper sticker that read: *Turtles? They Make Good Soup*. The van, on the other hand, was completely nondescript except for A-1 Pest Control which was lettered neatly across the back.

"Check that out," I said, pointing at a bumper sticker on the back of the van. "*Turn Lights Out for Turtles*. I don't suppose the guys in those trucks are good friends."

Ruthie squirmed. "Who cares? It's their problem. Give me the key, Penny. I've got to go. Now!" She was almost shouting.

Penny Sue arched a brow haughtily. A veritable cloud of gauzy cotton, she hurried to the oceanfront condominium with Ruthie close on her heels. I trailed behind, lugging the boom box and cooler.

As Penny Sue fumbled with her key ring, Ruthie reached over her shoulder and tried the door, which proved to be unlocked. Already starting to unbutton her shorts, Ruthie pushed past Penny Sue and ducked into the first bedroom. A man with a large spray canister flew out.

Penny Sue gave him the once over with an amused grin. About six feet tall, he had blond hair, a deep tan, and nice biceps. "A-1, indeed," she mumbled.

Oh, brother. I'd heard that tone a million times and knew where it was leading. An Atlanta Falcon and Atlanta Brave were not enough. Penny Sue was going after an exterminator.

I'd never understood her addiction to men. Though she'd packed on a few pounds over the years, as we all had (except Ruthie), Penny Sue had a lot going for her. Vivacious, connected, smart in an understated Southern-belle way, and very rich—owing to the huge settlement from her second divorce—Penny certainly didn't need a man, and could have virtually any one she wanted.

Yet, for some unfathomable reason she had a penchant for losers. Andy, her first husband was nice, but dumb. Real dumb. Last I heard, he was selling used cars in Valdosta. Her second, Sydney, had been artistic, rich and bisexual. Finally, there was Winston Brewer, an up-and-coming lawyer in Daddy's firm. Daddy had orchestrated that pairing, convinced that Penny couldn't tell a good man when she saw one. It seems, Daddy couldn't either. It was the Judge himself who caught Winston in a compromising position with a secretary on top of a copy machine.

Winston doesn't practice law in Georgia anymore.

"Excuse me." Hating to intrude on a romantic moment, not to mention that my bladder wasn't a high capacity model, either; I wedged by Penny Sue and the bug man into the bedroom that had swallowed Ruthie. I set my gear in the corner and perched on the end of the bed. Ruthie was humming, which meant I might be there a long time.

"Ruthie, you going to be long? I've got to go, too." She mumbled something that I couldn't understand. I leaned back on the bed to wait. There was no sense rushing Ruthie; she'd just get flustered and clam up, so to speak. Heck, now she was singing. Might as well get comfortable. I rolled to my side, checking out the layout of the room.

The decor was typically Florida: white-washed rattan furniture with pictures of birds and hibiscus. A pink flamingo lamp graced an imposing chest of drawers on the far wall. In any other setting, the piece would look hokey, but fit perfectly in this room. No doubt the ceramic fixture was rare, costly and decorator-picked. Penny Sue's mother, now passed, had always had impeccable taste. It ran in the family, I supposed.

Ruthie came out of the bathroom, and I rushed in. When I finally emerged, Penny Sue was waving goodbye to the bug man, Rick. Ruthie was in the great room, gazing out an expansive window that overlooked the ocean. I dropped the cooler on the kitchen counter and joined her.

Bladders pleasantly low, we could enjoy the scene. With Ruthie's help, I opened the sliding glass doors that had obviously not been moved for a long time, and stepped out on a wooden deck perched on top of a sand dune. Sea spray hit my face, dousing all thoughts of Zack, money, houses and children. I took a deep breath and let it out slowly. There is nothing like salt air to clear the mind and invigorate the spirit.

I surveyed the terrain. Storms had definitely taken their toll since my last visit. Though the beach was wide and flat as always, it was a good ten feet lower than I recalled, not to mention that an entire row of dunes was now missing. And, for a beautiful October afternoon with temperatures in the mid-eighties, the beach was surprisingly vacant except for a four-by-four square marked off by stakes and green tape at the edge of the sand dune.

"A turtle mound," Ruthie commented, pointing at the stakes below us. "The tour book said turtle season runs through the end of October. We must be careful to close the blinds and turn off all our beach-side lights after sunset. There's a strict light pollution ordinance, since bright lights disorient the hatchlings. Every year, hundreds of baby turtles are crushed by cars or die from dehydration and starvation because they are distracted by lights and never make it to the water."

Penny Sue appeared with paper cups of wine. "That's sad," she said, passing out the drinks. "You're in charge of the lights, Ruthie. We sure don't want any turtles dying on our account." Penny Sue stepped up on the low benches built into the side of the deck and looked out over the ocean. "We've had some good times here, haven't we, girls?"

Ruthie climbed up on the bench alongside her. "I'll say. Foot-loose and fancy free. Though, you never stayed footloose for long; you always got hooked up with someone," she said to Penny Sue. "Remember the guy you met the summer after our sophomore year? He had a funny name—what was it?"

Penny Sue giggled. "Woodhead. Woody Woodhead."

Ruthie sputtered, spitting wine. "That's right. What a name! Remember the commotion when Zack showed up. He'd come down to see Penny Sue, and was so ticked off—" Ruthie stopped abruptly, realizing what she'd said. She looked at me guiltily, apologetically ... when angry shouts from the front of the condo cut the air.

"You're a real ass," Rick barked.

"Stuff it," a male voice shouted back. Then a dull, slapping sound.

Penny Sue was off the deck in a millisecond. She grabbed her purse and raced to the front door. Ruthie and I were initially too stunned to move, though finally recovered, and chased after Penny Sue. By the time we arrived, the men were rolling in the drive-way, trading punches. Penny Sue was fumbling in her purse, and couples from the two-story duplex behind our unit had come out on their balconies to watch.

Rick seemed to be getting the upper hand, sitting on the stranger—the owner of the pickup truck, I presumed—until the stranger's hand found a large chunk of concrete in the driveway.

The man swung the slab toward Rick, missing his head, but catching his shoulder.

"Stop it," Penny Sue demanded loudly. They ignored her.

"Stop it! I'm not kidding," she shouted again, pulling a small, pearl-handled revolver from her purse.

I gasped so hard, I almost swallowed my tongue. Penny Sue'd always had a penchant for playing roles, but they usually took the form of a femme fatale—Scarlett O'Hara, Cleopatra, Marilyn Monroe. I'd never, ever, imagined Annie Oakley was part of her repertoire.

"That's enough, boys," Penny Sue yelled.

Rick landed a punch on his opponent's face.

"Stop! I'm not fooling." Penny Sue waved the gun in their general direction.

My heart flopped over with fear. Penny Sue was excitable; how far would she go? I grabbed Ruthie's arm and whispered, "Go call 9-1-1." She hurried off.

"Stay out of this, bitch," Rick shouted.

Penny Sue's eyes narrowed. "What did you say?" She aimed the gun to the side and pulled the trigger. The bullet hit the ground with a thud. Sand billowed. An elderly couple on the balcony scurried inside. My heart did a triple flip. "Would you like to repeat that last comment?" Penny Sue asked sweetly, beaming her fake beauty-queen smile.

Rick held his hands up and rolled off his adversary. "Calm down, lady."

"That's better. For a moment I thought you were talking to a dog."

Rick's foe took the opportunity to scramble to his truck. He sped off, spewing sand.

Rick glared at Penny Sue, hands raised. "He started it."

Penny Sue kept the gun angled to the side. "Maybe so, but that's no call for being rude."

"What planet are you from?" Rick asked, snickering derisively.

Penny Sue set her jaw, pointed the gun at the ground and squeezed the trigger. "Georgia."

Chapter 3

The New Smyrna Beach police arrived minutes later. Not only had Ruthie called 9-1-1, but so had both sets of balcony owners in the duplex behind ours. Sadly, the neighbors said nothing about the fight, only that a crazy woman was brandishing a hand-gun. I could tell from the police officers' line of questioning that the situation was serious. Fearing Penny Sue might end up behind bars, I snuck to the bedroom and called Judge Parker—had him summoned out of a meeting. He said he'd take care of it.

I found out later the Judge called a Florida Supreme Court Justice, who called the Attorney General, who called the local prosecutor. A half hour after my conversation with Judge Daddy, the Chief of the Georgia State Police was on the horn asking to speak to the local officers in charge. The New Smyrna Beach policemen were real polite after that.

It wasn't very long before the local prosecutor arrived. His name was Robert "Woody" Woodhead. Penny Sue almost fainted when she saw her old flame. Woody didn't seem particularly thrilled to see her, either. They eyed each other through the screen door like prize fighters waiting for the match to start. I stepped between them, beaming my most fetching smile and greeted Woody warmly. This was not the time to relive the past.

Woody listened with a pinched look as Penny Sue told her story for the third time. With each telling, her voice got stronger and the dramatics laid on a little thicker. This version ended with a haughty toss of her perfectly streaked hair and an emphatic: "I *was not* shooting at Rick. They were warning shots, nothing more. I know how to handle a gun; I can shoot the wings off a fly from twenty paces."

"I don't doubt that." Woody handed back Penny Sue's revolver and permit for a concealed weapon. "We'll see what Rick has to say. He may want to press charges." Woody stood to leave.

"Charges? For what?"

"Reckless display of a weapon, aggravated assault, discharge of a firearm within city limits, use of a firearm in the commission of a felony—there are lots of possibilities." Woody paused with his hand on the front door and grinned. "I'll be in touch. Don't leave town."

Woody smirked and jerked the door open. An attractive blonde woman—hand raised in the knocking position—pitched forward. A riot of shrieks, mop handles and pinwheeling arms, the young lady grabbed for anything—the anything she finally found being Woody's trousers, which she almost pulled off.

Jaws slack and eyes wide, Penny Sue, Ruthie and I were momentarily frozen by the sight of Woody—shirt tail and boxer shorts completely exposed—with a shapely young woman hugging his knees. I recovered first and stooped to help the poor girl.

Woody pulled his pants up, making no effort to tuck in his shirt tail, and stalked out. As the screen door slammed behind him, Woody shot Penny Sue a look of pure rage which said: *This is your fault*, and backed into a scruffy guy clad in jeans and a tee shirt. The stranger grabbed Woody by the shoulders and pushed him roughly.

"Pete, it's all right," the young woman said. Then to us, "I'm sorry, I didn't expect anyone to be home. I'm Charlotte, the cleaning lady."

Woody wriggled out of Pete's grasp and held up his briefcase to display the State Prosecutor's ID tag suspended from the handle. "Watch your hands, bud, unless you want to spend a night in jail." Shirt tail fluttering, Woody stormed past Pete to his car.

I handed Charlotte the mop. "That's all right. That man was in a sour mood before you got here."

"Sour? Pissy's more like it," Ruthie corrected, eyeing Pete who didn't seem exactly cheery.

The corner of Pete's top lip was puffy and misshapen, giving him the appearance of a permanent sneer or of a man who'd been in a fight. The guy had sun-streaked hair, a ruddy complexion, and wasn't unattractive, just hard and rough; the type you'd expect to pick fights in bars. In any case, he didn't seem to fit Charlotte, a tanned nymph who looked like she'd hopped off a surfboard.

Charlotte must have picked up our questioning look.

"My husband," she offered. "My car's in the shop."

Penny Sue was perplexed. "What happened to Mrs. Hudson? She usually does the cleaning."

"She's my aunt. I've taken over some of her accounts, now that she's gotten up in years."

"We just arrived; the place doesn't need cleaning."

Charlotte glanced over her shoulder at Pete and shifted nervously. "I'll do a light dusting. Everything on the beach stays dusty; it's the salt spray. It'll only take a minute." She turned to get the bucket and cleaning supplies which she'd left on the front porch.

"That's not necessary," Penny Sue insisted, holding her forehead with both hands. "Get my purse, will you, Leigh? All this commotion has given me a terrific headache." Then, to Charlotte who was standing on the other side of the screen door with a dejected look, "Wait a moment, hon."

I returned with the purse. Penny Sue found forty dollars which she handed to Charlotte. "Thanks, we can manage on our own. We'll be here a week or two. Do you have a card? I'll call you before we leave." Charlotte found a rumpled blue card in her pocket and started to speak. Penny Sue shut the door before anything got out. "Laa, I have a headache." She brushed past us to the kitchen for a glass of water and four ibuprofens.

Ruthie and I followed her into the living room where Penny Sue stretched out on the couch. No one said anything for a long time. Ruthie sat with her eyes closed and her hands in her lap— palms up, thumbs and forefingers lightly touching. I supposed she was trying to meditate and find her center.

I knew my center was hopelessly lost and there was no sense looking for it. My world in Atlanta was in shambles, and now Penny Sue was about to get me—us—locked up. *With friends like her, who needs*—I started angrily, then caught myself.

I glanced at her lying on the sofa, holding her head, looking like a pitiful little girl, and my anger dissolved. Penny Sue was an exasperating flake, but a person would be hard-pressed to find a better friend. She'd been there for me when the kids were born, when I broke my ankle, when Zack, Jr.'d almost died of pneumonia, and other times too numerous to count. Well, she needed me now and I was going to stand by her.

But, a gun? When in the world did she start carrying a revolver? And why? I broke the silence. "Geez, Penny Sue, I didn't know you carried a weapon. What brought that on?"

She answered without looking at me, her hand still covering her eyes. "I've carried one for ages, for protection. Daddy gets death threats all the time. He's locked up his share of druggies over the years."

I knew I should probably drop it and let her rest, yet couldn't. "What possessed you to wave your gun at those men? Why didn't you let them fight it out?"

"Rick seemed like a nice guy. After all, he's into saving the turtles and everything." She spread her fingers and peeked at me. "Of course, *that* has proven to be a gross misconception." She closed her fingers over her eyes. "I was merely trying to break up the fight. I thought the redneck was going to hit Rick in the head with that chunk of concrete." She sat up and folded her arms across her chest. "I wish I'd let him do it, now."

"I know." I moved to the couch and patted her shoulder. Penny Sue'd always had a weak spot for the underdog. In college she was constantly bringing stray cats, injured dogs and troubled men back to the sorority house. I'd hoped she'd outgrown it. Apparently not.

"What were the guys fighting about?" Ruthie asked.

"The turtles, I suppose. Rick said he was on the Turtle Patrol that ropes off the nests. They're an endangered species and the county has banned driving on the beach to protect them. A lot of old-timers are angry about the driving ban."

I nodded. "The 'turtles-make-good-soup' crowd," I said, remembering the pickup's bumper sticker. "Rick's certainly not the average environmentalist. Aren't they usually pacifists?"

Penny Sue's eyes narrowed. "Yes, and they generally don't have foul mouths. That's what set me off. *Bitch!* The nerve of that guy." She puffed up as she spoke, gaining strength from her indignation, then, just as quickly, deflated like a punctured balloon. "I don't suppose being called a bitch is much of a defense for aggravated assault." She pulled on her lip nervously.

Ruthie moved to the couch and hugged Penny Sue. "Don't worry, we'll stand by you."

"Thanks," Penny Sue said with a sigh. "I guess I can always claim PMS. I think it's a legitimate defense for murder, now."

Ruthie and I both did a double take. Penny Sue was serious.

* * *

The New Smyrna Beach police could not find Rick or A-1 Pest Control, for that matter. Woody Woodhead speculated that A-1 Pest was operating without proper licenses (a serious offense for a business utilizing dangerous chemicals), thus Rick would never come forward to press charges.

Another round of interviews with the neighbors also seemed to corroborate Penny Sue's story of intending to threaten, not kill or maim, thus Woody agreed to let Penny Sue off the hook. His reprieve was definitely reluctant; there was no doubt in our minds that Woody was still furious at Penny Sue for dumping him twenty-odd years ago, not to mention the incident where he'd dropped his drawers in front of us.

Following a stern lecture from the Judge the next morning, the three of us set out to do what we'd come to Florida for—have fun. But, first, we had to unpack. We'd been so bummed out the previous evening, we made no attempt to settle in the condo. We'd merely supped on snacks from the cooler, fished night-gowns from our luggage, and fallen into bed. Ruthie and I volunteered to stow our gear, while Penny Sue went for groceries.

With one suitcase apiece, Ruthie and I made quick business of getting ourselves situated. It was Penny Sue's belongings that offered the challenge. Three large suitcases, a small closet, and one chest of drawers presented a problem worthy of an industrial engineer. We decided to take the approach of an assembly line, where I unloaded the suitcases and handed the clothes to Ruthie, who put them away. The system worked fine until I found a stack of underwear at the bottom of the third suitcase. "Uh oh." I held up an amazingly small, iridescent blue thong with two fingers.

"More underwear?" Ruthie complained. "That screws up my whole system. I'm going to have to move everything." She jerked open the bottom drawer of the bureau and stared. "What's this stuff?"

I peered over her shoulder to see what she was talking about.

The drawer contained a heap of thermally sealed plastic bags of white powder, with a featheredged note card wedged between two packages in the center. Ruthie pulled the card out and held it so I could see. *Mark how he trembles ...* was embossed in bold letters across the top. Below that, *200 @ 6* was scrawled in small letters, followed by *Same time, same place* in ornate, handwritten script and a smiley face.

Ruthie ran her finger along the ragged edge of the stationery, then held it up to the light. "This is really expensive stuff," she observed, pointing to the watermark. "Italian Amalfi. Daddy used it years ago. The process for making this paper dates back to the 1300s."

As one who'd used Post-It notes for most of my correspondence since Zack and I separated, I was certain the embossing alone cost more than my annual paper budget. I pointed at the smiley face. "That Rick must be schizophrenic. A violent environmentalist, with a foul mouth, who uses fancy stationery and draws smiley faces. Go figure."

"Must be a Gemini," Ruthie replied matter-of-factly, lifting the bags out of the drawer and dumping them onto the floor.

"Be careful," I cautioned. "I'll bet those are Rick's pesticides. He probably treats the whole complex and stores his chemicals here. Penny Sue said no one had used this place in a long time."

"I'm going to throw them away. Rick won't be back."

"You can't put chemicals like that in the trash. There are strict laws about disposing of hazardous substances."

She stared at me, hands on hips, as if I'd lost my mind. "I'll flush them down the toilet."

"That's worse, you'll pollute the groundwater. Besides, we should keep them for insurance."

"Insurance?"

"In the event Rick tries to make trouble, we've got evidence." I'd learned the importance of evidence, but good, in my dealings with Zack.

"Well, what should I do with this?"

I grabbed a trash bag from the bathroom, scooped the packages into the bag, and started to drag them to the closet. The load was so heavy, I feared the sack would break. "This won't do." I dropped the bag and headed across the hall to search the utility room for a better container. A broom, vacuum, bucket, and rag mop were stowed in the space between the clothes dryer and the wall. "This is perfect," I said, lifting the trash bag into the bucket. "This way, if any of the packages break, the powder won't scatter all over the place." I returned the bucket to its place and put the rag mop on top.

Back in the bedroom, Ruthie had started to shift things around in the dresser in order to put the underwear in its *proper place.*

"Don't bother—"

"Yoo hoo," Penny Sue called from the front door. "I could use some help out here."

I grabbed Penny Sue's clothes from Ruthie's hands and stuffed them into the bottom drawer.

"Wait," Ruthie protested, miffed at me for screwing up her system.

"It doesn't matter." I slammed the last suitcase shut and swung it into the closet. "All this will be in shambles the first time Penny Sue changes clothes."

Ruthie harrumphed, but didn't argue. She knew I was right. Underwear would be hanging from door knobs and bras draped over lamps. That's just the way Penny Sue was, not one for details.

We finally made it to the beach a little after two. Laden with cooler, boom box, chairs, and other sundry comforts, we lumbered down the wooden walkway that protected the dunes, looking more like an African safari than middle-aged women on vacation.

"Crap," Penny Sue said, stopping abruptly. A large square of sand was roped off at the bottom of the stairs. "Another turtle nest. What now?"

I put the cooler down and peered over her shoulder. There was maybe a foot of space between the walk's railing and the staked off area. "We can make it. Here, give me that." I took the boom box and beach bag from Penny Sue. "Go through and we'll hand the stuff over the railing."

Penny Sue sucked up and sidled through the narrow opening. Though she ripped a hole in her new sarong—something she reminded us of all afternoon—we eventually got ourselves and paraphernalia to the beach without disturbing the nest, and thus committing a state and federal crime. The last thing we needed was another run-in with Woody.

The rest of the day proved pleasantly uneventful. We took a leisurely walk on the beach, sunned ourselves, gossiped, and generally acted like giggly college girls, less mature than our own kids. True to form, Penny Sue took center stage, entertaining us by comparing everyone who walked by to some form of bird or beast. She was amazingly good at it, had a real eye for the absurd. Of course, she never turned an eye on herself. Just as well, she looked remarkably similar to a chubby flamingo in her hot pink two-piece and feathered sun hat.

We capped off the evening with dinner at The Riverview, a picturesque restaurant on the Inland Waterway where we ate outside on the deck that overlooked a small marina of expensive boats. An imposing yacht named *Ecstasy* immediately caught Penny Sue's eye.

"That cost a bundle," Penny Sue said, waving her wine glass in the boat's direction.

Ruthie agreed. "*Lifestyles of the Rich and Famous* did a show on yachts. That one must have cost millions."

Millions for a boat? My house in Atlanta Country Club wasn't worth that much.

"I like sailing," Penny Sue said wistfully.

"It's not a sailboat, Penny Sue. No sails," I said, pointing at the radar scope rotating on top of the bridge.

She looked down her nose at me. "Sailing, motoring; it's all the same if the captain is good looking and the champagne's cold."

"What about the Falcon and the Brave?" I asked.

"They're in Atlanta." Penny Sue fingered her emerald necklace absently. "Ecstasy. Isn't that the name of a cruise line? I'll bet the owner is a shipping tycoon. Greek, maybe. Europeans are so interesting."

A busboy leaned forward to fill her water glass. "He's sitting at the bar over there."

"Pardon?"

The young man straightened, looking embarrassed. "I didn't mean to intrude. I overheard your comment."

"Never mind interrupting, sugar," Penny Sue snapped. "Please repeat what you said."

"The owner of the yacht is sitting at the bar. His name is Lyndon Fulbright." The busboy canted his head at a smartly dressed man in his fifties.

Ruthie pursed her lips impishly. "Is there a Mrs. Fulbright?"

"Haven't seen one."

Penny Sue smoothed the front of her dress and grinned. "Well, well, Lyndon. Things are surely looking up."

Chapter 4

I woke up early the next day with the stark realization it was time to get on with my life. For the last eighteen months I'd been busy getting divorced. I was finally free—now what? I couldn't live off my paltry settlement forever. I'd have to work; heck, I wanted to work. Then there was the issue of where to go when the house sold.

The kids were on their own. Zack, Jr. was in Vail trying to decide what to do with a degree in philosophy. Ann would graduate in December and already had an internship lined up at the American Embassy in London. I doubted that either would want to come back to Atlanta to live; at least, no time soon. The divorce had taken its toll on them, too. They'd come home less and less over the last year, the tension of having Zack in the house being more than they could bear.

I rolled over and looked at the clock radio. Six o'clock. Ruthie was sound asleep in the next twin bed, lying on her back, mouth open, snoring softly. I snatched my robe from the foot of the bed and crept out of the room. I put on a pot of coffee and drew the drapes in the living room. Instead of a sunrise, I was greeted by a thick mist. Fitting. The fog matched my mood.

I poured a cup of coffee and headed to the deck. The mist was cool and wet on my face with a faint fishy smell. Though I couldn't see the ocean, I heard it lapping gently. Low tide, the perfect time to look for shells. And, surely, no one had beaten me to it in this fog.

I hitched the belt on my robe tighter and started for the beach. My plans for the future could wait another hour or two.

I was happy to see that the turtle mound at the end of the boardwalk had been moved. Relocating nests from traffic areas was a key function of the Turtle Patrols. Evidently, they had come through the night before, saving not only the turtles, but Ruthie and me from extreme mental anguish. Penny Sue had groused about her torn sarong all through dinner. I made a mental note to compliment the patrol on their fine work the next time I saw them.

The fog was so dense, I was standing in the water before I saw it. I stopped ankle deep and turned slowly. I couldn't see a thing. I looked to where I thought the horizon should be, hoping to spy a glimmer of sunrise. Nothing. I took a long pull of my coffee. I didn't have a chance of finding a shell in this pea soup unless I happened to step on it.

Well, there was always tomorrow.

I turned around and headed back the way I came. But, the wet, turbid haze had become so thick I kept losing sight of my tracks in the sand. I stopped, a wave of panic welling in my chest. I couldn't see anything. For all I knew, I was walking north, parallel to the shore, in which case I could go a long way—in my bathrobe, no less.

I dropped to one knee, frantically looking for footprints and my way home. Thankfully, I found some close by. I followed the tracks, bent double to keep the depressions in view. A moist draft on my bare derrière told me vital parts were protruding from the short bathrobe. I tugged at the back of the robe, however, the cotton sleep set had not been designed for contorted movement. Or, maybe it had. I'd gotten it on sale at Victoria's Secret, my only thought at the time being the great price. It had never occurred to me I might be getting *less* than I bargained for.

I hadn't gone very far when the beach began to incline, which told me I was approaching the dunes and salvation. By following the dune line, I reasoned, I'd eventually get to a cross-walk and was confident I would recognize the rickety bridge to our unit. Simple. Success was certain; I couldn't have wandered very far from the condo.

I straightened up and took a sip of coffee, congratulating myself on brilliant scouting. Zack used to say I could get lost in the driveway. Of course, he used to make a lot of other stupid, cruel remarks. Well, Zack was wrong and Zack was gone. Good riddance. I smoothed the robe over my rear end and resumed my trek—upright, confident, dignified. Two seconds later I tripped and went sprawling. The coffee mug flew from my hand; my bed clothes went up around my shoulders.

"Damn." I levered up to my knees and brushed myself off. I was covered in sand. The moist grit clung to my skin like breading on a chicken. I had it on my thighs, my boobs, and everywhere in between. I spit. The stuff was even in my teeth. I brushed myself quickly and pulled down my gown.

Thank God for the fog. Now, if I could just find the mug. It was a wonder I hadn't spilled the coffee all over myself. That was my usual MO. It seemed I spent most of my life cleaning spots off my clothes, which gave me a lot of sympathy for little kids.

I saw it in my neighborhood all the time. Little kids covered in dirt, their mommies looming over them menacingly. "How did you get dirty?" Mommy always asked sternly. "I don't know," the kid whined. I understood.

I really didn't know half the time, spots appeared from nowhere. Ruthie said it was because I was always thinking—lost in thought and not paying attention. Penny Sue attributed the whole thing to hormones. "Memory loss, foggy-brained: first sign of an estrogen deficiency."

"Darn, where is that cup?" I pushed myself up into a squat. Sand grated in the folds of my crotch, and I was starting to itch all over. "One pass, that's it," I told myself, running my hands across the sand. "That cheap mug isn't worth it."

I rotated on the balls of my feet, patting the ground. Ninety degrees, one-eighty; I found nothing. I stretched my arms as far as I could manage and still keep my balance. Then, my fingertip touched something cold and hard. I leaned forward and grabbed ... *a cold, stiff foot!*

It was like a bad dream—the one where someone is chasing you, and you try to scream but can't. You open your mouth, straining, yet no sound comes out. You try and try, your heart thumping furiously until you finally wake yourself up. Only I didn't wake up. I was frozen in place, my mouth open, breath coming in staccato bursts.

I have no idea how long I stayed in that state. Seconds, a minute, an hour—it seemed like an eternity. Finally, a single note escaped from my throat. A woosey peep that even I could barely hear—a sound, nonetheless. And, if one could get out, why not two? That thought broke the stupor. My throat unclenched, and a cacophonous torrent emerged.

My screams woke up the whole neighborhood. Spotlights flashed on, and I could hear voices. I half crawled, half ran across the dunes toward the lights. Hell with my pantiless butt, let the whole world see it! I was getting out of there. Sand burrs embedded in my feet and legs, but I didn't care. "Call an ambulance. Call the police," I shrieked at the top of my lungs.

An EVAC ambulance arrived first, followed by a fire truck and police car. By then the fog had cleared, and the neighbors poured out of their condos and onto the beach. Penny Sue, Ruthie, and I watched from the deck. I was shaking so hard, my teeth literally chattered. Even two of Penny Sue's tranquilizers did not calm my racing heart. I sat on the lawn chair watching the commotion as Ruthie picked burrs from my feet with tweezers. Penny Sue sat next to me rubbing my back, then hugged me to her side as the EVAC crew carried a stretcher with a yellow body bag across the deck and through the condo to the ambulance.

"A helluva way to start the day," Penny Sue drawled.

By ten o'clock it was over. The police had carted off the body, taken my statement, and photographed the crime scene. My statement was brief, very brief, since I truly knew nothing. I had not even looked at the corpse. All I remembered was the bare foot. The big toe had a gash on it and the one next to it was bent at a crazy angle. It was a big foot, definitely a man's, since it was connected to a hairy leg. That was all I knew. Period.

For the second time in two days the police instructed us not to leave town. I collapsed on the sofa.

At ten thirty my realtor called. She was showing my house to a young couple for the third time. Things looked promising, could I stay close to the phone in case there was an offer? I said "Sure." I was too bummed out by the morning's events to do much, anyway.

We ate a light breakfast and stretched out on the deck for some sun. Penny Sue perused a *Cosmopolitan* magazine while Ruthie read astrology. I just lay there in a tranquilized daze, grateful for the peace and quiet, until Ruthie bolted out of her chair, shrieking. My heart all but stopped from fright again.

"I'm allergic," Ruthie threw her book down and dashed inside, a wasp hot on her tail.

Another bug appeared which went after Penny Sue. She swatted it with her magazine. By this time I was on my feet and saw the problem. A wasp nest was lodged in the space between the glass pane and molding on the sliding door. We'd knocked it loose when we opened the door and the wasps were none too happy about the intrusion.

"Om-m-m." Ruthie, safe behind the screen door, started to chant while Penny Sue batted the air wildly.

"What the heck are you doing, Ruthie?" Penny Sue screeched.

"Om-m-m. I'm setting up a protection field. Om-m-m."

"Protection for who? Us or the bugs? Scoot, scoot." Penny Sue grabbed her beach towel and put it over her head.

By then the vermin had started to buzz me. But I was calm, collected ... heck, sedated. "Your force field isn't working, Ruthie. Go get the Hot Shot Wasp Spray. I saw some under the sink." Still chanting, she found the insecticide. As Ruthie opened the door to hand me the can, Penny Sue bounded through, leaving me to face the vicious vespids alone.

"Kills on Contact from Twenty Feet," the container read in bright yellow letters. I intended to put it to the test. Draping a towel over my head, I backed up and pushed the button. A stream of foul smelling poison spewed forth. The bugs exploded from the nest like shrapnel as Ruthie's chanting grew louder and more frantic. I clutched the towel around me and dashed down the boardwalk toward the beach. When I returned a few minutes later, the wasps were writhing pitifully in the final throes of death.

Penny Sue emerged from the condo holding a fly swatter. "Great shooting, girl."

I didn't respond, just brushed dead bugs off of my chair and stretched out again. Yet, my head had hardly touched the chair when the telephone rang. Ruthie stopped chanting long enough to answer it. My realtor again.

Yes, the couple seemed very interested, but there wasn't any hot water. Was something wrong with the hot water heater? Could she hire a repairman to take a look at it? Although I suspected it was something simple like a pilot light, I said, "Go ahead, if it will help make the sale."

As I talked, Ruthie busied herself making sandwiches. I hung up the telephone and snatched a half. "Um-m, cream cheese and olive. I can't remember when I last had one of these."

Ruthie took one. "Me either, but they must be Penny Sue's favorite. Look at the size of these containers." Ruthie motioned at an extra large tub of cream cheese and an enormous jar of green olives. "What if you sell the house? Have you thought of where you'd like to live?"

I concentrated on my sandwich. I'd been so caught up in the mechanics of now, of details, of what had to be done, that I hadn't given any thought to the future. "I don't know."

"There are some adorable apartments in Vinings. That's a nice, eclectic area. Lots of cute shops, great restaurants."

I picked the crust off my sandwich. "I like Vinings, but I'm not sure I want to stay in Atlanta. There's nothing to hold me there."

Ruthie looked stricken. "What about the kids?"

"Ann's going to London in January, and Zack, Jr. seems happy in Vail. His old girl friend just moved out there to be with him. The kids went to Vanderbilt, so most of their friends are in Tennessee. Neither of them are particularly thrilled with their father. There's no need for me to stay in Atlanta for their sake."

"What about Penny Sue and me? We DAFFODILS have to stick together."

I patted her hand soothingly. "I'd always come back to visit."

"I would hope so," she said, looking sad.

"For the first time I can do whatever I want. Until now, my life has been one big obligation. School, then marriage, the kids, even the divorce. There were certain steps you had to follow, certain things you had to do; shoot, even certain stages of grieving. Duty has always determined my life. But, I have no responsibilities at this moment. It's a funny feeling."

Ruthie poured some tea and handed me the plate of sandwiches. I took one and started peeling the crust off again.

"What about you?" I asked. "Haven't you ever thought of moving, doing something else?"

"Sure," she said slowly. "Jo Ruth's been accepted to med school at Chapel Hill. I'd move up there if it weren't for Poppa; he's my responsibility."

"You're here." I swept my arm in a wide arc.

"Oh, I have lots of freedom. Mr. Wong and the housekeeper take care of Poppa's physical needs; I provide the emotional support. I owe him. After all, Poppa was there for me when I got divorced; it's my turn now."

I nodded. "An obligation. I'd feel exactly the same way."

"What are y'all up to? You look awfully serious." Penny Sue stood in the doorway, peering across the top of her Chanel sunglasses.

I held up the plate of sandwiches. "Having a little snack. Cream cheese and olive."

"Just what I need." Penny Sue perched on a stool at the counter and took a sandwich. "Hand me the pepper, please." She doused the sandwich liberally and took a bite. "Hm-m. Onion, it needs onion." She found a Vidalia in the refrigerator and cut a thick slice. "Delicious," she muttered between bites.

Ruthie watched with distaste. "Are you sure there's nothing wrong with *your* hormones?"

"I've taken care of that. I'm doing hormone replacement therapy." Penny Sue finished her half and took another. "You know what would be good on this? Jalapeño pepper jelly. Would you fetch it from the frig, Ruthie?"

Ruthie handed her the jar. "Maybe you need to cut back on the estrogen."

Penny Sue slathered a thick layer of jelly on the bread and tasted it. "Mmm-m. What, ruin all this fun? Not a chance."

I didn't hear from the realtor again that afternoon. We never left the deck, so I couldn't have missed the call. Truth be told, I was relieved. When the house sold, I'd have to make some decisions, and fast.

Ruthie brought out her laptop computer and cast my astrology chart. "You have Mars in Libra, so you hate conflict and have a hard time making up your mind."

No kidding. Tell me something I don't know. "Can you see anything about a job?"

"Well, your twelfth house shows a need to search for truth and wisdom. You'd probably be good at some kind of investigation."

Penny Sue sat up. "Isn't that what you did after graduation?"

"I worked for an accounting firm doing audits. I guess that was investigation of sorts."

"Ever thought of taking it up again?" Penny Sue asked, munching on her sandwich.

"It's terribly demanding. Long hours, lots of travel, I'm not sure I could keep up."

"There must be another way to use your expertise," Ruthie said.

I rubbed my neck. I was starting to get a headache. "I'm open to suggestions."

Ruthie smiled. "I've got an idea. Let's go to Cassadaga and get a reading—ask the spirits for guidance."

"What's Cassadaga?" I asked.

"A small village of mediums and psychics. It's not far. Momma used to go there every year to get a reading. Come on, it'll be fun."

I wasn't particularly anxious to go, since I doubted the spirits did job placement. But, Ruthie looked like an exuberant kid. *Mommy, Mommy let's go to the park, or the fair, or whatever.* How could I say no? "Okay, we'll go tomorrow."

We were dressing for dinner when the shit hit the fan.

There was a loud knock at the front door. It was Woody Woodhead, the local prosecutor, and a detective. Could they have a word with us about the body on the beach? Stone-faced and silent, the men sat in the living room while we assembled. As usual, Penny Sue was the last to arrive, her appearance heralded by a wave of Joy perfume which preceded her by a full minute.

"Good evening," Penny Sue said breathlessly.

"Evening, ladies." The detective slipped several eight-by-ten glossy photographs from a manila envelop and handed them to Penny Sue.

Her mouth dropped open as her hand flew to her chest. "Magod, it's Rick." She handed the pictures to me and covered her eyes.

Woody leaned back in the chair and steepled his fingers in front of his chest. "That answers our first question."

"What happened?" I asked.

"He was shot with a small caliber weapon, a .38. We figure he'd been dead for about six hours when you found him."

Ruthie glanced at the photos, then looked away. "Why? Who would do such a thing?"

Woody took the pictures. "Good question. Where's your gun, Penny Sue?"

She drew back with indignation. "Surely, you don't think I had anything to do with that."

"I'm not making an accusation. I merely want to know where your gun is. Would you get it, please?"

Penny Sue went to the bedroom and returned with her purse. Glaring defiantly, she retrieved her revolver.

"May I see it?"

She handed Woody the gun and snapped her purse shut. He gave the weapon a cursory examination, then handed it to the detective who placed it in a plastic evidence bag. "You don't mind if we take this in for a few tests, do you?"

"Well, no—"

I broke in. "You won't find anything. Penny Sue was with us all night. We went to dinner, then came back here and went to bed. All of us. We can vouch for her."

"In which case we'll find nothing," Woody replied. He nodded to the detective and stood. "Your neighbor saw a woman on your deck at about one o'clock this morning. The woman was wearing a bright red robe."

Red robe? Ruthie and I gaped at Penny Sue.

"I stepped out to smoke a cigarette. I couldn't sleep."

"I thought you'd quit smoking," Ruthie said, surprised. "I gave you that worry stone to rub when you got the urge."

Penny Sue shrugged. "I did quit, sorta. I sneak one now and then. Everybody makes such a big deal about smoking, I feel like a criminal. I was outside for all of five minutes."

Woody snorted, definitely unimpressed. "We appreciate your cooperation, ladies. We'll be in touch. Please don't leave town."

Don't leave town. The third time in two days.

Chapter 5

When I got up the next morning, Penny Sue was out on the deck smoking a cigarette in her red silk robe with an Oriental dragon embroidered on the back. I checked the time. Eight o'clock. Penny Sue was the world's latest sleeper. The fact that she was up at such an ungodly hour told me Penny Sue was a lot more worried than she'd let on. I poured a cup of coffee and went out to join her.

"Out of the closet?" I said, nodding at the cigarette.

Penny Sue blew a smoke ring. "This is my third. I want to make sure those nosy neighbors see me out here smoking. I hope they're watching. The nerve of them, pointing the finger at me." She panned the two-story buildings behind our condo. "I wish I knew which one it was. I'd give them a piece of my mind."

"That won't solve anything and will make matters worse."

"Don't worry, I'll stay cool."

I was worried. None of this would have happened if Penny Sue hadn't waved her gun around. What in the world possessed her to do it? I used to describe her as high-strung, even flighty; but her behavior lately had been down right erratic. Maybe it *was* a hormone problem. Perimenopause: that phase where a woman's hormones started the downhill slide. PMS run wild, and it could last for as long as ten years. The thought made me shudder.

"I know it's ridiculous. You know it's ridiculous. But the neighbors, whoever they are, don't know. As far as they're concerned, you could be a mass murderer."

Penny Sue stared at the building behind us where the balconies overlook the parking lot. "I'll bet it was one of them. Someone up there called the police about the Rick row, we know that. Nosy old bags, they're probably spying on us at this minute." She snuffed out the cigarette angrily.

I put myself in the line of view between Penny Sue and the building. I wasn't taking any chances. Under normal circumstances, Penny Sue was far too refined for angry outbursts, or God-forbid, rude gestures; but, these weren't typical times. "The best thing we can do is be ourselves; let them see what nice, normal people we are."

Penny Sue tilted her head back and looked down her nose. "Normal? As in average? Pu-leeze, I am *not* normal."

Brother, that was the truth. "Bad choice of words," I added quickly. "How about not dangerous? Not nutty? Not a homicidal maniac?"

"Better." She pulled her robe up around her neck and tightened the belt. "You're right, though. I didn't kill Rick, and I'm not going to let Woody intimidate me. He'll find out soon enough when they test the gun. He's jerking me around because I dumped him back in college. He's on a power trip now and lording it over me."

She lit another cigarette. That made what, four or five? To say she'd fallen off the no-smoking-wagon was an understatement. She hadn't fallen, she'd barreled over the cliff.

"Little twerp," she went on. "I won't give Woody the satisfaction of seeing me sweat. I absolutely won't allow that nerd to ruin our vacation. This is your time, Leigh. Your respite from worldly cares."

It certainly had taken my mind off my troubles, though I wasn't sure I'd call it a respite. Debacle seemed more fitting.

Penny Sue folded her arms, eyes narrowed, thinking. "So, the neighbors don't know me? Don't know what a nice person I am?" She took a long drag of the cigarette. "Maybe we should throw a little party. A mixer for the neighborhood, wouldn't that be fun? Apologize for causing a stir. Let them see how nice I really am." The last comment was uttered through gritted teeth, as if she wanted to bite their heads off. She took another pull on her cigarette, then grinned mischievously. "I think I'll invite Lyndon."

"Who?" Penny Sue'd always had a grasshopper mind, but that switch was too fast for me.

"Lyndon Fulbright. The good looking yachtsman we saw at The Riverview."

I stared at her, stunned. Under suspicion for murder, yet concerned about getting a date. I'd tossed and turned half the night worrying about her, and she was planning a party. "You beat all, you know that."

"What?"

"This isn't a game, Penny Sue; we're talking about a murder. Woody could make your life miserable. I think we should call your father."

She stomped her foot. "We are not calling Daddy. I'm not guilty, so there's nothing to worry about."

"Come on, innocent people get convicted every day, especially if they don't have good legal advice." It was hard to believe that I was suggesting that anyone see a lawyer. After my experience with Zack and PH&S, I put lawyers at the bottom of the human hierarchy, right next to rapists, child molesters and murderers. Murderers. Hm-m, it takes one to know one, we used to say as kids. "You absolutely need to consult a lawyer."

"I can handle it. I'm not going to run to Daddy like a child. 'You're a big girl, Penny Sue. Now act like one.' That's what Daddy said about the Rick mess. Anyway, it would embarrass him, again, in front of his important friends. I'm simply not going to do it. What he doesn't know won't hurt him."

Ah, the lecture from Daddy must have been tougher than she'd let on. Still, I hoped she wasn't being foolhardy. Ignorance might be bliss for the Judge; I just hoped it didn't have the opposite effect on Penny Sue.

She crushed her cigarette in a flower pot. "Come on, Leigh, let's go in. I need some more coffee."

Ruthie came out a few minutes later, and we had breakfast. Penny Sue acted as if she didn't have a care in the world. I studied her hard, trying to decide if she was putting up a front or really felt nothing. I finally decided she was on the level. She'd simply dismissed the murder from her mind.

Live in the present, the self-help books said. The past is gone, the future isn't here, and the present moment is all that exists. I guess that's what Penny Sue was doing. But how? My mind was a hopeless jumble of shoulds, if-onlys, and what-ifs. What happened to all that stuff in her mind? Was it simply forgotten? Had she always been this way, or was it an acquired skill? With three divorces, perhaps her brain circuits had been burned out. Or, maybe it was the hormone thing. Memory loss was supposedly one of the first symptoms. However it occurred, I found myself envying Penny Sue. For the first time in my life, I wished my mind worked like hers—and that was a scary thought!

I called my realtor before we left for Cassadaga. The water heater checked out okay; she guessed they didn't let the water run long enough to get hot. The service call cost fifty dollars— should she send the bill to me or Zack? The young couple was definitely interested in the house, but they were bothered by its age. Would we consider buying a major repair insurance policy? Though it would cost close to a thousand dollars, she thought a warranty would cinch the deal.

I said, "Fine, no problem." I picked up her card and paused. "Let Us Take The Worry Out Of Selling Your Home." Yeah, right.

Ruthie called, "Ready?" Then, I heard the twang of the rusty spring on the screen door. I pocketed the card and hurried out.

Penny Sue was waiting impatiently, car in gear, and started moving before I even had a chance to close the door. "What's the rush—" I started to complain, but caught myself mid-sentence. A New Smyrna Beach patrol car was parked at the edge of the lot, and a ramrod officer with a clipboard was talking to a sandy-haired man next door. That surprised me—I'd thought the condo was vacant. I hadn't seen any cars there since the red pickup truck on the first day, which I'd assumed belonged to a workman.

"Getting the daily report on our activities," Penny Sue muttered tightly, as she guided the car to the street.

"I'm sure it's routine; they're still taking statements on the murder," I said.

Penny Sue harrumphed and tuned the radio to a rock station which was playing Bob Marley's song "I Shot the Sheriff."

"Don't you dare," I said. We all laughed. Penny Sue's face muscles relaxed, and I could see she'd banished the incident from her mind. She amazed me—I would still be stewing.

We rode in silence for a while, Ruthie reading *Places to Go in Florida*, while I spotted license plates. Ontario, New York, Illinois, even a Missouri. While the season had not officially started, New Smyrna Beach was already bustling with tourists driven south by an unusually early winter. A tractor trailer pulled out at the New Smyrna Beach Speedway, a dirt-poor relation of its big time cousin in Daytona Beach, and we slowed to a crawl.

"What is Cassadaga, again?" Penny Sue asked Ruthie. "A bunch of astrologers?"

"It's a Spiritualists enclave. You know, mediums. People who channel information from entities on the other side."

"Dead people?"

"Yes."

Penny Sue chuckled. "Spooks speak, huh?"

Ruthie shook her head with disgust. "Stop that. You'll offend the spirits, and none of us will get a good reading."

"I was just kidding. Surely, the spirits are not so thin-skinned. They know we call them spooks. If they used to be human, they probably called spirits spooks, too."

Ruthie folded her arms. "Maybe so, but there's no sense in taking chances."

I could see that Ruthie was getting pouty, so rushed to change the subject. "How do these readings work? Do the mediums go into a trance, or can we ask questions?"

"Every medium has their own system, but they all give you an opportunity to ask questions."

"I'm going to ask if Lyndon Fulbright is married," Penny Sue declared airily. "I sure liked the looks of that boat. I can see myself sailing around on it."

"It's not a sailboat," I said.

"Sail, float, what difference does it make? It's the Lyndon and me going off into the great blue yonder that counts. Sail to Cancun. Cruise the Caribbean. Flit over to Monte Carlo."

"I don't think you flit to Monte Carlo. The trip would take weeks."

"I'm sure he'd hire someone to sail—"

"It's not a sailboat."

"—it across the ocean. We'd fly."

"My, you do think big," I quipped.

"Thoughts are things, right, Ruthie? You can't have what you can't imagine."

The comment stopped me. Just when I'd almost concluded that Penny Sue was a empty-headed hedonist, she'd come up with something profound. It happened every time, and she was right.

Thoughts and attitudes *do* determine our lives. Depressed people see a dismal world. Happy people see humor in almost anything. So, what did that say about me? What did I see? I thought of Penny Sue, the spirits, Woody with his pants around his ankles ... nuts. I must be nuts.

We parked the car in front of the Cassadaga Hotel. Typical of resorts from the turn of the century, the hotel was a stucco and wood structure ringed by a wide porch with white rocking chairs and worn wooden benches. Only a handful of people were outside, most having a cigarette. We entered through the front door, and Ruthie's face lit with delight. An ancient sofa and old-fashioned upholstered chairs complemented the lobby's polished hardwood floors and ornate tray ceiling. A wooden telephone booth, complete with folding door and corner seat, stood against the wall. A New Age shop offering books, incense, rocks and Indian paraphernalia was off to the right. To our immediate left was The Lost in Time Cafe, a pleasant room with lace curtains, a delicately carved bar and tables decked out with white tablecloths, small vases of flowers, and bottles of the house wine, Delicious Spirits.

Everything about the place was reminiscent of a long past, slower era. I could almost see women in long dresses having tea in the cafe. Or men with handlebar mustaches in white linen suits milling around the lobby. The place truly was lost in time, maybe that's what the spirits liked about it.

We went to the front desk and inquired about readings. Several mediums were available. Who was the best? we asked. The receptionist refused to comment, recommending that we use intuition to make our choice.

"I'll take Horace," Penny Sue said instantly.

Ruthie regarded her quizzically. "You get good vibes from him?"

"No. He's available now, and he's the only man. I like available men." Penny Sue smiled, counted out her money and sashayed across the lobby to find Horace.

Illumina, Sally Ann and Reverend Angelina were the other choices. Ruthie took a deep breath and touched each of their names, trying to divine their energy. A minute later her eyelids fluttered and she pronounced, "Angelina."

That left me with Sally Ann or Illumina. As Ruthie toddled off to her appointment, I stared at the names, hoping to hear a voice, feel a tingle, something. I got absolutely nothing. The reservationist started to fidget, and I felt like a dense putz. Choose one, I told myself, it's fifty-fifty. "Sally Ann," I blurted. Illumina sounded too much like a car.

After our sessions we had lunch; checked out several book-stores where Ruthie bought the book *Cassadaga, The South's Oldest Spiritualist Community*; and took a walking tour of the village. It wasn't until we were in the car headed back to the beach that we compared notes on our readings.

"I'm going to get married again. A man with light hair who's involved in sports," Penny Sue announced as she sped down Route 44. "A true Prince Charming, Horace said."

"Who fits the bill?" I asked. "The Falcon or the Brave?"

"Neither. The Falcon's bald; what little hair he has, he shaves off. Jimmy, the Brave, has brown hair. I think it's Lyndon. Yachting's a sport, isn't it?"

"Sure, they have races and stuff; it must be considered a sport," Ruthie replied.

"How about we go to The Riverview for dinner tonight?" Penny Sue said.

"Not wasting any time, eh?"

"Girl, I don't intend to let Prince Charming get away. What about you, Ruthie? How was your reading?"

She was looking out the window and didn't answer immediately. I held my breath with anticipation. Ruthie had been quiet all afternoon. I hoped the medium hadn't given her bad news.

"Angelina said I was a born sensitive, and my life purpose was to help people by becoming a medium myself. She said I'd move to Cassadaga one day."

"I can see that," Penny Sue said. "You've always been interested in spiritual stuff."

"I guess."

Ruthie's response was flat and lifeless. Something was bothering her. "What's wrong?" I asked. "I'd think you'd be thrilled at the prospect of becoming a medium."

"Oh sure, it's the move that bothers me."

"Why is that a big deal?"

"I'd never leave Poppa. Don't you see, it means Poppa's going to die." Her green eyes filled with tears.

A black cloud descended on all of us. I recovered first. "Your dad is eighty-four, Ruthie. You know he's going to go eventually. We all do ... sometime."

Penny Sue jumped in. "And there is no death, right? You told me that yourself when Momma passed. He's simply going to change form, drop his body. His spirit will live on. Shoot, maybe J.T.'s going to be your guide when you become a medium. You know how much he loves directing people, and that way you'd actually listen."

Ruthie brightened. "I hadn't thought of that. Lord, he'd hound me to death."

I looked out the window, thinking. Sally Ann told me I would be instrumental in getting a friend through a life and death situation. Initially, I interpreted the comment to mean the mess with Penny Sue and the murder. Now I wondered if she'd been referring to Ruthie. I hoped not.

"What did your medium say, Leigh?"

I took a deep breath. "Nothing much, she was pretty vague. You know, my health was good; the kids' health was good; I'd eventually have four grandchildren." I could see Penny Sue regarding me in the rearview mirror and knew she wasn't buying it. But Providence was on my side.

"There's a red pickup truck behind us. I think it's the guy that was fighting with Rick," Penny Sue exclaimed. "I recognize the spotlights on the bumper."

Ruthie turned around to see. "Don't look, he'll see you," I hissed, then caught myself. Why did I care if he saw us? Geez, I sounded like my mother. I turned around and looked myself.

"He could be the person who killed Rick," Ruthie said. "He had a motive: the fight."

"He hates turtles," I added. "Remember the bumper sticker? Rick's body was found next to the turtle mound."

"Yeah," Ruthie exclaimed. "He waited on the beach, knowing that Rick would come by to move the turtle nest, then killed him to settle the score."

I could see Penny Sue's eyes in the mirror.

"We need to find out if it's really him—get his license plate number," she said. "A passing zone's coming up, I'll slow down. You get the number when he goes by." Ruthie pulled out a pen and scrap of paper, poised to write, as Penny Sue slowed the car from sixty to forty-five. "Come on, buddy, the coast is clear. Pass." The truck slowed, too, dropping back several car lengths.

"What's wrong with him?" Ruthie asked.

Penny Sue's jaw tightened. "He's following us." She stepped on the accelerator. The truck matched our speed, though stayed a few car lengths behind.

"Following us? Why?"

"Maybe he's out to settle a score with us, too," I ventured slowly. Though Sally Ann did not specifically mention Rick's murder—

which made me doubt her abilities—she did foresee trouble with a man in the near future. At the time, I assumed she meant Zack. Was it possible Mr. Pickup was the guy in her vision?

We were approaching the New Smyrna Beach Speedway and the intersection with Route 415. Penny Sue gripped the steering wheel with both hands. "Hold on, girls." She took a hard right through a service station, onto Route 415, then looped back to Route 44. The truck went speeding by. Penny Sue pulled in behind him. She floored the Mercedes and got right on his bumper. There it was: *Turtles? They Make Good Soup.*

"Darn," Ruthie said. The license plate was splattered with mud, obliterating the numbers. – – N42 – was all that we could make out.

"Where did you learn to drive like that?" I asked, breathless from the evasive maneuver.

"Daddy and I took one of those anti-terrorist driving courses."

Defensive driving, carrying a gun; I hadn't realized that judging was such a dangerous profession.

We followed the truck past the city limits to the regional shopping center. It took a left into Gilley's Pub 44 parking lot. Penny Sue went one block further and made a U-turn.

"I want to make sure the same guy is driving," Penny Sue said. "We can chip some of the mud off his license plate."

Ruthie drew back, hugging the passenger-side door. "I'm not chipping any mud. That guy could be dangerous."

"Pooh, it's broad daylight. You'll be perfectly safe."

"If it's so safe, you do it."

"I have to drive the getaway car. Leigh, you'll do it, won't you?" I could see her face in the mirror. She was staring at me through those damned Chanel sunglasses and flashing the sweet, manipulative grin that I hated so much. The one that said: "This is such a simple thing, you're brain-damaged if you don't comply with my wishes." I bared my teeth and gave her a low growl. Childish and catty, I know, but she deserved it.

The fates were on my side, again. We circled the lot twice, but the truck was not there. "Damn." Penny Sue slapped the steering wheel angrily. "He must have doubled back while we were making our turn."

"Yeah," Ruthie said. "Maybe he took one of those driving courses, too."

Chapter 6

The Riverview was packed. We expected as much since a tour bus was parked by the door. Penny Sue insisted that we eat on the deck overlooking the marina even though it would entail a twenty-minute wait. She tried valiantly to finagle our way to the outside bar, but the hostess held firm. We found a table at the inside bar and ordered wine.

"Hm-m, this is good," Penny Sue commented after tasting the golden liquid. "I'll have to get some of this for the party."

The party. Penny Sue had hired Party Hearty Catering, an outfit specializing in fried catfish and kegs of beer. I was skeptical. I had a sneaking suspicion most of their business was done in Daytona Beach during Bike Week and Spring Break. Actually, Penny Sue didn't have much choice. The reputable services were booked for Saturday night—three days was not a lot of notice—and the only other available caterer's forté was pony rides.

I voted for that one. If Penny Sue wanted to show the neighbors that she was innocuous, the sight of her on a small pony would do the trick. But, considering her size, an animal rights advocate might see it as extreme cruelty, in which case the whole thing would backfire. A person who would torture a little pony was capable of anything, even murder, the reasoning would go. On second thought, Pony Parties was not a good idea, at all. Though, it sure would be a terrific ice breaker.

"Did you hear me, Leigh?" Penny Sue said.

I turned my attention back to the table. "Sorry. I was thinking of something else."

"The wine. Do you like this wine?"

I took a sip and held it on my tongue. "Dry, smooth. Yes, I like it," I said seriously. Then, stifling a chuckle, "It should go great with hot wings and catfish fingers."

Penny Sue grinned mockingly. "Shirley said traditional hors d'oeuvres were no problem. She's studied abroad and Continental cuisine was her first love."

"Which continent and whose tradition?" Ruthie was snickering, too.

"Give me a break. Negative. Y'all are just negative."

"There's a difference between being negative and realistic," I countered. "You don't think it's strange she was free on a Saturday night?"

"Shirley got a last minute cancellation. The groom crashed his Harley—"

I was really laughing now. "Like Ruthie said: Who's tradition and which continent?"

Penny Sue shook her head. "Negative and rude. For your information we're going to have steamed shrimp, Crab Rangoon, stuffed mushrooms, red caviar, artichoke dip, a fruit tray, and strawberries dipped in chocolate."

"And a keg of Budweiser?" I loved needling Penny Sue. She was so good at dishing it out, she deserved some flack. Then there was her reaction—always melodramatic, infinitely entertaining. Finally, I knew she rarely took any of it seriously. To say Penny Sue's self concept was intact was a monumental understatement. For her, jokes and gibes were like water running off a duck's back. I admired that trait in her and wished I could be more that way.

Penny Sue smiled impishly. "Billy Beer."

"Is that stuff still on the market?" Ruthie asked.

"It's long gone," I said. "In fact, it's probably a collector's item."

Penny Sue took a five dollar bill from her purse and waved for our waiter. "The only beer will be imported and in bottles." The waiter arrived and Penny Sue pressed the bill into his hand. "Hon, would you see if there's room for us at the outside bar? It's a little warm in here."

"Hot flash?" Ruthie asked after the waiter left.

"Or hot on the trail of Lyndon Fulbright?"

The waiter appeared in the doorway and motioned for us to follow.

"Both," Penny Sue said as she gathered up her purse, wine and hurried after the young server.

Napkins were draped over the backs of three stools at the corner of the bar with a perfect view of both the marina and the deck. Penny Sue nodded appreciatively and tipped the waiter another five. She settled onto the stool at the end of the counter and surveyed the marina. The *Ecstasy* was still docked. Penny Sue's spine stiffened with anticipation.

She sipped her wine demurely and scanned the area. Suddenly, her eyes locked on target like a laser-guided missile. I followed her gaze. Lyndon sat at a table on the far end of the deck, alone. Penny Sue checked her lipstick and misted her neck with a few squirts of Joy. As if she needed any more. I knew sweet smells are supposed to be a lure and aphrodisiac, but I'd contend Penny Sue had passed right through attraction and was well on the way to asphyxiation.

"What are you going to do?" Ruthie asked.

"Introduce myself, of course."

I said, "What? Saunter up and say: 'Hi, I'm Penny Sue, and my medium told me we're going to get married?'"

"Don't be silly, I'd never be so brash. I'm going to ask him about his boat. Tell him I'm thinking of buying one."

I scoffed. "Well, don't call it a boat. That'd be a dead giveaway."

"Uh oh," Ruthie said, putting her hand on Penny Sue's shoulder to hold her down.

"What are you doing?" Penny Sue shook loose.

"Look."

A waitress stood by Lyndon's table. Clad in the restaurant's uniform of Hawaiian shirt and white shorts, the woman was a stunning specimen of youth with shapely legs, a perfect tan and sun-streaked hair (the real stuff—not the exquisite, expensive variety Penny Sue so loved to toss carelessly.) We watched as she leaned over, exposing large breasts in the cleft of her shirt. We also saw Lyndon smile broadly.

"Now see what you've done," Penny Sue said, turning on Ruthie. "That girl beat me to the punch."

"Me?" Ruthie shot back. "I was trying to keep you from making a fool of yourself. But go ahead, do it your way. Race over there and shove her out of the way like Roller Derby."

"Wait a minute," I said as I took out my eyeglasses. "That's the cleaning lady, er, Charlotte."

Penny Sue squinted at them. "You're right." A smile stretched her cheeks. "This is perfect. I was going to ask Charlotte to help out with the party. Now I can talk to her and invite Lyndon at the same time." She took the last sip of wine. "When you get a table, don't wait on me to order." Penny Sue draped her purse over her shoulder and sashayed across the deck.

We watched as Penny Sue talked animatedly to Lyndon and Charlotte. A moment later she sat down and Lyndon was ordering her a drink.

Ruthie and I toasted her chutzpah. "She's got balls," Ruthie said.

"I guess that's why she always goes for the macho sports types. She'd run right over a normal guy."

"After three divorces, you'd think she be gun-shy."

"She's definitely not that."

Ruthie chuckled. "Right. Shy in any way, shape or form is not one of Penny Sue's shortcomings. But, you have to admit, she's made a royal mess this time. Do you think Penny Sue's truly under suspicion for Rick's murder or is Woody just jerking her chain?"

I took a sip of my Sauvignon Blanc. "I think she's on the list, though not at the top. Woody isn't going to do anything rash; he knows the Judge's connections. Remember, Woody got a call from the Attorney General over the brawl in the parking lot. A murder charge would bring the whole state down around his shoulders. Woody's no fool—he's going to be careful and thorough. The thing that bothers me is that pickup truck. I sure don't like the idea that we're being followed."

Ruthie signaled the bartender for another round of drinks. "Me, either. Maybe we should go home," Ruthie said nervously.

"We can't. We're stuck here until the investigation's over."

"I'd forgotten that. Did Penny Sue get in touch with Woody about the truck?"

"He was out, so she left a message."

The bartender arrived with peanuts and more wine. The nuts were a bad sign. I had a feeling we weren't going to eat any time soon. "No word on our table?" I asked hopefully, flashing a big smile.

He looked uncomfortable. "A few more minutes. A large party should be leaving shortly."

He was lying, I thought, remembering the bus parked by the front door. Twenty or so senior citizens were seated at a long table in the middle of the deck. They were eating dessert and having a high old time, so I doubted they'd leave soon. I downed a handful of peanuts.

"I think I'll call home and check on Poppa," Ruthie announced suddenly.

I nodded. She was still bothered by her psychic reading. The thought of losing a parent was unsettling, to say the least. I was fortunate that both of mine were alive and going strong. I was the oldest, and Mom had me when she was twenty. In their sixties, Warren and Barbara Martin weren't old by anyone's standards. In fact, a scientist on *Good Morning, America* said that one hundred forty would be the life span for our children. By that gauge, Mom and Dad weren't even middle-aged, and I was still a youngster. Zack, Jr. and Ann were mere infants. I liked that idea a lot.

Which reminded me that I needed to give the kids a call. I doubted they'd talked to their father, and I supposed they deserved to know the divorce was final. I had to tell them I was selling the house, too. I'd be happy to leave it, I had nothing but terrible memories from the last year—yet it was the only home they'd ever known.

Damn Zack. He cheated me out of my marriage, assets, *and* memories. The kids grew up in that house, yet I could hardly stand the sight of it. Ann took her first step there. Little Zack had his Cub Scout meetings. The kitchen had always been full of the kids and their friends eating cookies and discussing their troubles with school or sports or the bully down the street. Zack had robbed me of all that, for what? Money. Some legal-smegal nonsense about abandoning the home. Translation: Zack was terrified I'd end up with the house if he left. He didn't give a damn that it put me through hell, or ruined the kids' holidays, or anything else. Himself, that's all he thought about. How had I married such a selfish shit? Why hadn't I seen his true colors sooner? All the small—and not-so-small—indignities from our marriage flooded my mind. I gripped the stem of my wine glass tightly. If Zack had been there, at that moment, he'd probably have gotten the contents in his face.

A good looking guy motioned at Penny Sue's chair. "Is this seat taken?"

My first inclination was to take his head off. I was still wrapped up in my not-so-fond memories of Zack and the look I gave the newcomer must have been ferocious, because he backed away before I said a word. I caught myself and forced a smile. He was not Zack. He was harmless, and in fact, he looked kinda familiar. A quick glance at Penny Sue told me she was not returning in the near future. In any event, our table should be ready shortly, the bus people were finally preparing to leave. "Help yourself," I said, picking up the car keys from the counter.

He sat down, and ordered a beer. "Nice night, isn't it?"

I cut my eyes at him. Was this guy trying to pick me up? I took a sip of wine to buy time and gather my thoughts. Damn, what was keeping Ruthie? The ink on my divorce decree was barely dry, so a relationship was the last thing I wanted. Yet, that was making quite a leap. *Nice night* was hardly a blatant pass. It's not like he'd whispered: 'Hey, sugar, I want to jump your bones.'

"It's been beautiful all day," I finally replied.

"I hope it stays that way. I'm down from New Jersey. It was snowing when I left."

I remembered seeing something about a freak winter storm on the Weather Channel. "It's supposed to be warm here for the next few days."

"How about you? From the north?" he asked.

My antenna went up. Where are you from? What's your name? Want to come back to my hotel for a drink? Maybe this *was* a come-on, the guy was following the typical script. Though, I could be wrong. "Yeah, if you call Georgia north," I replied.

He laughed. A nice, full chuckle—something I never heard from Zack.

"Not unless it's snowing there. Al," he said, extending his hand.

"Leigh," I replied, accepting it. A crisp handshake—no fingering my palm or rubbing my wrist or other sleazy maneuver to indicate bad intentions.

"Do you live here permanently?"

I took a nervous sip of my wine. Where was Ruthie? I'd sure feel better if she were with me; it'd been a long time since I'd done the dating scene. "No, just visiting with some old friends. You?"

His beer arrived, and he took a drink. "Got a few days off and hated to schlep through snow so early in the season. I come here a lot, so figured this was the perfect time for a visit."

Ruthie appeared with a waiter in tow. "Our table's ready," she said.

Relieved, I took my wine and stood. "It's been nice talking with you. I hope you have a good visit," I said. As Ruthie and I threaded our way to the table, it hit me. Al was the guy next door, the one the police had interviewed that morning!

Our table was at the back of the deck, several stations away from Penny Sue and Lyndon, who seemed to be hitting it off fabulously. Every time I glanced that way, Penny Sue's hands were waving theatrically. I always said she couldn't talk if her hands were tied behind her back. We actually tried it once in college. She only managed two sentences before stopping cold. I thought she'd bust from frustration before we got her hands untied, and it was something I teased her about when she got particularly excited.

We'd finished dinner and our pie had just arrived when Penny Sue brought Lyndon over to the table. He was terrific looking up close. Lyndon had a perfect body, perfect teeth, perfect clothes, and the polished, understated assurance of the super wealthy. Penny Sue was in hog heaven. She introduced us; we made polite small talk; then he excused himself to place an overseas phone call.

Penny Sue ogled his back as he walked down the pier to his yacht. When he disappeared inside, she reached over and snatched my drink. "Mmmm-hmm, that is one fine specimen of manhood." She finished off the last few sips of the wine and grabbed Ruthie's, downing it as well.

"How much have you had to drink?" I asked.

She tossed her head. "You can drive."

"Did you ever eat dinner?" Ruthie questioned.

"I'll make a sandwich when we get home." Penny Sue snatched the spoon from Ruthie's coffee cup and helped herself to my coconut cream pie. I pushed the plate in front of her, obviously she needed it more than I did.

"Well?"

"Well, what?" Penny Sue said, mouth full of whipped cream.

Talking with her mouth full! That was completely out of character. Penny Sue must really be smashed. "What's the story on Lyndon?"

Pie demolished, she licked her finger and sat back. "He's in town to check on an investment. Condos or something. Will be here for at least a few days, maybe a week. He's coming to the party."

"And ..." Ruthie prodded.

"Charlotte's going to come over to clean and help with the party."

Ruthie leaned forward, elbows on the table. "Come on, Penny Sue, you know what I mean. Is he married? What does he do for a living? Are you going to see him before Saturday?"

Penny Sue flashed a goofy grin. "Divorced, don't know, lunch tomorrow."

"Did you tell him y'all were destined to marry?" I asked.

She tittered. "I'm saving that tidbit for another time. But, we're definitely in sync. Lyndon said he felt like he'd known me all his life."

"How much had he had to drink?" I gibed.

Penny Sue folded her arms and pursed her lips peevishly. "You're just jealous."

"I'm kidding. Though, it's an amazing turn of events. I get inducted into the DAFFODILS, and the president resigns a few days later."

"Who said anything about me resigning?"

"Well, if you get married ..."

"That doesn't make any difference. I'm still divorced and free of licentious scum." She chopped the air with her hand and knocked over the wine glass. Fortunately, it was empty. "DAFFODILS are allowed to remarry, as long as it's Prince Charming. Royalty's a whole 'nother matter."

Ruthie and I each took one of Penny Sue's arms. "I'm glad you clarified that, Cinderella. It's almost midnight, we need to get you home before your carriage turns into a pumpkin."

"Pumpkin—" She followed us out without protest. "—wouldn't a pumpkin pie taste good?" I unlocked the car and helped her into the passenger side. She laid her head back and closed her eyes. "Stop at Food Lion and get a pie, Leigh."

I guided the car out of the parking lot. I wasn't about to stop anywhere; a bed was what she needed.

Ruthie came to my aid. "I know, how about cream cheese and pepper jelly on toast?"

"Mmmm," Penny Sue mumbled. "With onion."

Chapter 7

"Do you think a guy should wear a dress to a school dance?"

I looked up from the cinnamon and raisin bagel I was smearing with cream cheese. Ruthie sat at the counter reading the newspaper. "Sure, as long as he doesn't look better than his date. That pro basketball player with the funny hair wore dresses. He even wore wed—" I stopped myself. I was about to say wedding dresses, Ruthie's favorite attire (complete with veil) to Kappa Alpha's Old South gala when we were in college. That subject was best left untouched, no sense starting the day on the wrong foot. I raised on tiptoes and peered at the newsprint. "What are you reading?"

Ruthie held up the paper so I could see the headline: *Local High School Bars Teen In Drag.*

I took a bite of my bagel. "What's the problem?"

"The principal won't let a gay boy go to the homecoming dance wearing a dress. The kid's broken-hearted, worked overtime for months to buy a red ball gown with matching shoes."

"What's the big deal?"

"A bunch of parents are upset." She scanned the article. "They say: No one should be allowed to make himself the center of attention by deliberately making a spectacle of himself."

I hooted. "As if that's not what every female is trying to do! Who are they kidding? Sounds like some mothers are afraid the guy will upstage their daughters."

"He probably would," Ruthie said. "I went to a bar in San Francisco that featured a stage show of female impersonators. I couldn't believe the performers were actually men. They looked fabulous, better than I do."

"Me, too." One of the talk shows did a segment on cross dressing. On my best day I don't look that glamorous. "I can't believe it's legal."

"Everything's legal in San Francisco."

"No, I mean barring the teen from the dance. Isn't that discrimination?"

"I'd think so."

I took a bite of the bagel. It wasn't the best I'd ever had; in fact, it was bland, very bland. I thought of the Jalapeño jelly. Why not? I pulled off a piece of bagel and slathered on the hot concoction. It was surprisingly good.

"Listen to this," Ruthie said. "Moving turtle nests can cause the eggs not to hatch or change the sex of hatchlings."

"Change the sex of hatchlings? How does that work?" I asked.

Ruthie scanned the article. "Doesn't say. But the number of nests is up, while hatchlings are lower. No one knows why. Vandalism has increased from here to South Florida."

I spread hot jelly on the other half of my bagel. "What kind of person would vandalize turtle nests?"

"The eggs are considered a delicacy and aphrodisiac. Bars in the Cayman Islands sell them in shot glasses with Tabasco. It says here that turtle eggs sell for as much as five dollars apiece."

"Ouch, that's steep."

"The price is nothing. It's a misdemeanor to possess the eggs of loggerhead turtles and a felony to destroy them. A guy in West Palm Beach was sentenced to five years for possessing the eggs."

"West Palm? Those rich people will try anything."

"Yeah." Ruthie took a sip of her coffee and gazed at me over the rim of the cup. "By the way, I know what you were thinking earlier."

Earlier? I blinked, baffled.

"There was nothing wrong with my wearing a wedding gown to Old South. It was a masquerade ball."

Oh, *that* earlier. I gulped down guilt. Fortunately Ruthie let the subject drop and went back to reading the paper. I nibbled my bagel, waiting for her next pearl of wisdom. A consummate news junky, if Ruthie wasn't reading something—even a cereal box—she was listening to talk radio or watching television newscasts. And, she delighted in sharing the knowledge so we would be informed. Where was she when Zack was running around on me? I wish she'd informed me about that.

"There were a record number of manatees at Blue Springs last year," Ruthie said a few minutes later. "Blue Springs isn't far, just past Cassadaga. We should go over there, don't you think? I'd like to see the manatees."

The mention of Cassadaga reminded me of our psychic readings and I realized Ruthie hadn't said anything about her call home. "I meant to ask, is everything all right in Atlanta?"

"Fine. Mr. Wong has things firmly in hand, including the housekeeper next door."

Mr. Wong had been in the Edwards' employ for as long as I could remember and had to be close to eighty himself. "Mr. Wong is having an affair?"

"I think so. He's always had an eye for the ladies, but he seems especially partial to Hilda, who works for our neighbor. Of course, it may simply be that Hilda's close. Mr. Wong doesn't get around as well as he used to. Poppa offered to buy him one of those motorized scooters, but he'd have nothing to do with it. Said he'd accept one when he stopped catching twenty-year-olds." She chuckled. "Big talker."

"They're all like that. It's testosterone." I thought of little Zack and his buddies. As mere toddlers boys swaggered around, bragging. Not to mention hitting each other over the head with their toys, running into walls, chasing dogs, and generally creating chaos. It was then that I realized there truly was a hormonal component to behavior. Little girls played quietly with dolls and tea sets. Boys? Get out of the way. "Did you talk to your father?"

"Poppa didn't have much to say. Poor thing, he's starting to get confused. He thought I was Jo Ruth, kept asking me how school was going."

I let out a long sigh. My parents were still in good health, though I knew my time was coming. "That's tough."

She looked sad, and I thought I saw her lip quiver. "He's in no pain, and actually pretty happy. I guess it's true that ignorance is bliss. It could be worse—"

"Nothing could be worse than this headache." Penny Sue rounded the corner holding her head, face contorted in an agonized grimace. "Ibuprofen, please," she whimpered pitifully. I found the bottle in her purse and handed her a glass of water. She swallowed four pills and shuffled to the sofa. I put a damp paper towel over her forehead. "I'm never drinking again," she said, holding the paper towel in place with both hands. "If I ever so much as mention wine, shoot me."

I grinned to myself. Ten bucks said she'd be having a glass by evening. Yet, I did feel sorry for her. Penny Sue liked her wine, but normally didn't overdo. If only she'd eaten something, she probably wouldn't feel so bad. "How about some toast or a bagel? You need to get something in your stomach."

"Oooo, I can still taste that coconut cream pie."

Good, she remembered the pie. There was hope.

She wiped her face with the paper towel and handed it to me. I understood the unspoken plea. I rinsed the compress in cold water.

"Wait," Ruthie stopped me before I could take it back. She ran to our bedroom and returned with a small dropper bottle. Ruthie squirted the liquid on the compress.

"What is that?" I asked.

"A flower remedy." Ruthie turned the bottle so I could see the name: Rescue Remedy. "It's good for grave situations: heart attack, stage fright, accidents—"

"Massive hangovers. Put on an extra dose." I eyed the small container, then glanced at Penny Sue. "Does it come in a larger size?"

"Like what, a gallon jug?" Ruthie chuckled.

I placed the compress back on Penny Sue's forehead. She smiled appreciatively.

"What time is it? I'm supposed to have lunch with Lyndon at noon."

"Eight-thirty," I said. Penny Sue groaned.

The phone rang and Ruthie leaped to get it. "Penny Sue, it's Woody. He's returning your call."

She struggled to a sitting position. "Oh crap, I think I'm going to throw up."

In fact, Penny Sue did not puke and actually managed to talk to Woody, although the call was remarkably brief. "Jerk," Penny Sue declared as she hung up the phone. "He told us to get the license number if we see the pickup again. Leigh, I think I will have some toast." She sat next to Ruthie at the bar.

"Did he say anything about the investigation?" Ruthie asked. "What about the test results for the gun?"

Penny Sue crossed her arms on the counter and lay her head down. "He didn't say. He's trying to torment me."

I slid the plate of toast in front of her. Woody wasn't the only one; Penny Sue was doing a good job of torturing herself.

The phone rang again at nine.

"Mars is conjuncting Mercury," Ruthie said, as if that pearl explained some deep, dark secret about Alexander Graham Bell's jingling invention.

It told me zip, zilch, nada. I answered the telephone, it was my realtor. Our house had made the cute young couple's short list. I got a strangely sick feeling at the news. I should be happy, right? Sell the house, get rid of Zack and all those rotten memories ... except, damn it, there was a whole raft of good memories there.

Who were these people? Did they deserve such a house with so many wonderful features? Could they take care of my crepe myrtle? Would they recognize that the evergreens in the back-yard were our Christmas trees from years-gone-by? Twenty-two, one for every year we'd been in the house. Did they know you had to prune roses and dust them for aphids and fungus? Would they smile at Ann and Zack, Jr.'s handprints in the cement on the patio?

The handprints! There was no way I was leaving those precious little fingers behind. I'd hire someone to remove that part of the concrete. Cement was cement, right? Cut it out and fill the hole. Though, it would probably look tacky. I could put in a decorative tile. Or, a carved flagstone with a sweet saying; I'd seen them at the garden shop. Something inspiring like: *Bless this Home*, *Seize the Day*, *Eat Shit and Die*. What difference did it make? Strangers weren't getting my babies' handprints.

"—throw in the refrigerator and drapes?" My realtor was saying.

That snot-nosed couple sure was greedy. They wanted everything. Well, they couldn't have it.

The realtor continued, "I've already talked to your husband. He has no problem with it."

My husband. My voice turned to ice. "Ex-husband. I'll include the refrigerator and drapes on the first floor, nothing more." Feeling furious, I hung up the receiver and turned on Ruthie. "What's this stuff about Mars and Mercury?"

* * *

"Penny Sue must have a liver the size of Texas," I commented under my breath.

Ruthie and I watched through the screen door as she got into the cab. Though we assured her we were not leaving the premises, she insisted on taking a taxi so we'd have use of her car. Penny Sue paused before shutting the door and wiggled her fingers in our direction. "Toodles."

"Toodles?" I echoed, rolling my eyes.

Ruthie waved as the Silver Bullet cab pulled out of the parking lot. "I think that's her aristocratic persona. Warming up for Lyndon."

I closed and locked the front door. "She never ceases to amaze me. This morning I would have bet money that she'd have to cancel her date. Then, a few pills, a little toast, and she's ready to boogie. What's her secret?" We picked up our beach bags and chairs, and headed out the back door.

"The secret is M-A-N," Ruthie explained. "She's a hopeless romantic. Penny Sue isn't kidding when she talks about finding Prince Charming; she's really looking for him. Her only problem is she thinks everyone she meets fits the bill. I can't tell you how many times I've heard her say that she's finally found her soul mate." We planted our chairs at the edge of the surf and sat down. Ruthie chuckled. "Best I can figure, Penny Sue was a man with a harem in a previous life."

"Do you believe in that?"

"Penny Sue with a harem? It fits."

"No, soul mates. Do you think there's a perfect partner for everyone?" Was there a perfect mate for me somewhere? At one time I thought it was Zack, but that had proven to be a gross mistake.

Ruthie pulled her T-shirt over her head. She was wearing a floral two piece which showed off her slim, pale body. Her stomach was perfectly flat. I folded my arms over my paunch self-consciously.

"Yes and no," she replied, smearing on suntan lotion. "I think there is such a thing as soul mates, although I don't believe everyone has one in each lifetime."

I dug into my beach bag for my own sun block. "Why is that?"

"I think each of us is born with an agenda. You know, something we need to accomplish or learn. For some the goal requires a helpmate—it's sort of a joint purpose. Others can do their thing alone. It doesn't mean those people won't have relationships, just that they don't need a partner to fulfill their destiny."

Destiny. I didn't have a clue what mine was. I looked out across the ocean, a vast expanse of ... what? Calm on the surface, movement underneath—a dolphin arched over the water—and life. Perhaps it *was* time for me to do something different. But what? And, how did one go about finding their purpose? "Do you know what your life purpose is?"

Ruthie sank back, eyes closed, and grinned. "Not sure. Perhaps I'll move to Cassadaga and become a medium."

I tilted my face to the sun. Boy, wouldn't that be something.

We dozed peacefully in the warm sun until the ocean got pissed. Or, so it seemed. One minute soaring euphorically on gentle breezes; the next, swallowed by a teeth-chattering swell. Clawing for life. Gasping for breath. Okay, clawing for life might be a slight exaggeration, but we did gasp for air. The water was cold, absolutely frigid! We blasted out of the chairs like we were jet propelled and dragged our stuff toward the dunes. A small group of mostly senior citizens were already there. They were placing a wreath on the turtle mound where I'd stumbled over Rick's body.

"Did you know him well?" I asked.

A small woman with short gray hair, probably in her seventies, answered. "Not too well; Rick had only been with us for a couple of months. New to the area. But, he loved the turtles. Volunteered to come out before dawn to relocate the nests. Too dangerous to do it in the daytime; the birds, you know. Besides, the hot sun dries out the eggs."

Daytime had its dangers, but night obviously had some too, I thought. "Any idea why someone would want to kill him?"

The little woman clenched her fists as tears welled in her eyes. "The H. M. don't need a special reason. They're just mean. They did it, they did it for sure."

"The H.M.?"

"Hate mongers. The turtle haters. Only, they don't just loathe turtles, they despise everything. Shoot arrows at sea gulls, leave them wounded to die. Kidnap pets and torture them. Race their trucks up and down the beach, belching smoke and tossing beer bottles in the ocean so little kids cut their feet on the glass." The woman grew more and more agitated as she talked until the veins in her neck stood out like taunt cords. Alarmed, I stepped back. "Why, I heard one of their gun molls was taking pot shots at people right over there the other day." She pointed to our parking lot. "I'll bet that hussy killed Rick."

Ruthie and I exchanged horrified looks. Gun moll? Hussy? The woman sounded like a 1940 detective novel, which would have been funny except that she was talking about Penny Sue.

"I tell you they're an evil menace to us, to everyone." She started to cry. "Murderers. The H. M. did it. Murderers."

Another woman from the group stepped forward to comfort her. "Calm down, Gerty. It'll be all right."

I smiled soothingly. I had to steer Gerty away from Penny Sue. "The H. M. Is that a gang or something?" I couldn't tell if the woman was talking in philosophical generalities or referring to a specific group.

A red-headed woman about my age replied, "It's not a formal thing, like the Hell's Angels. There's a small core of mean ones who whip up the locals with their hateful talk. You know, a lot of old-timers regard driving on the beach as an inalienable right."

Except for a few places in North Carolina, I couldn't think of other areas that still allowed that. "How does that fit in with the turtles?"

"The green, leatherback and loggerhead turtles are endangered," a gaunt man pushing eighty answered. "The cars and motor-cycles destroy their nests and crush the hatchlings."

"I wouldn't think the cars would be great for little kids, either," Ruthie commented.

"They're not. There's a death almost every year, but the driving advocates never talk about that. Anyway, the county banned driving on half the beach in a compromise settlement to a federal lawsuit."

I looked around at the wide, pristine expanse.

The red-head noticed my confusion. "Motor vehicles are out-lawed on this stretch of beach. The driving ban runs south from Twenty-Seventh Street. Walk north, past there sometime; you'll see wall-to-wall cars."

Ruthie motioned at the wreath the group had placed next to the mound. "Did Rick have family?"

"The police asked that," the elderly man answered. "Apparently they're having a hard time finding his next of kin. We don't know of any, Rick never talked about himself. The poor guy deserves a decent burial, though. If the Sheriff doesn't find his relatives, we're going to take up a collection. We figure it's the least we can do."

Ruthie nodded solemnly. "If it comes to that, we'd like to help out."

I glanced at the wreath and then to our condo at the top of the dune. A man was shot to death a mere hundred, hundred-fifty feet from our unit. Yes, I wanted to make sure Rick got a decent burial. But more than that, I wanted someone to find the killer and lock him away from us.

Chapter 8

Penny Sue returned a little after three. By then we'd moved to the deck so we could be closer to the bathroom. Ruthie was wearing herself out running back and forth. I was going to broach the subject of the pee-urgency pill that was advertised on television, but stopped myself when I realized that all the peeing and going back and forth was probably how Ruthie stayed slim.

Penny Sue bounced out to the deck, full of herself, grinning from ear to ear. She brushed my feet to one side and sat at the end of the lounge chair. I was reading *Midnight in the Garden of Good and Evil*. Though I'd seen the movie with Kevin Spacey, I'd somehow missed the book when it first came out. I'd gotten to the part where Joe Odom was hot-wiring the electric meter at his pilfered abode when Penny Sue sat down. She looked like the cat who'd swallowed the canary. I wondered how long she could last if we didn't ask about her date. I stealthily moved my arm behind the book so I had a view of my watch and winked at Ruthie. She caught my drift.

It took exactly one minute and ten seconds for the exciting details to bubble up and spew forth. "He has his own chef. A captain, first mate, and *chef*. Isn't that divine?"

I marked my place and lowered the book. "That explains why he didn't eat last night at The Riverview."

She let out a heavy sigh. I could tell she was winding up for high drama. "You wouldn't believe his yacht. All plush carpet, polished teak and marble. It's decorated in a South Pacific motif. The living room is huge with bamboo furniture covered in silk. The dining room has a gorgeous round table inlaid with mother of pearl. It seats ten. No telling how much that thing cost, Lyndon said it was an antique. There are three bedrooms, all king and queen-sized, and the master suite has a hot tub for two!"

"Only a hot tub? No indoor pool?" I needled. Considering she'd been on death's door hours earlier, I guess I should have cut her some slack. Though, she'd made a remarkable recovery. Perhaps Ruthie's Rescue Remedy really did work.

"Smart aleck." Penny Sue poked my thigh. Hard.

Ruthie gave me the don't-get-her-riled expression and changed the subject. "What did you have for lunch?"

Penny Sue reared back, squashing my feet. "A heavenly tarragon chicken salad on croissant, pasta medley, fruit cup (fresh, of course), a scrumptious chocolate mousse, and champagne." The last word was mumbled.

"You had champagne?" I extricated my feet and formed my thumb and index finger in the shape of a gun. "Pow. You said we should shoot you if you ever drank wine again."

Penny Sue folded her arms defensively. "I couldn't be rude. Thomas, the chef, had gone to so much trouble and, I didn't have much, just a few sips. Besides, champagne isn't wine, it's, well, champagne."

I shook my head. Penny Sue was incorrigible. "What's Daddy Warbucks do for a living?" I asked.

"I'm not sure. I suspect it's inherited wealth. Lyndon seems to have been everywhere, though he spends a lot of time in the Caribbean, especially the Caymans. You'll love this, Ruthie: he's into New Age. Traveled to most of the power spots. The pyramids, Macchu Picchu, Sedona, Easter Island—Lyndon's seen it all. He even knew about Cassadaga."

"Did you tell him about your reading?" Ruthie asked.

"Pu-leeze. I am many things, but stupid's not one of them. Think I want to scare him off?" Penny Sue stood up. I flexed my toes to get the circulation going again. "What's that?" She asked, pointing toward the wreath.

Ruthie admonished me with her eyes.

I understood. "The Turtle Patrol put it there in Rick's honor." I filled her in on the Turtle Patrol and Hate Mongers, conveniently leaving out Gerty's reference to the Hussy Gun Moll. "The Patrol plans to collect money for a funeral if Rick's relatives aren't found."

"I'd chip in. Did you get the names of the members of the patrol?"

"No, but they come by here every morning. All we have to do is get up early."

Penny Sue cut her eyes at me reprovingly.

Dumb comment. Penny Sue was the person who's favorite refrain was: Chickens get up early, civilized people don't. In college, she wouldn't take a class that met before ten o'clock even though it meant she had to go an extra semester to get enough credits to graduate. She was late to her first wedding because she'd overslept. (An eleven o'clock wedding, what was she thinking?) No, if the Turtle Patrol was going to be contacted, Ruthie or I would be the ones to do it. Besides, it was probably advisable that we keep Penny Sue and Gerty as far apart as possible.

"I went to one of those parties." Penny Sue bent forward and thumped the back of my book.

"What?" Another one-hundred-eighty degree turn. The workings of Penny Sue's mind were a marvel. Either a few neurons were missing or her lobes had connections and cross connections that nobody else possessed.

"Jim Williams' Christmas party. Sydney knew him," she said smugly.

Jim Williams was the subject of *Midnight in the Garden of Good and Evil*, played by Kevin Spacey in the movie. Renowned throughout Savannah for his lavish lifestyle and impeccable taste, invitations to Williams' parties were a coveted prize. That Jim murdered his gay lover made no difference. Right up until Jim's death from a heart attack, Savannah's privileged elite clamored to be among the chosen few at Williams' parties. Sydney had apparently been chosen. He was Penny Sue's second husband, the movie producer who turned out to be bisexual.

Ruthie broke in, "Before or after the murder?"

Penny Sue stroked her forehead as if trying to conjure up the memory the way a stranded castaway might summon a genie from a bottle that washed up on the shore. Maybe that was the answer to Penny Sue's mind, I thought. There was someone else inside her head!

"In the middle, I think. Seems like the murder had taken place, but everyone still thought Jim was innocent."

"Was he as charming as they say?"

Penny Sue smiled—that thin, crooked smirk that said she was thinking of something devilish. "Absolutely. But he had this friend, Attila, who was the master courtier." Her smile grew wider.

"Come on, Penny Sue. What happened?"

"I had on a particularly low-cut dress. That was during the period when I couldn't understand why Sydney wasn't more affectionate. I'd bought a lot of sexy underwear, wore tight clothes, rented porno flicks—generally made a fool of myself trying to get his attention. Little did I know Sydney preferred three-piece suits. Anyway, my dress had a plunging neckline and I had on one of those push up bras ..." She stopped, a wide grin plastered on her face.

"And ..." I prodded.

"I guess Attila had had a few drinks. He leaned over to kiss my hand, but licked my breast instead." She giggled. "That man was a real trendsetter. Before the night was over men were licking women's boobs left and right. One of the best parties I ever went to."

"Which reminds me, I've got to call Party Hearty to see if they have the invitations. Shirley was going to have a high school student take them around to our neighbors. They need to get them out. Two days isn't much notice for a party, though this is only cocktails. It's not like a Jim Williams do." She turned to go into the house.

The party. I'd forgotten all about it. "Wait," I called after her. "What are you going to wear to the party?"

She replied over her shoulder, wiggling her fanny. "Something low cut."

Every ocean resort has to have a few seafood restaurants. New Smyrna Beach is no exception. On beachside (the narrow strip of barrier island sandwiched between the ocean and Intracoastal Waterway) there are two longstanding favorites: Norwood's Fine Seafood and JB's Fish Camp. The names say it all.

The first thing visitors see when they hit the island from the South Causeway Bridge is Norwood's, a sprawling stucco and stone structure with a tin roof nestled in a stand of pines, palms, and oaks. Known for its extensive menu and 1,400 varieties of wine, Norwood's is almost ways packed with patrons who drive Buicks, Continentals, Mercedes and SUV's. Further down Highway A1A in Bethune Beach, JB's Fish Camp is perched on Mosquito Lagoon. It, too, is a sprawling building with a tin roof, though it is known for its ample selection of beer. The parking lot is littered with oyster shells (whole) and typically full of motorcycles, pickup trucks, boat trailers and utility vans.

We decided on JB's for dinner. Penny Sue wanted to go back to The Riverview (wonder why?), but Ruthie and I convinced her it would look like she was chasing Lyndon and desperate to boot. Desperate was the word that finally won her over. Thank goodness. I, for one, had enjoyed about all the rich food I could stand for a while. Plain, simple fare; that's what my system needed.

And I got it. JB's decor was old time, fish-camp rustic. We sat at a picnic table covered in Kraft paper with a roll of paper towels in lieu of napkins. Tartar sauce, ketchup, and cocktail sauce in plastic squirt bottles rounded out the traditional setup of salt, pepper, and hot sauce. Our wine was served in plastic cups. Greasy fingerprints dotted the menus.

"Food must be good," Penny Sue observed.

"How can you tell?"

She held up her menu which was mottled with thumb prints and streaks of a brown substance, probably cocktail sauce. "The person who had this was really chowing down. Wonder what they had."

"Probably seafood," I said dryly. Penny Sue curled her lip in a mock sneer.

The meal would have been perfect except for two inebriated rednecks at the next table who kept trying to flirt. One had dark curly hair pulled back in a pony tail, the other had stringy blond hair, brown teeth and needed a bath in the worst way.

"Whew, that boy is stinky," Ruthie said under her breath as she scooted as far away from him as possible.

"The catfish is the best thing on the menu," Stinky declared loudly. We all pointedly ordered something else.

"Where are you girls from? There's a good band down at the Breakers. How long y'all staying? Wanna take a ride on my motorcycle?" There was an endless stream of inane remarks. We started out responding with clipped, polite statements. Then,

"You look like a girl who loves hush puppies," that said to Penny Sue. I was glad she didn't have her gun. She shot Stinky a look that would have killed a sober person. That's when we started ignoring them all together. But it was hard.

The food was greasy and good. I pressed my thumb on the Kraft paper when I finished. It left an oily spot in spite of the fact that I'd already gone through a half dozen paper towels.

We finished eating and called for the check. Penny Sue disgustedly counted out two twenties and a ten. "I think you'd better cut them off," she whispered to the waitress as we pushed past.

We made a quick stop in the ladies' room (Ruthie absolutely could not pass one without going in) then headed out the door. The parking lot was packed. Rows had appeared where none existed before and we paused to get our bearings. Clearly none of us had had past lives as Indian scouts, because it took a fair amount of wandering around for us to find the bright yellow car.

Penny Sue hung a left on A1A/Turtlemound Road and headed back toward the condo. We were chattering happily when Penny Sue broke in with a "Crap!"

"I've got two motorcycles right on my bumper," she said angrily. "People talk about cars following motorcycles too closely, half of them are just as bad. Idiots. If I were to suddenly stop those guys wouldn't have a chance."

Ruthie was sitting in the front seat and turned around to look. "One's pulling out. I think they're going to pass."

"Good," Penny Sue said. The motorcycle pulled alongside and stayed there. Penny Sue slowed down, but rather than dart ahead, the bike held back. "What the—" She glanced at the bike from the corner of her eye. "Darn. It's the redneck with the pony tail from JB's."

"The restaurant must have taken your advice and cut them off," I said.

"And now they're ticked off," Ruthie added.

Penny Sue tightened her grip on the steering wheel and set her jaw. The motorcycle traveling abreast of us had started to drift toward the car. Penny Sue edged over. The cycle moved closer still. "He's trying to run us off the road," Penny Sue said and floored it. The Mercedes lurched ahead, yet the bike kept pace. Stinky, on our bumper, pulled alongside, too. They were hooting and hollering and acting like drunken fools. Our speedometer crept up to sixty-five.

Then, four bright lights appeared from gods-know-where, illuminating the back of the car. I turned around and squinted to see. It was a pickup truck with spotlights mounted on the bumper. And, the truck was red! "Oh no, that red truck is behind us," I exclaimed.

"Oh, God. Oh, God," Ruthie cried nervously. Then, "Om-m-m. Om-m-m." The sound bounced around the interior of the car. Ruthie was chanting.

"What the heck are you doing?" Penny Sue demanded.

"Setting up a protection field."

"Tone it down, will you? I need to think."

"Let her think, Ruthie. Let her think." My heart was racing, pounding in my throat. Turtlemound was a two-lane road with numerous cross streets. At any moment a car could pull out and at our velocity—the speedometer was approaching seventy—we'd all be goners.

Stinky must have thought the same thing. He pulled in front of us and started to slow down. Pony Tail was still beside us, and the truck was on our bumper. We were hemmed in; we had to slow down. "They're making their move," Penny Sue said through gritted teeth. "Hold on." She pulled the steering wheel right. I braced for a crash.

"OM-M-M," Ruthie screeched.

The car skidded across a side street and into the unpaved lot of a bait shop. Caught off guard, the motorcycles and truck flew by. A wave of relief swept through me, then my eyes grew wide. We were headed for the front door of the store! Spewing a rooster tail of sand, the car pulsed spastically as the antilock brakes battled to halt our forward progress. I braced myself for the second time—the glass storefront was coming up fast. But Penny Sue drove like a stock car pro. She took her foot off the brake pedal and jerked the steering wheel hard left. The car did a three-hundred-sixty twirl and stopped dead. Ruthie squealed.

Before I'd even caught my breath, Penny Sue had punched the emergency button on the cell phone and was heading the car back to JB's. The emergency operator would have the police meet us there. We parked close to the front door and waited. A few minutes later, a Volusia County Sheriff's car showed up. A stocky officer in his forties ambled over to the Mercedes. Thankfully, he was not one we'd met before.

Deputy Ted Moore took our statement and seemed genuinely concerned. "Let me get this straight. The driver of the red pickup had a fight with the man found murdered on the beach, one day before the body was discovered?"

We nodded.

"You think that same truck was following you a couple of days ago, and you reported it to Mr. Woodhead." I thought I detected a suppressed sneer when he mentioned Woody's name, which told me that Woody wasn't one of his favorites, either. "The men riding the motorcycles had dinner here tonight and harassed you. Did you see the driver of the truck in the restaurant?"

"He may have been there, though we didn't see him," Penny Sue responded. "The place was crowded."

Deputy Moore made a notation, then called the station to request a back-up. "I'm going to interview the staff here at JB's to see if I can get a make on those bikers. They sound like locals, so there's a good chance someone knew them. In any event, they might have paid their bill with a credit card. I'll have the other car escort you ladies home, since the guy in the pickup knows where you live."

The blood drained from my face. That possibility had never entered my mind. Judging by Ruthie's slack jaw, she hadn't thought of it either. Penny Sue was stoic, showing no emotion at all.

Our escort arrived a few minutes later, and we pulled out of the restaurant's parking lot for the second time. "So, what do you think?" I asked Penny Sue.

She stared straight ahead. "Deputy Moore's kinda cute, and he isn't wearing a wedding band."

Chapter 9

We had just stepped out on the deck with our morning coffee when the old woman screamed. Penny Sue almost swallowed the cigarette she was about to light. "Magod, someone's hurt."

There was a moment of indecision where the three of us stared at one another like wide-eyed fools, each trying to calculate the danger quotient and decide whether we should scurry inside and pretend we hadn't heard anything, or go to investigate. There was also the problem that each of us knew the other had heard the scream. While we might get away with feigning ignorance to outsiders, we couldn't fake it with ourselves. It was one of those crazy situations where each knew the others knew, and the others knew we knew they knew ... So there we stood, stuck in fear and circular reasoning.

The second howl jolted us into action. We raced down to the beach where four members of the Turtle Patrol stood forlorn. The sand was littered with dozens of leathery orbs, pinkish-tan in color and slightly larger than ping pong balls. The wreath the group had placed in Rick's honor the previous day lay twenty feet away; battered, waterlogged, and half buried in the sand.

Gerty, the little old lady who'd told us about the Hate Mongers, was the one doing the wailing. I said a silent prayer she wouldn't say anything about the Hussy taking pot shots.

"They killed Rick, and now this. I told you they were evil—" Gerty said something else that was garbled by a sob "—call the media."

"That'll only make matters worse, Gerty," the older gentleman we'd met the previous day responded. "We've discussed this before. It will alienate the authorities, make them look bad."

She swept her hand at the scattered remains of the turtle nest. A seagull had grasped an egg in its beak and was shaking it violently, trying to get at the precious little critter inside. "Make them look bad? What about my babies, Robert?"

"Some nests simply never make it," the man said. "We all know that. This is just one of them."

Fists clenched, the old woman backed away. "Look the other way, turn the other cheek, again? Those hoodlums are slaughtering the turtles, wiping them off the face of the Earth. Now, they're coming after us ..."

I held my breath, fearing her next statement would be about the Gun Moll.

"We've got to take a stand. If we don't, where will it end?" Gerty planted her feet defiantly.

I exhaled. Safe. For now.

Robert shrugged. He had the presence of a man who'd been a mid-level executive, who'd seen his share of conflict and strife, which he'd hoped to escape by coming to Florida and ministering to turtles. Exercise, sun, doing a good deed; idyllic, he'd probably thought. Now Gerty was throwing a wrench in the works. "The news media blows things out of proportion, we've talked about that. We've finally found some allies in government, but they won't be allies long if we sic reporters on them. No, Gerty, we've got to take the long view, follow the path of least resistance."

They glared at each other; two stubborn septuagenarians, each intent on running the show. I imagined this wasn't the first time Gerty and Robert had squared off. The fact that no one else in the group uttered a word spoke volumes: they knew better than to get caught between these two.

Ruthie broke the impasse. She dropped to her knees and scooped up a handful of sand with an egg on top. "Can't we put them back?"

"They will never hatch now. The nest was already moved once, they've been exposed too long," Gerty replied.

Robert followed Ruthie's cue. "Maybe not. At least they'll have a chance."

I could tell Gerty was annoyed by Robert's opposition, yet couldn't argue with his logic. She reluctantly agreed. "Don't touch them if you can help it."

We all went into action scooping up the leathery spheres. I was crawling around on my hands and knees, shooing birds and gathering eggs, when a big foot appeared out of nowhere. A big foot, just like Rick's. To say I almost fainted is an understatement. My heart did a triple flip followed by a belly flop.

"Hey, you all right? I didn't mean to startle you," a male voice said.

Crouched on all fours, I forced my face skyward. It was the guy from the bar at The Riverview, our next door neighbor. I let out a long sigh and sat back in the sand. My heart was still racing. "I'll be okay," I mumbled.

He squatted beside me. "We met at the bar the other night, right?"

I nodded. My pulse was finally beginning to slow.

"What are you guys doing?" he asked, looking around.

Penny Sue answered. "What does it look like? We're reburying these turtle eggs."

The man stood to face Penny Sue. "Al Maroni," he said, offering his hand. "I'm staying in the condo next to yours."

Her demeanor changed instantly. Penny Sue brushed her hand on her shorts and smiled demurely. She took his hand and answered in her sultry, Southern voice, "Penny Sue Parker. These are my friends Leigh Stratton," she motioned at me, still sitting in the sand, "and Ruthie Nichols." She swept her arm in a wide arc at the rest of the crowd, "And this is Gerty, Robert and the Turtle Patrol. Vicious vandals destroyed this nest. We're trying to save the poor little critters."

"Can I help?" Al asked.

"That's very kind." Penny Sue knelt in the sand. "Scoop up the egg with sand under it, so you don't touch it. See." She plunged her hand into the sand and carefully lifted an egg which she placed in the nest.

Al nodded and did as instructed. With his help, we finished in less than five minutes. Robert thanked us for our assistance, and the patrol headed up the beach. Al said goodbye and jogged off in the other direction.

"Nice guy," Penny Sue mumbled, watching his trim form retreat into the distance.

"Yeah, I just hope this isn't an omen for the rest of the day," Ruthie said when we got back to the deck.

"Why?" Penny Sue countered. "He's good looking and nice."

"I didn't mean Al—I meant screams and disasters," Ruthie said.

"I for one have had about all the excitement I can stand. Much more and I'll have to take up smoking." I nodded at Penny Sue who'd just blown out a long drag of her cigarette.

Ruthie frowned. "It's almost like we're cursed. There's a dark, heavy feeling around this condo. Negative vibes."

Penny Sue flicked her ash and took another long pull. "That's your department, sugar. Can't you do an exorcism or something?"

Ruthie's brows knitted. "I'd need a smudge stick."

"An eyeliner? I think I have a brown one by Chanel."

"Not an eyeliner—incense. It's a Native American tradition for purifying places. Sage removes negative energy, and cedar attracts positive."

"We need a barrel of both. Check the kitchen, Leigh. Maybe there's some sage in the spice rack. Would that work?"

"Yes, though it would be good to have the cedar, too. I've seen combinations of cedar, sage, and sweetgrass; we probably could have gotten some at Cassadaga. A shame we didn't think of this earlier."

I returned to report that oregano was the only spice in the kitchen and it looked dried up.

"Naa," Penny Sue said. "That would probably only work for Italians. We don't have to go all the way to Cassadaga, I saw a New Age incense and candle shop on Flagler Avenue when I went to Lyndon's for lunch. We'll try there first, it's only a few miles away."

The rest of the morning was a blur of piddling stuff. Ruthie said it had something to do with Mercury, Mars, Uranus, and gravitational fields like the Moon's effects on tides. The explanation was too deep for me so early in the morning. The discussion was definitely one which required a drink, or two, to make sense.

A call from Deborah, my next door neighbor in Atlanta, was the first manifestation of the mischievous planetary alignment. We'd been friends for years and had always made a point of keeping each other informed of our respective whereabouts, in case of an emergency. Everyone that mattered knew to call Deborah if they needed to find me. And that's what my daughter, Ann, had done when she couldn't reach me and I didn't return her messages.

"Sorry to bother you so early," Deborah led off. "Ann just called sounding pretty upset. She said she'd been trying to reach you for days. I told her you were vacationing with your old sorority sisters and gave her the phone number down there, but you may want to ring her up."

The dreaded phone call—I couldn't put it off any longer. The kids knew the divorce was imminent, yet it was still going to be hard to tell them it was final. Eighteen months of sadness, shame, and regret were all jumbled up in making that admission. I'd discussed this with one of my therapists, who'd pointed out that Zack was the one who had ended the marriage. He had broken the marriage vow, I hadn't, so I had no reason to feel ashamed.

But I did. I felt responsible for not making the marriage work. The nagging doubt that something I'd done or hadn't done had driven Zack over the line and deprived the kids of their happy home remained, no matter how much I tried to convince myself otherwise. My rational mind knew that wasn't true—if anything I'd been far too deferential with Zack. Yet, that female, old-fashioned, role-conscious, guilt-ridden part of my brain didn't buy it and gave me no peace, at least until recently. Truth be told, the craziness of the last few days had actually been a relief—

That realization hit me between the eyes. What was so special about the last few days? Chaos, danger ... my mind was off myself!

"While I've got you," Deborah went on, "I think there's something wrong with your sprinkler system. I haven't seen it running, and your lawn is beginning to turn brown."

The sprinkler? It had been running when we left; in fact, we'd had to dodge water as we loaded the car. What could have gone wrong? *The realtor.* "I think I know what happened. I'll take care of it. Thanks for calling, Deborah. I owe you one."

Ruthie noticed the exasperated look on my face. "Everything all right?"

"Can we smudge my realtor?"

The call to Ann went better than I expected. She wasn't the least bit shaken by the news that the divorce was final. If anything, she sounded relieved. Figuring I should finish it all while I had momentum, I dialed Zack, Jr.'s number in Vail, catching him before he left for work. I eased into the subject on the pretense of telling him where I was and how I could be reached. I'd given him the phone number when he took the bull by the horns.

"Isn't the divorce final yet?" he asked.

"As a matter of fact, it is. Last week."

"So you're down in Florida celebrating? Good for you, Mom. Gotta run, or I'll be late for work. Love you." He hung up. I sighed. I had great kids—why didn't I give them credit?

The next call was to my realtor. "That young couple is still on the hook," she bubbled. "It's down to your house and one other. But there's a small problem. They drove by the house yesterday and noticed the lawn was awfully brown. Do you think you could have cinch bugs?"

The positive wave I'd been riding crashed into a wall. I wanted to reach through the phone and grab her scrawny neck. At the very least I wanted to jump down her throat verbally. Fortunately, I remembered Ruthie's admonition about Mars, Uranus, and being hasty. I swallowed my initial response (It's brown, you fool, because *you* turned off the sprinkler) and opted for, "My neighbor called to say the sprinkler wasn't running. Is it possible," butter-melting-in-my-mouth sweet, "someone turned it off by accident?"

"Oh my, I don't know how that could have happened," she said in a sing-songy voice. "I do recall that Todd, the husband, was looking at it. I'll try to check into it today."

"Thanks, you do that."

Todd was looking at it. That was the last straw. I called Barkley Home Improvement, a Marietta outfit that had always done the repairs Zack never had time to do. Adam Barkley was a prince of a guy, a real Southern gentleman. I asked him to cut out the handprints on the patio and repair the hole. Adam said he'd get on it right away. Satisfied, I hung up the phone. Whatever happened, no one was getting my darling children's little hands.

The door bell rang as Ruthie emerged from our bedroom fully dressed. "Mars and Mercury," she said portentously.

I checked the clock. It was almost eleven, and I was still in my sweats. I scurried to the bedroom as Penny Sue answered the front door. It was Shirley from Party Hearty with the leftover invitations.

I showered and dressed in record time. I'd gotten some color on my face, so a little mascara and lipstick was all the makeup I needed. I pulled my hair back in a headband and put on a peach-colored, cotton short set. Reef Rider sandals completed my casual ensemble, as Penny Sue would say.

Though Penny Sue's concept of casual and my idea, like most other things, were as different as night and day. By Penny Sue's standards I was almost naked. No scarves, hats, or fancy belts. A gold chain and modest sapphire ring were my only jewelry. Accessories, accessories, Penny Sue harped at me all the time. It wasn't that I couldn't afford those niceties, all that stuff just bugged me. Superfluous clutter; things to clean, keep up with, pack, and haul around.

I stuffed my lipstick and powder into a blue leather bag and went into the living room. Penny Sue regarded me as if I'd just dropped in from outer space. "What?" I asked.

She motioned from the purse to the sandals.

Mercy me, they didn't match. "It's the beach, Penny Sue. Nobody cares."

She pinched her nose up in that haughty *I care* expression.

I stuck my tongue out at her and went to change purses. I hated giving in, but knew she'd hound me to death if I didn't. A small concession for a large return in peace-of-mind. I changed to a woven straw shoulder bag which earned a nod of approval from Her Highness, when the doorbell rang again. Ruthie was right—Mercury, Mars and Uranus were certainly in high gear today. Now what? I wondered.

It was Federal Express with a large package for Ruthie. She opened the box on the dining table and stared at the contents.

"What is it?" Penny Sue and I asked in unison, peering over her shoulder. The box contained what looked like a child's toy water cannon—the pump action kind kids play with in pools and on the beach. Only this one was gray and made of a material that was definitely not cheap plastic.

"What is it?" I asked again.

Ruthie opened a neatly folded letter with the corporate letterhead of Taser Technology, Inc. She read the letter, then let out a loud sigh. "Mr. Wong and Daddy are worried about our safety," she said quietly. "I mentioned Rick's murder to Mr. Wong. He promised not to tell Daddy, but apparently did. This is for our protection."

"We're supposed to protect ourselves with a Super Soaker squirt gun, a child's toy?" Penny Sue said.

"Not a squirt gun—a state-of-the-art liquid Taser. According to this," Ruthie thumped the letter, "this thing is cutting edge technology. Instead of shooting barbed probes on wires which deliver a shock that knocks attackers on their butts, this gun uses an electrified saline solution. That means it has multiple shots, a range of 25 feet and can stun more than one person. It's a prototype that isn't even on the market yet."

Penny Sue took the letter from Ruthie's hands, read it quickly, then handed me the letter and took the gun from the box. It was about a foot and a half long with a typical water cannon nozzle, trigger and bulbous reservoir for the fluid. She hefted it to test its balance. "This is really neat." Penny Sue's eyes shown with excitement. "How did your Dad get his hands on it?"

"Daddy supplied the start-up capital and was on the company's board. He must have called the president to ask this favor."

"The letter *is* signed by the company's president," I confirmed. "He says all you have to do is fill the reservoir with the enclosed bottle of saline, insert the rechargeable battery pack, and you're ready to go. No permit is required as long as it's used to protect one's home."

"How does it work?" Penny Sue asked.

I consulted the brochure in the bottom of the box. "This says the gun's low amperage charge is not enough to do permanent damage, but does scramble electrical signals from the brain. An attacker will be partially paralyzed as well as confused and unbalanced."

"Neat-o, let's load it." Penny Sue reached for the bottle of electrolyte.

"No," Ruthie said with uncharacteristic force. "I have bad feelings about this. We're in enough trouble already."

"Come on, Ruthie, it's a defensive weapon." Penny Sue slapped the battery pack into its slot and started to unscrew the bottle of electrolyte solution. "Since Woody still has my gun, I'd feel a lot safer with this around. The good thing about this gizmo is that it doesn't kill. Even Woody can't find fault with that."

"I don't know ..." Ruthie mumbled doubtfully.

"With all that's happened, I don't mind having it," I said sincerely.

Ruthie studied me, pulling on her ear, considering. "I guess it wouldn't hurt," she allowed slowly, "as long as we keep it here. We're not carrying it out with us."

"Sure," Penny Sue agreed, siting the Taser like it was a rifle. "We'd look like fools lugging this big thing around."

We put the Taser on the middle shelf of the linen closet in the hall, gathered our purses, and prepared to leave. We had just locked the front door when Deputy Moore arrived.

"Morning, ladies," he said with a smile that was movie star quality.

Penny Sue's bossy, hurry-up-girls demeanor instantly shifted to demure Georgia Peach.

"I wanted to make sure you were all right. No more problems last night, I hope?" he said casually.

Penny Sue gushed in the negative.

"I'm afraid I came up empty handed at JB's," Moore said. "Your bikers paid their bill in cash. No one recalled seeing them before, which means they're not locals. Most likely, they were passing through, and you'll never see them again."

"But the truck," I objected. "That was definitely not a chance encounter."

Deputy Moore smoothed down his thick, wavy hair; a nervous gesture which told me that he wasn't entirely committed to what he was about to say. "I've been giving that some thought. Red pickups with spotlights are very common in this area and the truck actually didn't do anything. It was the bikers that tried to run you off—"

Penny Sue's spine grew stiffer and stiffer as he spoke. The Georgia Peach was morphing into a Steel Magnolia.

"—the road. There's a good chance the truck was not the same one you saw before and may not have had anything to do with the bikers. The pickup could have been an innocent bystander."

"That was riding right on our bumper," Penny Sue said pointedly.

Deputy Moore met her eyes. "That was following too close."

Penny Sue folded her arms. "So, where does that leave us?" she asked icily.

The deputy looked away and cleared his throat. Another tell-tale sign he wasn't comfortable with the situation, I thought. Though, who wouldn't be antsy under Penny Sue's glacial scrutiny. If thoughts were things, as Penny Sue was fond of saying, Deputy Moore had just been hit by a bone-chilling blizzard.

"You need to be careful," he said, his voice softening. "Call me immediately if you see the bikers or truck again." He opened Penny Sue's car door for her, then closed it firmly. She started the car as we got in the other side. Penny Sue backed away slowly without another word, leaving Deputy Moore standing in the parking lot.

"What do you make of that?" Ruthie asked as we turned onto the main road.

"I think our friend Woody got to Moore and convinced him we are a bunch of hysterical women imagining things," Penny Sue said.

"That's a good sign."

"How so?" I asked.

"If Woody convinced Deputy Moore we are hysterical crackpots, then Woody must not believe we're dangerous criminals," Ruthie said.

"Yeah," Penny Sue said brightly.

Now, that was an entry for my diary: *On this day, Penny Sue Parker freely acknowledged she was a hysterical crackpot.*

"Which probably means the gun test results have come back negative, proving Penny Sue's innocence," Ruthie continued.

"Right," Penny Sue said. "And Woody hasn't had the decency to let me know or return my gun. He is small, you know that, small."

An image of Woody in plaid boxer shorts with his pale, knobby knees exposed popped into my mind. I laughed out loud.

"What's so funny?" Penny Sue asked.

"I was thinking of Woody with his pants down. That's the real issue, you know: Woody's afraid we do think he's small." There was a pause as the meaning sunk in, followed by a wave of hysterics. "Our problem is that one or more people are after us for some unknown reason, and the police aren't going to lift a finger to help."

Ruthie objected. "I think Deputy Moore would help. The emphasis on calling him was pretty obvious."

"I picked up on that, too," I said. "The key is that we have to call him with something. He won't or can't pursue the matter on his own—that was pretty clear. Which all boils down to one simple truth: If anything's going to be done, we'll have to do it ourselves."

But then, I thought, wasn't that the way it always happened?

Chapter 10

We stopped at Chases for a grouper sandwich, then swung by The Riverview on the way to the incense store so Penny Sue could deliver Lyndon's invitation. It was amazing how The Riverview seemed to be "on-the-way," no matter where we were going. Lyndon was not at home, much to Penny Sue's chagrin and my relief, yet Chef Thomas promised to personally place the calligraphic invite into his boss' hand.

We left the marina and took a right on Flagler, heading east toward the ocean. We hadn't gone far when we met a swarm of dancing soap bubbles. "The store's over there," Penny Sue said as she backed the Mercedes into a parking space across the street from the source of the bubbles. We paused at the window of Chris' Place which featured a variety of New Age paraphernalia, including smudge sticks and candles.

"Just what we need," Penny Sue said, starting for the door.

"Wait," Ruthie ordered, pointing to the brick sidewalk. Flagler Avenue, like many restored districts, had apparently sold commemorative bricks to help finance the street's restoration. While most bricks contained family names and proclamations of undying love for people and New Smyrna Beach, two positioned in front of the shop were real standouts. The first proclaimed "Starpeople Landing Zone!" while a second said "Good Vibes." Ruthie grinned. "This is a sign. I think we'll find exactly what we need in this shop."

We stepped through a cloud of bubbles into a world of sweet smells, lilting music, and a wide array of incense, oils, candles, books, imported coffee and New Age accessories. The shop was empty except for a pleasant blond who identified herself as Chris, and a round-faced, gray-haired woman standing by the window sniffing candles. As Chris helped Ruthie with smudge sticks, Penny Sue and I gravitated to the candle display.

"Smell this." Penny Sue thrust a wax cylinder into my face.

I took a whiff. The sweet scent of gardenias. "Nice," I responded, consulting the candle's label. "'Sensual Nights.' Who do you plan to share this with?" I asked, handing the candle back.

Penny Sue tittered. "Lyndon, who else?"

Who else? I didn't respond. We'd been in New Smyrna Beach less than a week and already Penny Sue had shown interest in an exterminator (rest his soul), a policeman (briefly), a yachtsman, and a neighbor on the beach. All the while, she had an Atlanta Brave and a Falcon on the hook back home—although with Penny Sue, it was hard to tell who was the hooker and who was the hookee. However that worked, she had two big jocks in the picture.

The gray-haired woman smiled at us. In her mid-sixties, the woman was slightly stooped, yet still cut an imposing figure. Her short gray hair and pixie bangs fringed a full face of porcelain skin. She wore a flowing lavender blouse over black stretch pants; and though her upper body was substantial, her legs looked child-like in the tight-fitting slacks. "That scent fits all of you, you're like sisters," she stated in a knowing tone.

"Sorority sisters," Penny Sue corrected.

The lady replied, "You've been together before—a harem in the Middle East." She turned away to study the book display. Penny Sue did a double take.

There's a good come on, I thought. Throw out a pithy comment, then look away. Reverse psychology. Make the unsuspecting mark ask for more. From the look on Penny Sue's face, she was about to do just that. "Are you going to buy any?" I asked Penny Sue to distract her from the strange woman.

"Sure," she replied, keeping her eyes on the old lady as she raked the entire stock of Sensual Nights off the shelf.

Ruthie appeared with an armful of what looked like broom straw bound with blue twine. "These are our smudge sticks," she announced. "Guaranteed to ward off hexes, evil spirits and other nasty stuff."

"Visualize a white light surrounding your condo when you smudge it."

It was the strange old lady again. Condo? That remark got our attention. The woman smiled sweetly and went back to perusing the books.

Ruthie looked to Chris and mouthed the words, "Is she psychic?" Chris winked and nodded in the affirmative. Ruthie wasted no time in introducing herself. "I'm Ruthie Nichols," she said, juggling the smudge sticks to offer her hand.

"Pauline Gilbert," the woman answered, taking Ruthie's hand in both of hers. She stayed that way for almost a minute before she released Ruthie with a sigh.

The gesture was not lost on Penny Sue, who rushed to Pauline's side, almost knocking over a display of Egyptian Pharaohs in the process. "Have you used smudge sticks before?"

Pauline raised her chin to bring her eyeglasses into focus on us. "From time to time."

"Do you think they work?"

"They do if you believe they will."

Penny Sue smiled complacently. "See. Just what I always say: you create your own reality. Right, Ruthie? Thoughts are things. What man can conceive, man can achieve. Shoot, we could probably burn oregano and get the same result."

"No, you couldn't. Oregano wouldn't have the same vibration," Pauline stated imperiously, shutting down Penny Sue's self-congratulatory prattle.

I was impressed. Anyone who shut down Penny Sue couldn't be all bad. Ruthie flashed Penny Sue an I-told-you-so smirk.

Ruthie wasted no time trying to drive home the advantage. "Don't cedar and sage have a higher vibration which bridges the gap between the Earth plane and the spirit world?"

Pauline shook her head. "I don't know about it being higher; cedar and sage are pleasing scents to the kind of spirits who will help you out. With oregano, you'd probably get a bunch of Italians."

Penny Sue elbowed Ruthie smugly.

Pauline went on, "Not that Italians wouldn't help you, especially if you're making spaghetti. It's just not the mind-set for clearing negativity. With the murder and all, you need some powerful spirits ..."

Our jaws dropped as one. None of us had mentioned the murder.

"... Have any candles with jasmine and sandalwood? That combination stimulates the pineal and pituitary glands, which strengthens intuition and the connection with the angelic realm. That would be good, especially now."

Penny Sue dumped her armload of Sensual Nights on the counter and consulted Chris, who led her to a shelf of cream-colored candles. Penny Sue added all of them to her pile.

While Penny Sue'd focused on the jasmine and sandalwood, Pauline's last statement struck me. "What did you mean by 'especially now?'" I asked.

"There are discordant forces around you. They come from a light-haired man. He's angry." Pauline closed her eyes, then nodded and frowned as if talking to a phantom.

"What do you see?" Ruthie asked anxiously, as a group of chattering tourists entered the shop.

"Can you get his name?" Penny Sue pressed.

Pauline's eyes popped open, and she consulted her watch. "There's too much commotion here for me to get a clear picture, and I have to get home. I'm teaching a class in less than an hour." She hooked her purse over her arm. "I have something that will help you with the smudging, if you want to walk over to my place."

Penny Sue snatched the smudge sticks from Ruthie and plopped them on the counter. "What do I owe you, Chris?" she asked in a rush. Then to Pauline, "Yes, any help you can give us would be terrific."

I was surprised by Penny Sue's intensity, not to mention her sudden interest in the occult. Though she continuously parroted Ruthie's sayings, I'd never taken Penny Sue seriously. I figured metaphysics was simply another lark, a colorful eccentricity, a fun role to play. Yet, I began to doubt that judgment as I watched her fumble with her wallet and credit card. Maybe Penny Sue did believe in metaphysics, or perhaps she was more concerned about the murder than she let on.

Pauline stood by the door, shifting from foot to foot impatiently.

"Be right there," Penny Sue called as she gathered up her purse and purchases.

Pauline walked out the door. We caught up with her on the street.

"Sorry to hold you up," Penny Sue said with uncharacteristic humility.

Pauline waved off the apology. "I figured I'd get a head start." She shifted her oversized macramé purse to the other arm. "My legs get stiff when I stand too long, start to have spasms. I knew you girls would catch up."

We followed her down the street for a couple of blocks. Pauline waved and traded niceties with everyone we met along the way. They all greeted her with a reverent, almost deferential, tone. They also gave us the blatant once-over as if we'd just dropped in from Mars. Little wonder—even I got a surreal feeling from the spectacle. Pauline lead the procession like a pontiff dispensing absolution. I was close on her heels, followed by Penny Sue and Ruthie who bore a striking resemblance to native bearers in an African safari with their colorful clothes and voluminous cargo of purses and packages.

"Here we are." Pauline pointed to a blue bungalow in need of a coat of paint. We followed her up splintered steps into the small house and another world. It was then that I knew we weren't the aliens, she was!

To our left was a kitchen that was unremarkable except for an old-fashioned chrome and Formica table (it had to date back to the fifties) and the fact that the counter was lined with dozens and dozens of jars: Mason jars, mustard containers, catsup bottles—an incredible hodge-podge of half-filled vessels with hand-lettered labels.

"Bat wings, eye of newt ..." I whispered. Penny Sue glared: *shut-up*.

To our right was the living room and unequivocal alien territory. A faded colonial-style sofa occupied one wall, with a threadbare recliner angled alongside. A coffee table covered with rocks and candles was in the center of the room, while a miniature waterfall gurgled on a table in front of the side window. In the far corner, a four-foot blond angel stood like a sentry. Probably a remnant of a Christmas long past, the angel held an electric candle which she raised and lowered rhythmically as her head rotated with a swishing sound.

I cut my eyes at Pauline, half afraid her head might spin around too, like the blond angel or the kid in *The*

Exorcist. I measured my distance to the door. Two steps, three at the most. If the old lady started throwing-up green slime, I was out of there. Penny Sue and Ruthie were the ones who wanted to come here; they could deal with vile vomit, pernicious puke, and Belial belch.

I shook myself out of my musing and looked up ... into Pauline's steel gray eyes. She was grinning with amusement. My cheeks flushed with the realization she knew what I'd been thinking.

"That's Alice," Pauline said, cocking her thumb toward the angel. "My roommate. Good company. Quite a conversationalist."

Alice. So this was Wonderland?

"Keeps an eye on things when I'm away," Pauline continued. "Likes to cook; bat wings are her specialty."

I smiled sheepishly, certain now the old lady had picked up my rude ruminations. Thankfully, she let it drop. Pauline's disdain was bad enough. If Penny Sue had read my thoughts, she would have poked my arm so hard, the bruise wouldn't fade for a month. Pauline probably knew that and was giving me a break. Fairness dictated that I return the favor. I made up my mind at that moment to suspend snide judgments of Pauline and the hereafter.

Pauline shuffled to a pine sideboard laden with all manner of stuff, and retrieved a pink piece of paper. It was an article entitled "Smudging with Sacred Herbs." She handed it to Penny Sue. "This should help. Like attracts like, you know. Your condo is negative, it's drawing bad luck to you. Smudge it with cedar and sage. But be sure to purify yourselves first."

Purify ourselves? Prune juice was the first thing that came to my mind. I tried not to make a face.

"Start by picking up feathers on the beach," the woman instructed.

Penny Sue scrunched her brow. "Feathers? Any particular kind?"

"Feathers take your wishes to heaven. Anything you find around your condo will do."

I wanted to interrupt, ask how Pauline knew we were staying in a condo—it was the second time she'd mentioned it—but thought better of it. The grand dame had given me a reprieve; no sense pushing my luck with questions and skepticism. Any of that would have to come from Penny Sue or Ruthie, I wasn't going to open my mouth. I was definitely having foot karma in a big way.

"Use the feathers to fan the smudge stick and direct the smoke. Rub your hands in it and massage it over your body. That cleanses your aura."

Good, no prunes. I hadn't been able to stomach them since I was about five, when I mistook them for big raisins and ate a whole box.

"Then take the smoldering smudge stick around and through your condo. Be sure to get everything: under furniture, in closets and cabinets."

"Should we chant or something?" Ruthie asked eagerly.

"That's okay, though not necessary."

Ruthie looked disappointed.

"The key is to hold pure thoughts. It's your pure intention that will eradicate any—" there was a knock at the door, "—evil." She glanced at her watch. "Sorry, it's time for my class."

"Wait," Penny Sue pleaded. "You said we were in danger from a light-haired man. Can you give us some details? Where would we find him?"

There was another rap on the door. Pauline reached in her pocket and retrieved a card. She paused a moment before giving it to Penny Sue. "At a bar; I see drinks, you know, like beer and wine. And, there's a coin with two heads … and a wheel. A shiny wheel, spinning."

* * *

"A double-headed coin. Shiny, spinning wheels. What do you make of that?" Penny Sue asked, once we returned to the car.

"I think the wheels refer to those motorcycles and it's that greaser who's angry," Ruthie said after a moment. "We gave him the cold shoulder and had his drinks cut off."

I nodded. "A light-haired man. Everyone we've run into has light hair—Zack, Lyndon, Rick, Pete, Stinky. Why, even the guy next door, Al Maroni, has sandy hair with gray streaks."

"Rick's out, unless we're getting bad vibes from the other side," Penny Sue said.

"And Zack's not here. Though the two-headed coin—two-faced—fits him to a tee."

"Which leaves us with Lyndon, Pete, Stinky and Al."

"It's not Lyndon," Penny Sue declared with a saucy wink. "No bad vibes there, and Pete and Al have no reason to be mad."

"Which takes us back to Stinky—and maybe the guy in the red pickup. I don't care what Moore says, I think Mr. Pickup Truck's a pal of the two guys from JB's," Penny Sue said. "He was trying to run us down, there's no doubt in my mind."

"Maybe Al knows who he is. After all, Mr. Pickup was at Al's condo when we arrived. He's probably a maintenance man or something," Ruthie offered.

"That's worth following-up." I turned to Penny Sue. "Was Al invited to the party?"

She replied, "Sure, all the neighbors were."

"Good. Ruthie and I will work on him. Now, what about the bar?"

"It has to be JB's," Penny Sue said.

I shook my head. "I don't know. We followed the pickup to Gilley's Pub 44. That's a big bikers' hangout."

Ruthie's brows knitted with concern. "Why do we want to find them? I think we should steer clear of those hoods."

"Just wait for them to track us down? No one's going to help us, Ruthie," I reminded her.

"Deputy Moore—"

"If we get something and take it to him. He's not going to lift a finger to help us on his own." Like Max Bennett, my worthless attorney. Or Woody. Or even my realtor. I felt my face grow hot. I was sick of being used, stewed, and abused. Not again, I vowed. "I, for one, am not going to roll over like a squashed bug," I said through gritted teeth, shaking my finger for emphasis. "We're going to track those guys down and see that they get what they deserve. What are we, Docile-dils or DAFFODILS?"

Penny Sue started the car and slapped it into gear. "Damn straight. Let's run over to Pub 44 right now."

Chapter 11

It was a beautiful October afternoon, so we found a table in the back room of Gilley's which overlooked a pond. I'd insisted. We'd spent so much time eating in dark restaurants, I was starting to feel like a roach. Sunlight was what I needed—and no more wine. I was also beginning to feel like a lush.

A cute girl in short shorts, popping gum, came to take our order. Her name was Haley, like the Comet, she said. I led off with the orders. "A beer mug of ginger ale. No ice. Diet, if you have it." Penny Sue looked at me like I'd lost my mind. "On duty," I explained before Penny Sue could say anything. "We need to stay sharp."

Penny Sue reared back with a glint in her eye. An instant later she'd transformed into Nancy Drew or Jessica Fletcher or ... Austin Powers. "I'll have one of those non-alcoholic beers," she said in a no-nonsense, I-mean-business tone.

Ruthie glanced up from the newspaper she'd purchased from a box by the front door. "Perrier with a twist of lime."

The waitress leaned forward. The front of her floral shirt gaped open, exposing a black leather bra. "Sorry ma'am," gum popping, "we don't have Perrier. In case you didn't notice, this is a pub." She cut her eyes at Penny Sue and me. Apparently, Comet hadn't been too impressed with our orders, either.

Ruthie smiled sweetly. "Sorry. Club soda on the rocks in a short glass with a twist of lime. Think you can handle that?"

Comet glared contemptuously as she scribbled Ruthie's request. "It may take a while. We're kinda busy," she said over her shoulder as she sashayed toward the bar.

Actually, sashay might have been a slight understatement. Bump and grind was more like it. What a snide thought, I chastised myself, still watching Comet wiggle across the room. Perhaps the poor girl had on leather panties to match her bra which were digging in the wrong place.

A young man in jeans and a tee shirt came up behind her and patted her butt. Comet beamed. I thought of Ms. Thong and realized I'd unconsciously clenched my fist.

"Look, there's Jonathan McMillan," Penny Sue said. I followed her gaze to an older man sitting at the bar. The gentleman in question sported holey jeans, a tank top, a kerchief tied around his head, and a big tattoo on his arm.

"How do you know him?" I asked incredulously.

"He's president of a bank in Marietta. Yoo hoo, Jonathan." Penny Sue stood up and waved. The man turned around and grinned. The next thing I knew he was standing at our table.

"Penny Sue Parker," he drawled. "How're ya doing?" They exchanged hugs.

A moment later a woman our age appeared beside him. She was dressed in stretch jeans and a red leather halter top. "Marie," Penny Sue gushed. More hugs. "You look smashing."

Marie's lips stretched into a wide smile, revealing movie star teeth (at least eleven millimeters, obligatory for photos according to my dentist) and non-crinkled eyes. An eye-job I presumed, and a good one. Considering her flat abdomen, I suspected a tummy tuck had been part of the package. "It's been ages, Penny. What are you doing here?"

"Vacationing." Penny Sue introduced us and relayed the story of her daddy's condo. "What brings you to these parts?"

Jonathan grinned self-consciously. "Can't make Biketoberfest this year; have a conflict with a board meeting. So, we thought we'd come down early for our semi-annual bike getaway. Our chance to dress up and pretend we're still young characters in *Easy Rider.*"

Penny Sue patted the tattoo on his arm. It was a skull and cross bones surrounded by roses.

"Fake," he offered before she could say anything. "I got it at the Harley Davidson dealership next door. A hoot, isn't it? This is the first one I've had. They're always sold out during Bike Week."

I looked to Marie. "Y'all rode motorcycles down from Atlanta?" Talk about crotch rot; I shivered at the thought of eight hours on a motorcycle.

She rolled her eyes. "Oh no, we drove down in our car and pulled the bikes in a trailer."

Smart lady. If I had those teeth, I wouldn't want them peppered with gnats, either.

We went on to discuss where they were staying, old friends, old memories (at our age, why does everyone dwell on what was?) and finally the party Saturday night. They promised to come after Penny Sue assured them it was casual. They'd only brought biker garb.

A man—the manager I presumed from his polite, authoritative demeanor—arrived with our drinks soon after they left. He sat a chilled mug of ginger ale in front of me and a glass of ice. "I know you didn't want ice," he said, "but the ginger ale is warm. I put it in a cold mug, but I'm not sure that'll be enough."

The contrast was startling. "What happened to Caustic Comet?" I blurted before thinking. Ruthie's mouth dropped open, and my cheeks flamed. "I'm sorry," I said. "That came out the wrong way."

"That's all right," the manager said. "Haley's new, and she didn't get a lot of training. Seems to have missed the lesson on customer service."

I nodded. A shame more managers didn't watch their employees and insist on common civility. I looked around the sun-filled room. I liked this place after all, although I wasn't sure I could go as far as wearing a leather bra.

While this was going on, Penny Sue sipped her O'Douls and surveyed the room for suspects—or hot men. Ruthie was engrossed in her newspaper.

Penny Sue leaned toward me suddenly and whispered. "Quick, look. No, don't look, he'll see you," she added hastily. "I think that's Al Maroni behind you at the far side of the bar."

"Should I look or not look?"

Penny Sue scanned the room casually, her rendition of surreptitiousness. Unfortunately, the stealthy maneuver came across as a woman trying to work out a crick in her neck, or perhaps having a slight seizure. A second later, Penny Sue glanced sidelong at the bar.

"Darn, he's gone."

I turned around to see for myself. "Are you sure it was him?"

Penny Sue sank back dejectedly. "No, I'm not sure. The guy had on sunglasses, and his hair was combed differently. Sort of down in front, instead of brushed straight back."

"Never mind that, listen to this," Ruthie interrupted with a look of revulsion. "Four loggerhead sea turtles have washed up on the beach in the last few days. One was a female. They all had their heads and flippers cut off."

I thought of Robert, Gerty, and the Turtle Patrol. "Magod. The Hate Mongers?"

"Doesn't say. Some speculate it was commercial fishermen. Since the turtles weigh 250 to 400 pounds, they're the only ones capable of catching them with their huge nets."

"Why would they cut off their heads and flippers?" I asked.

"Meanness," Penny Sue said without hesitation. "There are just a lot of mean sickos in this world."

"Sea turtles are endangered; it's illegal to mess with them."

"Says here the perpetrators are subject to state penalties of 60 days in jail and a $500 fine," Ruthie said. "Federal law is worse: two years behind bars and a $50,000 fine."

"Which means nothing to sickos. I've learned that much from Daddy. Penalties have no effect on those people. They get a perverse thrill from seeing how far they can go, how much they can get away with."

My thoughts turned to Rick, Gerty and the defiled turtle nest. Then an image of Rick's stiff, mangled toes. I put down my ginger ale and fought back a wave of nausea.

Coming up empty-handed at Gilley's, we headed back to the condo for a short nap and change of clothes before continuing our investigation. Since Pauline saw the killer in a bar, JB's was our next, best prospect. We arrived at the restaurant at about seven and waited outside on the deck for a table. We had our eye on a booth in the corner with a clear view of both doors, the bar, and part of the back room. We ordered drinks (the real stuff this time, since teetotalers get no respect) and stood along a wooden railing overlooking Mosquito Lagoon. Two manatees rolled and splashed at our feet. The sun hung low on the horizon. For once, the lagoon's buzzing namesakes were inexplicably absent. It seemed like heaven instead of a stake-out and murder investigation.

"I want to make sure we're coordinated," Ruthie said. "What do we do if we see Stinky?"

Penny Sue gave her an exasperated look. "Get his name. Find out where he works, who his friends are, as much as we can. We need something to give to Deputy Moore and Woody."

Woody's name seemed to stick in her throat. Penny Sue still hadn't heard anything from him about the gun. I figured no news was good news. If she were really a suspect, they'd have taken her into custody by now. Of course, we'd all have felt better if someone—anyone but Penny Sue—had been arrested for killing Rick.

No such luck. Ruthie combed the paper every day, partly because she was a news freak, but mostly to search for articles about Rick's death. For a small town, there had been surprisingly few. There had been a short piece on Monday when Rick's body was found and a longer article on Tuesday which quoted the police as saying they were following several leads. Since then, nothing. Not a peep from the press in a place where DUI's and domestic disputes made the front page. Strange, to say the least.

"How, exactly, are we going to get his name?" Ruthie asked. "I thought we were working incognito."

"We are," Penny Sue said, perplexed. She swept her hand down her body in a motion worthy of Vanna White on *Wheel of Fortune*. "Why else would I be dressed like this?"

Penny Sue had on beige shorts, a white sleeveless shirt, and casual sandals. Her hair was pulled back in a pony tail, and she had on approximately half the makeup she usually wore. And, for the first time in her life, she wore no scarves, belts, jackets, shawls, caps, or jewelry except, of course, the two-carat diamond ring, which didn't count, since it had been her Momma's. For Penny Sue, that truly was incognito. Heck, she looked like me. Or Ruthie, whose drab, baggy, designer clothes would go unnoticed by all but the most discriminating eyes. Which meant Ruthie had nothing to worry about from Stinky. Discrimination of any kind did not appear to be one of his faults.

The fact that Penny Sue had stooped to looking plain was lost on Ruthie. "Yeah, but how do we find out who he is?" she asked again.

At that moment a waitress tapped Penny Sue on the shoulder and pointed toward the corner table that was being vacated. "Don't worry, we'll think of something."

Penny Sue and I took the side of the booth facing the room, which left Ruthie looking out the back window. She didn't mind. Although she was concerned about our situation, Ruthie was definitely not gung ho about our undercover exercise.

Ruthie kept remembering Pauline's prediction that we'd meet the angry light-haired man at a bar. When Pub 44 had turned out to be a dead end, Ruthie'd grown increasingly anxious about coming to JB's. In fact, she recommended that we hire a private detective and volunteered to pay for it herself. She called two P.I. agencies whose yellow page blurbs boasted FBI connections, but got no answer. After five on a Thursday, what did she expect?

I wasn't thrilled about playing detective, but only half-believed Pauline's prediction, so I wasn't on tenterhooks, either. I definitely didn't intend to do anything crazy like confront Stinky, or even follow him. I was willing to make a few inquiries; that was all. Period. No matter what.

A tall man appeared at the table a few minutes after we sat down. While virtually all men, except Zack, Jr., were on my shit list at that moment, I had to admit that this guy was a real hunk. With a deep tan, chiseled jaw, and solid build packed on a six-foot-four frame, this man would stand out in any crowd. "Your waitress is up a tree." The guy ripped a large piece of Kraft paper from a roll on the wall and slid it over our table top. "Can I get you ladies something to drink?" he asked.

Penny Sue lit up like a firefly spying a flame. She had the inside seat, next to the wall, and nearly pushed me off the bench as she leaned toward him. Batting her lashes several times, she answered "Chardonnay" in a syrupy, Southern drawl. Ruthie and I ordered the same.

"Three Chardonnays. It'll just be a minute." He smiled (nice teeth) and left.

Even I watched his back as he strode away, and Ruthie actually turned around in her seat.

"What a Titan," Penny Sue mumbled.

"Titan was the son of Uranus and Gaia," Ruthie said softly, eyes riveted on his retreating form.

"Whoever he's kin to, he's got nice jeans," I said, grinning. Neither of them got the drift. So much for genome wit, I thought wryly.

To our extreme disappointment a waitress, Joanne, delivered the wine. She was about our age and nice enough, but a letdown, nonetheless. Titan was a tough act to follow.

In order to prolong our surveillance, we'd already decided to stretch out dinner as long as possible by ordering a succession of appetizers. If we did that again and again, eventually we'd be full and a couple of hours would have passed. We started with one order of Buffalo Shrimp, to split. Penny Sue assured the waitress we were big tippers, hoping to assuage the woman's natural desire to turn the table. The server nodded politely, as if she'd heard the line more times than she could count.

We settled back, eating, chatting, and trolling the restaurant with our eyes. I couldn't help but notice that Penny Sue homed in on the Titan bartender after each pass of the room. About a half hour into the gig she got a bite.

"Look who's talking to Titan at the bar," Penny Sue whispered suddenly. "That's definitely Al."

I squinted in their direction. It was almost eight, and the room was getting dark. "I think you're right," I finally said.

"Should we say something to him? Ask if he got the invitation to the party?" Ruthie asked.

"No. We don't want to call attention to ourselves. We'll track him down tomorrow to make sure he got it."

Our second appetizer, clams, arrived. We ordered another round of wine and some water, but our waitress was not listening. Her eyes were fixed on the television at the far end of the room. I repeated our request.

"Sorry," Joanne said. "I was checking out the storm. I live on the beach. New Smyrna has never taken a direct hit. Even so, hurricanes always make me nervous."

"Hurricane?" Ruthie echoed, turning toward the television which was tuned to the Weather Channel. Jim Cantore was pointing to a swirling blob west of Puerto Rico. A moment later, arrows appeared indicating the storm's projected track. New Smyrna Beach was in the red, high probability zone.

"A hurricane," Penny Sue wailed. "It will ruin our party."

"Yeah," I said sarcastically. "A hurricane might put a damper on things, especially if they evacuate the island."

"Evacuate?" Ruthie moaned. "We can't leave."

"Surely, Woody wouldn't make us stay in a hurricane," I said.

Penny Sue shook her head. "I don't know. We'd have to have his permission first, that's for certain. Otherwise, we could be charged with fleeing from a murder investigation. I know that's serious."

"So is being blown away," Ruthie countered.

"We'll get permission," I said emphatically. "I'm not staying here in a hurricane."

My eyes wandered back to the Weather Channel at the exact moment Stinky walked by. The pony-tailed guy from the previous night was with him, as well as a balding man in a tee shirt with *Marines* in glitter across the back. The trio sat a few feet from the television at a table that had just been vacated.

We hunkered down and took big gulps of wine.

"Pauline was right," Penny Sue said, a trace of awe in her voice. "She said we'd find the angry man in a bar. There he is."

"Now what?" Ruthie asked.

"For starters, we should eat." I speared a clam. "We need to stay calm and act naturally." I looked askance at Penny Sue. Natural for her encompassed a lot. Perhaps I'd better clarify. "Normal," I added hastily. "We want to look like normal people on vacation."

Penny Sue raked several clams onto her paper plate. "Okay, how do normal people act?" She doused her clams with hot sauce.

They both stared at me, expecting answers. "They eat," I said.

"We covered that already," Penny Sue said.

I scanned the other tables. The couple next to us was watching the Weather Channel. Some kids behind Ruthie were drawing pictures on the Kraft paper covering their table. Young men in the kitty-cornered booth were drinking long neck beers and arguing sports. One of them had a head cold and kept wiping his nose with the back of his hand. Yuck. There was a whole roll of paper towels on their table, so why didn't he use one?

What was normal? I recalled my conversation with Penny Sue where she equated normal to being average. That being the case, normal was definitely not something she aspired to be. Neither did I, come to think of it. While I actually might be normal, it wasn't something I was particularly proud to claim. The terms "normal" and "boring" had an unusual affinity.

"Normal people don't do anything in particular," I said. "Virtually everything goes as long as it doesn't create a stir."

"No chanting, Ruthie," Penny Sue said mischievously.

Ruthie folded her arms defensively. "Or getting smashed." She nodded at Penny Sue's empty plastic cup.

Oh boy, I didn't want to get into that subject, and I could see they were both getting tense. "We should be ourselves ... in a low key way. Right?" I glanced from one friend to the other.

"Right," Penny Sue finally allowed. "Let's not forget that we're here to get the names of those bikers who killed Rick and tried to run us off the road."

That was an unexpected leap. "Killed Rick?" I asked.

"The guy in the red pickup killed Rick, but Stinky and his buddy are in cahoots with him."

I blinked. "You're sure of that?"

"Pretty sure. Why else would they try to kill us? Mr. Red Pickup knows we can link him to Rick."

I'd actually had the same thought myself. Gerty said the turtle haters were mean, and the guy in the red pickup was clearly a turtle hater, judging from his bumper sticker.

Ruthie broke in. "Which brings us back to square one. We must get some names for Deputy Moore."

"Let's ask Titan," Penny Sue said with a big grin.

I noticed a plaque hanging next to the bar. *Do you want to talk to the man in charge or to the woman who knows what's going on?* "Let's start with our waitress. Here she comes now."

Joanne sat a plate of potato skins in the center of the table and passed plastic cups of wine and water all around. Penny Sue glanced defiantly at Ruthie and took a big swallow of wine. I rolled my eyes. Honestly, Penny Sue acted like a kid sometimes—a headstrong, devilish one at that.

"Joanne, see those three guys sitting by the wall?" I nodded toward Stinky and crew. "The table with the bald guy."

"The one with *Marines* on his back? What about them?"

Good question. What about them? Why was I interested in those skuzzy slobs? I needed to be careful in case she knew them. Three of us; three of them. I sure didn't want her to think we wanted to pick them up and, God forbid, have her help us out by telling them. No, I had to have a reason to keep our interest secret.

"I think the guy with the pony tail might be the ex-husband of a woman I know. A bad situation; he used to slap her around. If that's him, I want to warn my friend that he's back in town."

Joanne frowned as she studied the men. "They don't look familiar; I'll ask the other girls."

"I don't want him to know I'm interested," I said quickly. "If that's Tom Jones, I sure don't want to mess with him."

"I understand." Joanne left and went to the bar.

I sat back, feeling satisfied with my ingenuity. It only lasted a moment.

"Tom Jones?" Penny Sue cackled. "Is that the best you can do? Talk about fake names! You might as well have said John Doe!"

"What's wrong with Tom Jones? It's a nice, normal name."

"It-t-t's not un-US-u-AL ..." Penny Sue sang off key. Ruthie giggled.

"It was the best I could do on short notice. Joanne didn't think it was funny. Look, it seems to have worked." I inclined my head toward the bar where Joanne was whispering with the other waitresses and motioning toward Stinky's table. "We'll have their names in a matter of minutes."

"I know how to get their names," Penny Sue blurted. The young guys drinking the long-necks looked over at us. Penny Sue leaned forward and lowered her voice. "I'll throw my panties at 'Tom Jones' and ask for an autograph!" She was laughing so hard, tears streamed down her face.

"Your panties aren't big enough to write on," I countered, thinking of the lacy thongs Ruthie and I had unpacked for her.

"Whoo-o." Penny Sue took a deep breath to calm herself and wiped her eyes. "Okay, a bad plan. Those guys probably can't write anyhow. But, Tom Jones? You must have had a brain cramp to come up with that oldie, goldie."

"Brain cramp? Don't start in on the hormone stuff. I'm not in the mood."

Penny Sue was getting wound up. The best policy was to ignore her. So, I turned my attention to the bar and watched as Joanne sidled up to Titan. The handsome hunk had just served a drink to a well-dressed, gray-haired fellow. Titan stooped to hear what Joanne was saying, glanced toward Stinky, then toward us. The gray-haired fellow turned around, too.

"Uh oh. Talk about goldie oldies," I said. "There's Lyndon Fulbright."

"Lyndon?" The look on Penny Sue's face was one of pure horror as she slid down into her seat.

Chapter 12

"*What's he doing* here? I don't have on any makeup." Penny Sue moaned as she rummaged in her purse for a compact. She was hastily applying lipstick when Lyndon arrived at our table.

"Ladies." He nodded politely. "I'm sorry I missed you this morning. It was so kind of you to personally deliver the invitation. I'm looking forward to your party, wouldn't miss it for the world."

Penny Sue stuffed the makeup back in her bag. "Lyndon, what a surprise. Join us, please," she said in her aristocratic tone, waving at the space beside Ruthie.

Ruthie's eyes widened into an unspoken: *What the heck are you doing?*

I had the same thought. One look at Lyndon, and Penny Sue'd forgotten all about the murder, Stinky, and our personal safety. Our big chance to get the thugs' names, and she was going to mess it up by flirting.

"I don't want to intrude," he protested lamely.

"You wouldn't be," Penny Sue bubbled. Her foot brushed me as it went for Ruthie under the table. Ruthie scooted to the side of the booth peevishly.

Lyndon sat down. "I returned minutes after you left; barely missed you. I had half a mind to jump in the car and try to find you. Alas, there were some pressing matters I had to attend to."

"The condos?" Penny Sue asked, gushing sympathy.

"That and other details. The storm has thrown a wrench in my plans. If it makes landfall, I may have to cut my stay short."

"Oh ..." Penny Sue couldn't contain her disappointment.

Fortunately, Joanne arrived at that moment. Conscious of Lyndon's presence, she spoke to me in a confidential tone. "The guy in the Marines shirt is a local fisherman. His name is Randall Stroski. No one knows the other guys, but they've been in here before. Chuck—"

She must have noticed my confused expression.

"—the bartender—"

Ah, Titan had a name.

"—says they're the same guys who created a scene last night. Had too much to drink, then went out and had a wreck or something. The police came here asking questions about them. You probably should warn your girlfriend. Those guys sound like bad news."

"Thanks, Joanne," I said, relieved she hadn't connected us to the ruckus with Stinky. Perhaps our no makeup, dressed-down disguises were working, or she hadn't been on duty then. "If they happen to pay with a credit card, do you mind getting the name?" I added hastily, "I'm not interested in their account number or anything, just the name."

Joanne winked. She tapped the table and turned to leave. "I'll get you a plate," she said to Lyndon.

He hardly noticed. Penny Sue was babbling merrily about Pauline and our past life in a harem.

I mouthed *bathroom* to Ruthie who was finishing up a potato skin. She excused herself and followed me out the side door and around to the front of the building. I wanted to stay as far away from Stinky and company as possible. Anyway, the place had become so crowded, a trip outside and around the building was the quickest route to the bathroom. We lingered at the corner of the deck to confer. A cacophony of televisions and voices wafted from inside, providing the perfect cover for our conversation.

"Marine's name is Randall Stroski. He's a local fisherman," I said.

"A fisherman?" Ruthie's hand flew to her throat. "Fishermen were supposedly responsible for decapitating the turtles."

I got a fluttery feeling in my chest as thoughts of Gerty, the Hate Mongers and Rick's foot raced through my mind. I took a deep breath to force down the panicky wave. I'd learned the technique from one of my therapists—the frustrated spinster, I think. She said slow, deliberate breaths would diffuse all but the worst anxiety attacks. It had worked pretty well for me. In fact, I'd wondered if Ruthie's chanting was the Far Eastern version of the same thing. She made a lot of noise, and I didn't, but otherwise, what was the difference?

"Let's not jump to conclusions," I said, as much for my benefit as Ruthie's.

"What kind of a person would murder a defenseless turtle?"

The same kind that would murder a person, but I didn't say it. Lord knows, I didn't want Ruthie to get nervous and start chanting. "A mean one," I said. "A Hate Monger. Yet, that's for the police to deal with. Our job is to generate leads, nothing more. We're making progress. We know the identity of one guy, and Joanne promised to get the name if they pay with a credit card."

"Okay." Ruthie nodded stoically. "What if they pay with cash? We still won't know anything about Stinky and Pony Tail."

I glanced through the window. Penny Sue was talking animatedly, her hands going a million miles a minute. The young men drinking long neck beers were still at it, though their discussion had taken on a lot of head shaking and table pounding.

And the little kids at the table next to ours had made a game of connecting dots with the greasy fingerprints on the Kraft paper.

What if they did pay cash? I stared across the room and watched as Stinky and Marine stood and counted bills out on the table. Damn, no names. I grabbed Ruthie's arm and pulled her out of sight as the men ambled onto the porch. We peered around the corner as they got on motorcycles and rumbled off into the night.

"Now—" Ruthie started.

I didn't give her time to finish. "Get the car keys from Penny Sue," I ordered. She hesitated only a moment, then rushed through the side door. I ran across the deck and in the front entrance. The waitress was clearing Stinky's table. I shoved the last plate onto her tray and whipped the Kraft paper off the table. "I need this," I said, heading for the front door, trailing the paper like a flag. The stunned waitress didn't say a thing.

Shrouded in darkness, I waited for Ruthie in the parking lot. I draped the paper over my extended arm like a sheet. Ruthie arrived just as I thought my shoulder would break from the strain. She handed me the car keys and took the paper.

"What are you going to do?" she asked.

I unlocked the car and snatched the cell phone from its cradle. "I'm going to call Deputy Moore."

It took some doing, but the switchboard operator patched me through to the officer who was miraculously on duty. He agreed to meet us at our condo.

Penny Sue stomped over as I hung up the phone. "Are you all right?"

"I told her you were sick—throwing up in the parking lot," Ruthie explained.

"You're not sick?" Penny Sue asked with annoyance, looking first at me, then at Ruthie.

"How else was I going to get you away from Lyndon?"

"Get me away from Lyndon? Why, he wanted to take us—" Penny Sue stopped mid-sentence, noticing the huge sheet of paper for the first time. "What is that?"

I opened the trunk and slipped the paper in, being careful to keep it as flat as possible. "Drive, Penny Sue, drive. Deputy Moore is meeting us at the condo."

"Deputy Moore. What is going on?" she demanded.

I slid into the backseat. "While you were sparking, we were gathering evidence. Now, drive!"

She did. Deputy Moore was waiting when we pulled into the parking lot. A thick cloud cover obscured the three-quarter moon making the night as dark as pitch. Even so, I noticed there was no car at Al's place.

"We should have left the porch light on," Penny Sue said.

"I did," Ruthie protested. "The bulb must have burned out."

We took Deputy Moore and the paper inside where there was light. I spread the paper on the floor, half holding my breath, not sure how many of the spots had been water that had now dried, and how many were greasy fingerprints. Deputy Moore watched with a combination of interest and amusement.

"Turn on the reading light; will you, Ruthie?" I pointed to a lamp beside the fireplace.

She headed for the lamp, stumbled on something, and almost went down. Luckily, Deputy Moore was close enough to catch her.

"Thanks," she muttered, turning on the light.

Deputy Moore stooped to pick up a long, thick pole. "Don't tell me. This is your security system, right?"

Penny Sue smiled sheepishly. "It goes in the track for the sliding glass door. Keeps it from being opened."

He went to the door and fit the stick in its place. "I know. Everyone on the beach uses these things. They work pretty well," he looked up at Penny Sue, "if you use them. You ladies should be more careful. All the evidence in the world won't do any good if you don't keep your doors locked."

I changed the subject before Penny Sue or Ruthie started sniping at each other. I could tell they were winding up for a volley of recriminations. "Do you think you can lift any fingerprints from this?" I pointed at the Kraft sheet spread across the floor.

As he squatted beside me to examine several of the spots, I caught a whiff of Aramis cologne. I used to love the scent—Zack had worn it in his sane days. Later, when he took up with Ms. Thong, he's switched to some trendy cologne like Drakkar or Chanel or High-Testosterone. That should have been my first clue, I realized; wish I'd paid attention.

"You might have something, there," the deputy said, indicating two spots next to a glob of grease. "These prints look fairly good." He grinned at me. "You're pretty sharp."

I stood up, feeling self-conscious. He rose, too, and took a notebook from his back pocket. "Okay, let's get the details."

We filled him in on Randall Stroski and the fact that the three men all left on motorcycles. Then I helped him take the paper to his car which we carefully spread across the backseat.

He paused to look at us standing on the front stoop, silhouetted by the light from the hall and shook his head. "You ladies must be careful, understand? Keep your doors locked. Under no circumstances should you open the door to anyone you don't know. Don't have pizza delivered—that's a favorite ploy." We all nodded dutifully like first-graders getting instructions for a fire drill. I guess we looked pitiful, or at least contrite, because Deputy Moore sighed and said, "Do you have a light bulb?"

While Penny Sue rushed inside to find one, he reached up into the dark plastic cylinder suspended from the porch ceiling. A moment later the fixture glowed yellow.

"A loose bulb," he commented, just as Penny Sue returned with a new bulb. "Here on the beach, bulbs get corroded if they're

not screwed in tightly, and wind gusts can shake them loose."
He brushed his hands off and strode to his cruiser. "Now
go inside and lock the door. Keep the front light on ... and be
careful! I'll call as soon as I find out about these prints."

"Thank you, Deputy." Penny Sue's voice dripped honey.
"We're so grateful for your concern."

He tipped his hat and left. I shut the door and threw the
deadbolt.

"I think he likes you, Leigh. He was giving you the look,"
Penny Sue said airily.

I ignored her comment and headed into the living room where
Ruthie had turned on the Weather Channel.

"Uh oh," Ruthie said. "Dr. Steve's on. This hurricane must
be serious."

Penny Sue came from the kitchen with a glass of ice tea and
sat on the arm of the sofa. "Jim Cantore's my favorite."

"Dr. Steve's the hurricane expert," Ruthie said. "It's nearly
eleven o'clock. If he's up at this hour, the storm must have
gotten worse."

I sat on the end of the loveseat and watched. Hurricane Lizzie
had indeed gained strength. A pressure drop and shift in upper
level winds meant it posed a serious threat for Puerto Rico.
A graphic of the strike zone flashed on the screen. New Smyrna
Beach was smack, dab in the center of the high probability range.

"The waitress said that New Smyrna Beach has never taken
a direct hit from a hurricane," I said.

Penny Sue nodded. "That's right. I think it's because the
coast here curves northwest. Storms tend to hit south of here or
north of Jacksonville. As I recall, the chance of a direct hit is
higher for the Carolinas than it is for this area. That probably
explains why Cape Canaveral, which is only thirty miles south,
was chosen for space launches."

"What would we do if the hurricane does come this way?" I asked. Living in Atlanta, which was 250 miles inland at an elevation of over a thousand feet, I wasn't used to worrying about hurricanes. They usually petered out before they got close to the city.

"I certainly don't want to stay here," Ruthie declared.

Penny Sue pulled out a cigarette. "Would y'all be awfully mad if I smoked? Just one. I don't want to go out on the deck now that the place is all locked up."

"Wait." Ruthie went to our bedroom and returned with one of the scented candles we'd purchased at Chris' Place. "Sandalwood and jasmine," she announced. "We might as well chase away evil spirits while we cover up your smoke."

"That's right, we have to smudge the place. That'll take care of any smoke residue." She lit her cigarette.

"American Indians used tobacco as a sacred herb. The cigarette smoke may actually help the vibes in here."

Boy, I wished Ruthie hadn't made that statement. Penny Sue didn't need encouragement. At the rate she'd been puffing since Rick's murder, she'd be a chain smoker before the vacation ended. Except, I had an idea how I could squelch that trend. "There was a piece on the news this morning about smoking. New studies show it causes impotence. Even second-hand smoke can have a big effect on men."

Penny Sue stopped mid-drag and exhaled forcefully. "You're making that up."

"No. Everyone's talking about it. Causes early menopause and wrinkles, too."

She narrowed her eyes at me, trying to gauge my sincerity. I suppose I passed the test, because she took one more drag, then snuffed out the cigarette. "Lord, I hope that storm doesn't ruin our party. I guess we should put together a hurricane box just in case."

"A hurricane box?" Ruthie repeated with trepidation.

"Sure, supplies—food and water. We probably have the candle front covered. What did you think I meant?"

"I thought you were talking about a panic room like the one in the film with Jodi Foster. I'm claustrophobic, I can't stand being confined." Ruthie went to the kitchen and got a glass of water. "Why do you call it a hurricane box?"

"You keep the stuff in a box so it's easy to carry in the event you have to evacuate."

"Where would we go?" Ruthie groaned.

"If it's only a Category One, I don't think we need to go any-where. More than that, well ..."

"There are shelters," I said quickly, remembering what I'd seen on the news in previous years. "Schools, government buildings, hotels. We'd go to one of them."

Ruthie sighed heavily. "Some vacation this has turned out to be."

Though Ruthie would not intentionally hurt a fly, I could tell her remark cut Penny Sue deeply. But, she covered her feelings so well in brazen bluster, it was sometimes easy to forget Penny Sue had them at all. She did, and they ran deep.

"It has been an adventure," I said brightly, trying to salve my friend's injured feelings. "A little NASCAR-style driving, a hurricane, and an eccentric psychic sure took my mind off the divorce."

Penny Sue perked up. "Pauline may be eccentric, but she was right. We did see Stinky at the bar tonight."

"She's a hoot, all right," I said. "Wouldn't you love to be a bug on the wall and hear Pauline's conversations with Alice?"

"She was pulling your leg, putting you in your place. She heard your impudent remark about bat wings and eye of newt," Penny Sue said, back to her old, sassy self.

"I was kidding. Though, you have to admit her place was a little ... strange," I said. "It's a shame we don't have an Alice to keep an eye on things for us. We could use some help."

Arching a brow, Ruthie smiled smugly. "I know where we can get something just as good."

Chapter 13

"A Furby?"

Penny Sue arrived at the tail end of our conversation. It was eight o'clock on Friday morning. Ruthie and I had been up for an hour, sipping coffee and watching the Weather Channel. Strong westerly winds had knocked the top off Hurricane Lizzie; it had been downgraded to a tropical storm. Good news for us and the party.

Penny Sue notched her red robe tighter and shuffled to the kitchen for coffee. "So, what's this stuff about a Furby?"

Ruthie took a bite of toast. "I think we should get one to watch the place."

"This is a joke, right?" Penny Sue was baffled. "A Furby is a furry little child's toy."

"That talks," I added.

"That learns to talk," Ruthie corrected. She grinned smugly and picked up the newspaper, pretending to read.

Penny Sue sat at the bar, stirring her coffee. "All right, I'll bite. How can a Furby watch this place?"

"Well," Ruthie sat forward excitedly, "Furbies are like children, they learn language by imitation. They listen to the people around them and pick up phrases."

"Don't chant around it," Penny Sue teased. "You'll have the poor thing completely confused."

Ruthie turned the page of the paper noisily. "Do you want to hear my idea or not?"

"I do." She had me confused, that was for sure.

"We'll get a Furby and turn it on when we go out. If anyone comes in and speaks, it will pick up their conversation. That way we'll know if someone was here."

"Yes-s," Penny Sue enthused after a moment's thought. "Let's get one today, so we'll have it for the party. We'll put it in the corner where it can eavesdrop on everyone."

"That could be dangerous," I cautioned. I wasn't sure Penny Sue was ready to hear everyone's private thoughts. I knew I wasn't!

"Oh, it's a joke. It'll be fun—an ice breaker."

Pony Parties was a safer bet, especially since I didn't think the Furby idea had a chance of working. I turned to Ruthie. "I'm not sure Furbies are on the market anymore. Everything now is robotics."

Ruthie waved off my objection. "I'll bet they have them at the discount stores. There's a Dollar General over by the movie theater."

"I don't believe Furbies truly learn. I know they're supposed to learn English, but it's all pre-programmed. I'm certain they don't pick up words from their surroundings."

"Sure they do," Ruthie said. "Why else would the NSA ban them from government offices? They were afraid they would pick up classified information."

"NSA?" Penny Sue asked.

"National Security Agency. You know, the government's super spies."

I did remember hearing something about that years ago. Yet the kids on my block had Furbies, and I'd never seen signs of real intelligence. Of course, maybe that was more of a comment on the kids than the Furbies. "I guess it couldn't hurt," I said.

"Charlotte's coming to clean this afternoon. I need to pick up a few things for the party anyway, so we can run by Dollar General for some Furbies. It's worth a try. Nothing ventured, nothing gained," Penny Sue said.

"Do you believe someone has been in here?" I asked Ruthie, following up on her earlier comment.

"I'm certain I put the pole in the track to the sliding glass door before we left yesterday."

That had bothered me, too. Though, I'd tried to write it off as Penny Sue sneaking out for a cigarette when we weren't looking. "Have you noticed anything else?" I asked.

She glanced up from the paper and thought. "Nothing specific, it's just a feeling."

"That's the negativity you sensed before," Penny Sue said, pulling bagels from the freezer. "We never did smudge this place. We should do that as soon as we finish eating; I don't want any bad vibes for the party. We've got to clear it all out. Now, ladies, how about some melon and a bagel?"

I clicked off the television, and Ruthie brought her newspaper to the counter as Penny Sue dished up the food. The melon was good, a refreshing contrast to the heavy appetizers from the night before.

"The Pierson student will be allowed to wear a dress to homecoming after all," Ruthie said. "The superintendent reversed the principal's decision."

"A dress? What's wrong with a dress?" Penny Sue asked.

We filled her in on the controversy surrounding the gay student.

"The county attorney told the superintendent they were on shaky legal ground," Ruthie said.

"Quicksand is more like it," I remarked.

"He's going to wear a red gown with spaghetti straps."

"Red? That reminds me," Penny Sue said between bites of bagel. "Marie's leather halter top was cute. Let's look for one while we're out."

"You're not going to wear a leather bra to the party, are you?" I asked. "Remember, the whole point of the shindig is to show people that you're normal."

Penny Sue rolled her eyes. "Marie's normal. Her husband's a bank president for godssakes."

"Don't do it, Penny Sue," I warned.

She took a cigarette from her purse and headed for the deck. "We'll see."

While Penny Sue smoked a cigarette, Ruthie and I prepared to smoke up the house. We pulled out the smudging instructions Pauline had given us. As Ruthie unwrapped the candles and other paraphernalia, I read.

"Hmm, native American people burn herbs to cleanse the energy," I read out loud. "The botanical name for sage is Salvia, which means 'to heal.' It's used to drive out bad feelings and negativity. Some tribes spread it on the ground in the sweat lodge."

"Have you ever been to a sweat lodge ceremony with all the drumming?" Ruthie asked as she unwrapped one of the smudge bundles.

I once chaperoned a Cub Scout outing where the kids danced around a campfire with tom-toms, but I didn't suppose that counted. "No, have you?"

"A retreat at Stone Mountain. It was a powerful experience— really puts you in touch with your inner goddess."

Which deity was that? All that came to mind was the chubby comedienne with her Domestic Goddess skit. After twenty-odd years of marriage, I'd had a lot of experience with that Muse. Too much. My Domestic Goddess was one sleeping dog I hoped would slip into a coma.

"Cedar is burned while praying," I continued reading, "its smoke carries wishes to heaven. Indians in the Pacific Northwest believe it attracts positive energy. Sweetgrass also draws good influences and benevolent spirits.

"The procedure is to burn the smudge stick, and let the smoke permeate our auras first; that makes us a pure channel for the good energy. Then, we take the smudge stick all around the place, making sure the smoke gets in every nook and cranny. Finally, we flood the condo with candle light, to light up the place, so to speak.

"As we're doing all this, we should pray silently ... or aloud. It doesn't matter." I personally opted for silence.

Ruthie thought otherwise. "Chanting is a form of prayer. I know y'all think I'm crazy, but I'm going to do it. Sounds are important, they set up sympathetic vibrations. After all, the Mozart Effect has pretty much been proven."

I glanced sidelong at her. "What's that?" I asked, almost dreading the answer.

"You know, classical music. Music therapy. Psychiatrists have used it for decades. Upbeat music stimulates depressed patients. Soothing music can calm hyped-up types and rap music actually creates a predisposition to violence, drug addiction, and materialism. Universities have done studies on it and found that classical music, particularly Mozart, synchronizes brain waves. It also seems to have a beneficial affect on Attention Deficit Disorder."

ADD, I'd often wondered if that could be part of Penny Sue's problem, the way she flitted around at a million miles per hour. I thought of our trip to New Smyrna Beach on the interstate. Perhaps we should buy a Mozart CD before we started home. It couldn't hurt. "If you want to chant, it's fine with me. I just don't know any—"

"Vowel sounds." Penny Sue strode in from the deck holding a feather, having purified her system with tobacco. "Plain old vowel sounds are as good as anything. Deepak Chopra said so."

Penny Sue knew about chanting? How did I miss it? Where had I been? In a depressed funk, I guess. Made me wonder what else I'd missed. "Vowel sounds? You mean A, E, I, O, U, and som-metim-mes Y-Y-Y," I crooned, mimicking her gibe about Tom Jones.

Penny Sue poked my arm as she breezed into the kitchen for a diet soda. "Not sometimes Y, smarty. Just A, E, I, O, U. Deepak says it will harmonize your *chi*, revitalize your body. So, where do we start?"

Ruthie raked an armload of candles off the counter and started placing them around the condo.

Penny Sue pulled out a pack of matches. "Which candles are jasmine and sandalwood? Pauline said they worked on the pituitary or something. I think we want that stimulated before we start. Doesn't hurt to have the old MoJo working," she said, wiggling her fanny.

I wasn't sure whether the heinie action had to do with her reference to MoJo, pituitary, or stimulate. In any event, I decided against an anatomy discussion. Who knew where Penny Sue's pituitary might be. Ruthie, busy distributing our prodigious stock of waxware, was oblivious to the whole thing. She merely pointed to candles on the coffee table and an étagère beside the front door.

"We have to visualize a white light around this place," Penny Sue called out as she lit the taper in the hall. "And, be sure to keep a pure mind."

A pure mind? That from Ms. Leather-Bra-Swishy-Butt. If the exercise depended on her thoughts, we were doomed. Hopefully, Ruthie was sufficiently imbued with "The Force" to compensate.

"Okay, let's do it," Penny Sue called.

We gathered in the living room and held hands. I glanced out the window at the walkway to the beach.

"Wait," I said. "I don't think we want anyone to see this. We're trying to look normal, remember?" I ran around the condo and closed the blinds. Except for the flickering flames of two candles and a few shards of sunlight which slanted through the shades, the place was completely dark. Eerily so, for nine o'clock in the morning.

We joined hands again. Ruthie gave a brief invocation, then nodded at Penny Sue to light the smudge wand. I intoned A-A-A-A.

"Hold it," Penny Sue broke the spell. "Which end do I light? The pointed side or the fat one?"

She handed the straw bundle to Ruthie who shrugged ignorance and passed it to me. I took a whiff of each extremity and pointed to the blunt-cut end, which seemed more fragrant. We bowed our heads solemnly and started over. Penny Sue lit the smudge stick and fanned it with the feather. Ruthie and I started chanting the vowels. The smoke curled around our circle, spiraling up, up ... my nose. I whirled away, sneezing.

"Darn," I exclaimed. "That stuff smells like marijuana. We'll stink up the whole place."

Penny Sue sniffed the air. "It does, doesn't it? Do you suppose it'll make us high?"

I couldn't tell if she hoped for a yes or no response to the question.

Ruthie interrupted, "It's the sweetgrass you're smelling. Burning grass is burning grass; the scent's pretty much the same for all of them."

I watched the smoke coil toward the ceiling. "Do you think we should continue? We're in enough trouble without people thinking we smoke dope. All we need is to be raided for drugs! Your daddy would be real thrilled with that."

Penny Sue bit her bottom lip, considering. "No, let's keep going. Pauline said it would help. We'll air the place out later. We're going to burn all the scented candles to light up the place, anyway."

So we smudged. AA-A, EE-E, II-I, OO-O, UU-UUU. A conga line of middle-aged women, we snaked through the apartment, chanting softly and fanning smoke into all the corners. After everything had been thoroughly smoked, including ourselves, we assembled in the kitchen and ceremoniously plunged the smoldering wand into a beer mug of water. The straw hissed and sizzled, and Ruthie let out a loud OOM-MMM.

My heart did a swan dive as, for a brief moment, I wondered if an evil spirit had emerged from the straw and taken possession of Ruthie. The look on Penny Sue's face told me she'd had the same thought.

Thankfully, Ruthie grinned, returned to normal. "That was nice, wasn't it?" she said serenely. I mumbled a banal affirmative as she passed out candles. She lit hers and called to the ceiling, "Let light replace all darkness."

Ruthie angled her candle toward mine and nodded. I ignited my taper from her flame and racked my brain for an appropriate incantation. I finally whispered, "Let there be light," and tilted my candle toward Penny Sue. She didn't respond. Her face was screwed up in excruciating thought. My candle started to drip on the tile floor. I finally reached over and lit Penny Sue's candle myself.

She stared at the flame until a twinkle appeared in her eye. She snapped upright. "This little light of mine, I'm going to let it shine," Penny Sue warbled, snapping her fingers. "This little light of mine ..." she quick-stepped out of the kitchen.

I fell in behind her and picked up the song. "I'm going to let it shine."

Ruthie paused long enough to beseech the spirits for indulgence, then let out a loud trill, "Let it shine, let it shine, let it shin-ne." All that done with a terrific rendition of a barefooted time-step.

We danced and sang our way through the condo, lighting candles and shedding light in every crack, corner and closet—even under the bed. We ended up in the living room, breathless and giddy, our candles mere nubs getting dangerously close to skin. We reformed our circle and stood quietly. Ruthie thanked the spirits and gave a final invocation for world peace. On cue, we all blew out our flaming stubs ...

... and Penny Sue started singing *Kum Ba Ya*.

She'd just hit the verse about someone's praying Lord, when there was a knock at the front door. Our mouths dropped open, each of us wondering what to do. The place smelled like a drug den, the dozen or so scented candles having little impact on the smudge stench.

"Open the windows," I whispered. Penny Sue turned on the exhaust fan in the kitchen as Ruthie and I drew the blinds and threw open the windows. In the daylight we could see a thick haze of smoke.

Penny Sue surveyed the scene and realized the situation was hopeless. The choice was to answer the door and explain the peculiar odor or ignore it and hope the intruder would go away. "What kind of a person would drop in unannounced at," Penny Sue consulted the clock over the credenza in the dining area, "ten in the morning? It's positively uncivilized."

Ruthie nodded. "I hate it when people come over without calling first. They invariably arrive when I'm in the middle of a terrific meditation. So rude."

"There's no excuse for it in this day and age; everyone has a cell phone." I jumped on the rationalization bandwagon.

"You're right," Penny Sue said emphatically, as if she needed encouragement. "I'm not going to answer it." She set her lips resolutely.

We were all feeling justified and smug when the stranger banged on the door again. The whole wall shook.

Penny Sue's resolve turned to ire. "Who is that? Can't they take a hint?" She stomped down the hall and unlatched the front door, creating the perfect draw for the open windows. A thick cloud of smudge smoke blew through the screen into Woody's face. He coughed and covered his nose.

"Good morning, Penny Sue." He eyed her robe. "Did I interrupt something?"

Chapter 14

Woody didn't know anything about American Indian purification ceremonies we found out. Though Ruthie showed him the charred remains of the smudge stick, he remained skeptical. In fairness, all the hacking and sneezing made it hard for him to do much of anything; Woody was clearly allergic to the smoke. An interaction between the sage and his mean streak, Penny Sue whispered to me. Whatever the reason, we benefited, since his visit was short and to the point.

He handed Penny Sue a plastic bag with three bullets and her tagged .38. "Tests were inconclusive," he choked out. "You can have this back-k for now."

"Inconclusive?" she repeated. "Come on, Woody, you know I didn't kill anyone. Admit it."

He covered his mouth and nose with a handkerchief. "Inconclusive. In light of your clean record—"

"Clean record? I have *no* record," Penny Sue snapped.

"There's the matter of disturbing the peace … but, semantics aside, make sure your record stays clean," Woody inclined his head, indicating the hall and the dopey smell.

"Get serious." Penny Sue reared back preparing for a sally.

I interrupted. "I assume we can leave town now."

"Let me know first," he mumbled through the handkerchief.

Ruthie piped in. "What if there's a hurricane? There's a storm in the Caribbean."

"Let me know before you leave. Good day, ladies." Coughing, Woody left the condo and headed to his car.

Al, from next door, appeared a second later, waving the party invitation. "Thanks—" he started, then paused to take a deep breath, a knowing grin stretched his lips. "—for the invite." His eyes caught the bagged gun in Penny Sue's hand. He continued without missing a beat. "I'm looking forward to the party. Can I bring a bottle of wine or something?"

"Just yourself," Penny Sue answered cheerily, starting to shut the door. "It's a casual get together, mostly neighbors."

Al backed away, taking the hint. "I look forward to it," he said, eyes riveted on the gun.

"So do we, it should be fun." Penny Sue shut the door and threw the deadbolt. "We've got to get rid of this smell."

Ruthie turned on the exhaust fans in the bathrooms. Penny Sue found an old fan in the owner's closet which she positioned in the middle of the back door, blowing outward. She even donated her Sensual Nights candles to the cause, but the place still stunk to high heavens.

It was after eleven by then, and Charlotte was due at one o'clock to clean. So I threw on some clothes, smeared on lipstick, and headed to Food Lion for air freshener. It was on special, two for one, so I bought six cans of the heavy duty stuff for bathrooms—the kind that supposedly kills odors in addition to scenting the air. I also purchased two cans of Lysol spray as a last resort. If all else failed, we'd mask the odor with a stronger one.

I left the store confident I had the problem licked and was about to step into the parking lot, when I noticed a scruffy guy standing beside Penny Sue's daffodil-colored Mercedes.

It was Stinky. I rushed back into the store and watched from the cart area.

Stinky circled the car once, then approached the driver's side. The car's proximity alarm went off. He jumped back out of range and shrugged innocently at a couple walking by. He scanned the parking lot, looked back at the Mercedes, then strode to a motorcycle parked a few spaces away and roared off. I lolled in the store until I was sure he was gone.

I debated calling Deputy Moore, but had only brought my wallet, so didn't have his phone number. What good would that do, anyway? Stinky was long gone. And, even if he'd intended to burglarize the car, he hadn't touched it, so no laws had been broken. Best to let the incident slide, I figured, not wanting to push my luck with the one person in authority who seemed sympathetic to our plight. Besides, I sure didn't want Deputy Moore coming to our marijuana-reeking digs.

Penny Sue was waiting impatiently when I got home. "I thought the hogs had gotten you," she said, taking the bag from me and putting it on the kitchen counter. She reached in with both hands and came out with cans of Lysol and air freshener. "What's this?"

I explained my deodorization plan.

"Always thinking," Penny Sue said, giving me a can of air freshener.

"That's why she was president of the sorority," Ruthie said matter-of-factly.

"That's why she's always covered in spots." Penny Sue sniggered, pointing to a splotch on my shirt.

I angled my freshener in Penny Sue's direction. "Watch it, or I may be forced to use this on your mouth."

"Kidding, kidding." Penny Sue twirled away, spraying the air as she went. Ruthie and I followed suit, *sans* twirling. We expended all six cans and reconvened in the living room.

"What do you think?" Ruthie asked, sniffing.

Penny Sue replied, "Smells like a sweaty French prostitute."

I saw my opening and jumped in with both feet. "Gee, Penny Sue, I didn't know you spoke French."

Penny Sue puffed up like a blowfish, her mind searching for a witty response. Finding none, she finally grinned. "Touché."

We showered and dressed in record time; at least Ruthie and I did, and we were sharing a bathroom. Penny Sue was another story. Alone in the spacious master suite, her clothes neatly stored, Penny Sue could not manage to get ready in the hour before Charlotte arrived. At one point we heard some knocking around and low cursing. Ruthie and I exchanged knowing glances; the place would be a wreck when she emerged.

Charlotte arrived right on time, and I answered the door. To my dismay, her scruffy husband was with her.

Judge not according to appearance, I could hear Grandma Martin say as I held the screen door open for Charlotte and Pete to enter. A staunch Southern Baptist with a photographic mind, Grammy could, and did, provide Biblical guidance in virtually every situation.

The appearance quote came up often since Grammy's closest neighbor, Mr. Dinks, was the homeliest man we kids had ever seen. His hair, cut short, grew at bizarre angles—one big cowlick. His small eyes were set close together, and his chin didn't exist. His lips were puffy and twisted like Pete's, but worse, and they didn't move when he talked. Mr. Dinks tried to be nice, giving us candy and strawberries and wanting us to ride on his shoulders, but I never trusted him. No matter how hard I tried to be a good Christian, to walk in the ways of Jesus like Grammy said, the guy still gave me the creeps. And, I had the same creepy feeling about Pete. There was something about him that wasn't right, something I simply didn't trust.

"Why don't you start in the kitchen? Penny Sue hasn't finished dressing." I refrained from saying Her Highness, my first inclination, since Grandma Martin was fresh on my mind.

A jewel of gold in a swine's snout, so is a fair woman which is without discretion. From Proverbs, the quote was another one of Grammy's favorites which was applicable to a wide range of situations like fibbing, staying out past curfew, smacking my younger brother for beaning me with a baseball, or making snide remarks about people. Though, snide remarks were a two-quote infraction which typically earned a *Judge not, that ye be not judged,* too. Fortunately, Penny Sue fluttered by in her cotton gauze, squelching the Biblical groundswell building in my head.

"Hi, Charlotte," Penny Sue said, plopping her purse on a bar stool. She turned to Pete who was languidly dusting the dining room table. "And my bartender. I'm going to the liquor store now. What should I get?" She took a notepad and went to confer with Charlotte's seedy partner.

I nearly fainted. I couldn't believe Penny Sue had hired Pete to tend bar. If his liquor knowledge extended beyond beer and whiskey, I'd be surprised. (Sorry, Grammy.) On the plus side, his pugnacious puss would surely keep alcohol consumption in check. I for one would think twice before asking him for a refill. Perhaps that was Penny Sue's plan. Or, maybe she wanted him there to make herself look good. The contrast was striking.

"Ready girls?" Penny Sue chirped. "We've got a full afternoon of shopping ahead."

I picked up a bag of garbage from the kitchen and followed her to the car. "We need to stop by the Dumpster," I said, swinging the trash bag into the trunk. The Dumpster was tucked in the midst of a small clearing in the palmetto scrub next to the highway. As condo complexes go, it was one of the best treatments I'd ever seen for the smelly receptacles, because the green Dumpster blended perfectly with the green underbrush, making it all but invisible.

Penny Sue backed the car in so the trunk was next to the bin's lid. As neither Penny Sue nor Ruthie showed any inclination to move, I finally got out and heaved the bag into the container. I was closing the trunk, when a flash of red caught my eye on the highway. A red pickup truck had stopped on the shoulder of the road; a moment later, a Volusia County Sheriff's car pulled in behind. My heart skipped a beat.

Penny Sue's window went down. "What are you doing back there?" she called.

"Shh-h." I slinked around the car to her window. "A sheriff's car just pulled a red truck over," I whispered, pointing to a small opening in the brush.

Penny Sue switched off the engine. "Is it *the* red pickup?" she asked anxiously.

"Is it Deputy Moore?" Ruthie piped in.

I stood up slowly to get a better view. I could see two men standing at the back of the truck, but couldn't make out their faces through the brush. "I don't know. I need to get closer."

Crouching low, I skulked to the edge of the clearing and knelt behind a bushy palmetto. Though I couldn't distinguish words, I heard the muffled sounds of men talking, and one had the familiar, deep timbre of Deputy Moore's voice. Maybe we were wrong about Deputy Moore, and he was working our case, after all. I had to see. I shifted from side to side until I found an opening in the brush with a view of the highway. Both men were leaning against the truck with their backs toward me. Their slow, sweeping hand gestures told me it was a casual conversation, the type one might have with an old friend.

My shoulders slumped with disappointment. I'd really hoped it *was* Deputy Moore who'd come to our rescue, like a white knight, by tracking down Rick's killer and our stalker. I sighed dejectedly and glanced down at the very moment a lizard started to scamper up my leg. I yelped and batted the little reptile away, rustling the bushes. The men turned in my direction. I hunkered down, afraid to breathe. They stared for a second, then, seeing nothing, resumed their conversation. Yet, that moment was enough. I saw them both clearly, full face, and it *was* Deputy Moore and Mr. Red Pickup!

I stayed motionless in the brush until the men shook hands and drove away, then raced to the car and fell into the backseat, panting.

"What? What?" Penny Sue demanded, seeing the horrified look on my face.

I told them what I'd seen, how the men acted like old friends.

"That's why Moore tried to play down the truck angle," Penny Sue stated. "He was covering for his buddy."

"Do you truly believe Pickup Man killed Rick?" Ruthie asked with an edge of panic.

"He's the best candidate," Penny Sue replied matter-of-factly. "The question is whether Moore is in cahoots with him."

"Cahoots on what? The murder? Turtles?" I asked. Ted Moore had seemed like such a nice guy. He'd screwed in the light bulb on the porch for us, shown concern for our safety, and generally been a first-class gentleman. Surely, my judgment of character wasn't that bad. I thought of Zack. Maybe I *was* off base, again. "I guess there's no one we can turn to, no one we can trust," I muttered gloomily.

Penny Sue regarded me in the rearview mirror. "Sure there is—we have each other," she said blithely. "After all, we're the Daffodils." She smiled impishly. "Come on, we're jumping to conclusions about Deputy Moore. That," she waved at the highway, "doesn't mean a thing. We have a party to think about. Don't let this ruin the day."

I gave her a thin smile. "You're right. It's a small town. Everyone knows everyone—it's to be expected. There's nothing to worry about."

"Yeah," Ruthie agreed weakly.

Penny Sue started the car and slapped it into gear. "Perk up, now. This incident means nothing; forget it ever happened. We have a million things to do before the party."

Our first stop was the liquor store. Scotch, vodka, gin, bourbon, wine in every color, champagne, and imported beer; we had so much stuff I was surprised we didn't need a special permit to transport it. From there we went to Dollar General where we found the Furbies.

Ruthie rubbed the stomach of the display model. The furry critter laughed and said "Big fun." Delighted, she stroked its head. It made a smooching sound and declared, "I love you."

"Watch this," Ruthie continued. She stuck her finger in the Furby's mouth.

It went, "Yum-m," then said, "Hungry."

"Isn't it cute?" Ruthie asked as she reached for a leopard-spotted model with blond hair. I picked up another box and started reading.

"Absolutely the most precious thing I've ever seen," Penny Sue gushed. She put her finger in the display's mouth as Ruthie had done.

"Yum, very hungry. Again, please," it said.

"The poor little thing's starving to death," Penny Sue said. She stood there with her finger in its mouth, the critter going, "Yum, again. Yum, again. Please." Nearby shoppers drew close. "If only it were this easy with men," Penny Sue quipped loudly.

A gasp went up among the throng, and a petite black lady in her eighties went into hysterics. "You got that right, honey. Don't take much to get the 'again, again.' It's the 'yum, yum, please' that's always missing. I need one of them." The little woman lunged in front of Penny Sue and snatched a silver Furby.

Penny Sue quickly grabbed the only remaining toy and hugged it to her chest. "Ruthless," she whispered, watching the old lady toddle away. "Lord, this is as bad as the after-Christmas sale at Saks."

"Penny Sue," I said, as I put my Furby back on the shelf. "It doesn't really pick up words from the surroundings. It won't work."

She pouted. "I don't care. I'm getting one anyway, he's darling."

"Me, too," Ruthie exclaimed cradling her Furby. "Come on, let's get out of here before we start another riot."

We picked up batteries and headed through the Express Check-Out lane with two Furbies.

The next item on our To-Do List was a leather bra or halter top for Penny Sue. We sat in the car, air conditioner running, Ruthie engrossed in powering up her Furby.

"Where do you suppose we'd find one of those halter tops?" Penny Sue asked.

If I knew, I didn't want to tell her, even though our need to appear normal had diminished with Woody's return of the gun. Despite his protests to the contrary, Penny Sue was obviously not a suspect in Rick's murder. Still, it wouldn't hurt to be cautious and show a little decorum in front of the neighbors. After all, we weren't completely in the clear as evidenced by the fact that Woody wouldn't let us leave town without his permission.

"I'll bet you'd have to go all the way to Daytona Beach to find one," I replied with all the credence I could muster, hoping against hope that Penny Sue would drop the matter until after the party. No such luck.

"Motorcycle people wear them," Penny Sue went on, oblivious to my comment.

Ruthie's Furby came to life, laughing. "Ha, ha, ha—"

"Harley," Penny Sue exclaimed, slapping the car in gear. "I'll bet they carry them at the Harley Davidson store over by Pub 44."

They did. Thankfully, no bras; but the dealership had a good selection of black leather halter tops, short shorts, slacks, you name it. Penny Sue chose a halter top with a Harley emblem in the center, below the boobs. She wanted to buy leather shorts to match, but Ruthie convinced her otherwise.

"One continuous yeast infection," Ruthie pronounced quietly.

Those four words eclipsed all my arguments about propriety and image. Too bad I couldn't think of something similar for the top.

The final stop was at Publix supermarket for limes, mixers, ice, a bag of salad and Stouffers' lasagna. It took some doing, but Ruthie and I convinced Penny Sue that we should stay home and rest up for the party. (Guess where she wanted to go? It starts with an R.)

We finally got home at three-thirty. Charlotte was cleaning fingerprints from the sliding glass doors to the deck, and Pete was dusting Penny Sue's bedroom. Penny Sue enlisted Pete's help with the liquor which he arranged on the short side of the L-shaped bar next to the sink. I watched his preparations with interest. It was clear he knew what he was doing. I also noticed for the first time that he walked with a limp.

"What did you do to your leg?" I asked.

He hiked up his pant leg far enough to reveal the bottom of a walking cast. "Motorcycle accident. Got banged up pretty bad; broke this leg in three places. Almost healed now, this cast is the last of it."

An accident. So that's what happened to his lip. *Judge not according to appearance*, Grandma Martin's admonition came to mind. She was right again, bless her soul. Pete would probably be a splendid bartender.

Charlotte and Pete finished up and left with a promise to return the next day at two. Ruthie helped Penny Sue unpack her Furby. For all the effort it took, you'd have thought they were doing brain surgery. I knew better than to get in the middle of that fray and contented myself with the Weather Channel.

Former Hurricane, now Tropical Storm Lizzie remained stationary, though was gaining strength. If an approaching front held together, it would steer the storm out into the Atlantic, away from land. If the front fizzled, Lizzie could go anywhere. Stay tuned for the latest coordinates at eight.

"Me tah Lu Nee." A little voice heralded Ruthie and Penny Sue's success.

"That means her name is Lu Nee," Ruthie said, looking up from the instructions.

"Lu Nee?" Penny Sue asked. "My baby's name is Lu Nee?"

Lord, a chip off the old block. I could hardly keep a straight face.

"Little Lu Nee." Penny Sue positioned the toy in the crook of her arm and stuck her pinkie finger in its mouth. It responded with a stream of yums and gibberish, punctuated by a loud burp. Then, it snored and went to sleep.

We headed for the beach. We walked south toward the public entrance at Hiles Boulevard, which, counting the trek back, would give us a nice mile stroll. The weather was perfect and the beach virtually deserted at this time of year. We hadn't gone very far when we encountered Gerty and Robert standing between two turtle mounds.

"Good evening," I called. "How's the turtle business today?"

Gerty glared at us, clearly not realizing who we were. Luckily, Robert did. He put a hand on Gerty's shoulder as if to restrain her and replied with a jaunty, "Very fine, thank you. A new brood's about to hatch."

We rushed toward him. "Now?" Ruthie asked, excitedly.

Robert nodded. "Both nests are due. We came to dig this one up, but it's already cooking." He pointed to a tiny flipper emerging from the sand. Looking like a brown Brillo pad with feet, the reptilian tyke struggled free of its eggshell and turtle-toddled toward the ocean. Fortunately, the tide was high, so it didn't have far to go. Yet that short distance seemed like an eternity. First, he (Penny Sue claimed it was a male because of its pig-headedness) ran headlong into a piece of driftwood. The hatchling bounced back, paused, as if dazed, then plowed right back into the obstacle. The little booger did that four times before he found a path around the barrier.

"Can't we help him?" Ruthie asked after what looked like a particularly painful head butt.

"No," Gerty replied sternly. "A certain amount of flailing is good; it builds up their lungs. This little guy's developing the coordination he'll need to survive in the ocean."

"Like a child learning to walk," I observed.

"Exactly," Robert said.

By then the nest had transformed into a pot of boiling, roiling sand as miniature heads and flippers struggled free. Each struck out across the sand. Most seemed to sense the ocean and headed for the surf. Some went in circles, while others struck off in the wrong direction. Contrary to Gerty's stern admonition that we not touch them, I saw her stealthily nudge a few toward the ocean with the toe of her shoe. Eventually, all but one had made it into the water.

The straggler had had a particularly rough time of it, wandering in circles and being rammed and trampled by his siblings. Several times Gerty nudged him with her toe; each time he started out toward the ocean, but veered off course. We watched in horror as his motion got slower and slower.

Tears welling in her eyes, Ruthie dropped to her knees beside the hatchling. "He's too exhausted to go on. Can't we help him?" she looked up at Gerty. The old woman shook her head grimly. A tear streaked down Ruthie's cheek.

"We're going to let him die?" I asked, feeling a lump form in my throat.

"We can't pick them up," Robert responded stoically. "We can't interfere."

Penny Sue had watched the exchange in silence, hands on hips, her jaw getting tighter and tighter. Robert's comment sent her over the edge. "Horse hockey," she exploded. "There's more than one way to skin a cat." She dropped to the ground and plunged her hands into the sand. "Damn, I broke a nail." She paused, sucking her finger. "Well, help me. Are y'all just going to sit there?"

"What are you doing?" Ruthie asked, blotting her cheek with the back of her hand.

"I'm digging a canal, what does it look like? If we can't take the turtle to the water, we'll just have to bring the water to the turtle."

Brilliant! She'd surprised me again. Ruthie and I started scooping sand. In a matter of minutes the trench was finished and filling with water.

"Come on, sugar," Penny Sue purred to the hatchling. "Get in the water." A seagull swooped low, circling our heads, clearly anxious to intervene in his own way.

Ruthie covered her mouth, eyes welling up again. "I think we're too late."

Penny Sue glared defiantly—the same mixture of anger and determination I'd seen on her face when she tried to stop Rick's brawl. Lord, I was glad she didn't have the gun. If she had, the seagull was a goner and possibly the Turtle Patrol, too. Not that Penny Sue would shoot them; I was confident of that, unless of course, her hormones are seriously out of whack. But, she might *warn* them, which was the same as a threat with a deadly weapon, according to Woody.

"Come on, baby cakes; move it," Penny Sue called to the turtle. "Get in the water." The critter still didn't budge. Penny

Sue's face got red. "Get out of here," she shouted to the seagull, waving her fist overhead. Gerty, Robert, and I all took a step back.

And then the universe intervened. (At least, that's how Ruthie would have explained it.) A big wave overflowed the trench and splashed the baby turtle. He sprang to life, stroking frantically. The water washed over him, and he started to float.

"That's it, baby. Swim," Penny Sue cheered.

The receding wave sucked him into the trench. We followed him, shouting encouragement, as the tiny tyke paddled furiously toward the ocean. Another good wave, and our baby was gone. Gone to find his mother, his brothers, and a big meal, we hoped.

"Live long and prosper," Ruthie whispered.

Penny Sue yelled, "Stay away from fishermen."

Gerty checked her watch and nodded to Robert who removed the stakes from the now empty nest.

"What about the other nest?" Ruthie asked as they started to leave. "I thought you were going to dig it up."

"It's late. We'll give that nest another day. If they haven't hatched by Sunday morning, we'll dig it up. Six o'clock, if you want to watch."

Ruthie and I did; Penny Sue had other ideas.

"Six," Penny Sue mused as we headed back to the condo. "That's awfully early; we would hardly have gotten to bed."

"I thought the party was only cocktails: three to seven," I said.

"Oh sure, but we won't get home from the movie until three or four in the morning."

"Movie?" Ruthie asked, looking peeved. "What movie?"

"*The Rocky Horror Picture Show*. There's a special showing at the Beacon. Lyndon invited us all to go."

"Lyndon? When did you talk to him?"

"At JB's last night. I meant to tell y'all earlier, but it slipped my mind in all the commotion. I told Lyndon how we used to dress up and act out the movie with the water pistols and toast. Remember? Wasn't that fun?"

It was. A camp, cult flick about transvestites from outer space, *Rocky Horror* was the midnight show at the campus theater every Saturday night. For our first two years of college, until we all got hooked up in serious relationships, a huge sorority contingent would go to the show each week. People would dress like their favorite characters and recite dialogue with the cast. They would join in dance numbers and sing off-key. Basically, it was a big, boisterous bash that took our minds off heartbreaks, frizzy perms, and failed exams. The elixir of life, we used to say ...

... and why hadn't I thought of it sooner? It was the perfect antidote for divorce, treachery, and murder. Now that Penny Sue was off the hook, what better way to clear the air and jump start our vacation?

Chapter 15

"You bought that leather halter top to wear to *The Rocky Horror Picture Show*, didn't you?" I said to Penny Sue the next morning.

She arched a brow and chewed her cream cheese and pepper jelly bagel without comment.

"You did it to upstage Ruthie and me. Admit it: a sneaky tactic to impress Lyndon."

She finished chewing, swallowed and took a sip of coffee.

It was hard to believe the three of us were eating breakfast, and it wasn't even seven o'clock. Judge Parker could be credited with the early gathering. He had called at six to tell Penny Sue he was going fishing. His cell phone would probably be out of range, he said, so she should call the office if she needed to reach him.

"I wish you'd told us sooner. Ruthie and I don't have anything to wear, at least not a costume." Back in college I'd always dressed as Nell, a top-hatted, tap dancing vixen. I had a gold sequined top hat and silver tap shoes with heel braces: the real things. Walking shorts and leather sandals just wouldn't be the same.

Ruthie glanced up from the newspaper. "I'll bet only a handful of people come in costume. This is a resort, tourists don't pack for a masquerade. But, we could run out and get a water pistol, just in case."

"And umbrellas." A shield against water pistols.

"Better yet, slickers," Penny Sue said. "I'm sure they have them at Walgreen's. Why don't y'all take my car and pick some up," Penny Sue replied. "You'll have time. No one will get here until one-thirty."

"The party's supposed to go from three to seven. What if people don't leave?" I asked.

Penny Sue shrugged. "They will; the invitation clearly states that it's only cocktails. And, if they don't leave, well, I'll kick them out." She smiled over the rim of her coffee. "I don't have to impress anyone now. I can be myself."

She'd said that to torture me. Without the pressure of impressing the neighbors, I knew Penny Sue might do anything. I suppressed a shudder, recalling her story about the Jim Williams' party—the one where she'd instigated (no matter what she said, I knew she was responsible) a whole flurry of boob-licking instead of hand-kissing. I looked sidelong and saw her watching me expectantly. Well, I refused to react. I snatched a discarded section of the newspaper and started to read. "Federal agents in Miami busted another international drug ring. This one used young Hasidic Jews as couriers."

"Is that the group that wears black hats and sidecurls?" Ruthie asked, oblivious to my concerns about Penny Sue.

"Yes," I answered, pointedly avoiding Penny Sue's gaze. "That's precisely why they were recruited by drug lords. The young men looked so innocent and demure, custom agents never suspected a thing."

"That's unusual," Penny Sue said, waving a jelly-smeared piece of bagel. "I think most drugs come into the country by water; you know, in those cigarette boats they used on *Miami Vice.* Drug runners bury the stuff on the beach and no one's the wiser."

I skimmed down the article. "It says here that the Navy and Coast Guard have just about closed down that activity. Drug prices are beginning to soar."

"Let's talk about something else," Penny Sue said, picking up her Furby. "That drug stuff is depressing. Daddy's in constant danger, you know." She stuck her finger in the Furby's mouth; it went, *Yum-m.* "Is little Lu Nee hungry?" Penny Sue cooed to the fuzzy toy. "Have you fed yours, Ruthie? They'll die of starvation if you don't feed them."

While they played with their *children,* I checked the Weather Channel. Hurricane, Tropical Storm, now Hurricane, again, Lizzie had merged with another tropical wave and was gaining strength. Although it was currently spinning over open water, Lizzie was expected to begin moving toward the Eastern seaboard. Where and when it would come ashore was anyone's guess. Stay tuned for more details. Great, a hurricane in addition to an uncensored Penny Sue. That's all I needed!

Ruthie finished with her Furby and joined me on the couch. "I hope that storm doesn't come here," she said nervously.

"It won't," I said with more confidence than I felt. "You want to shower first?" I asked, trying to change the subject. Given half a chance, Ruthie would sit there all day, watching the Weather Channel.

She took the bait. "Okay."

I studied my wardrobe. I planned to wear a black cotton dress to the party. A scooped neck, sleeveless number, it was one of those indispensable dresses that would fit in anywhere. By changing accessories, it could go from the grocery store to a night on the town. Besides, Penny Sue wanted us all to wear our DAFFODIL pins, and the black dress was the only thing I'd brought that remotely suited the ornate brooch.

The Rocky Horror Picture Show was another matter. I leafed through my side of the closet twice. I needed something garish that wouldn't be ruined in the event audiences still acted out the rain scene with water pistols. I settled on a pair of tight fitting capris and a very wrinkled tank top.

I checked the utility room for an iron and ironing board, but came up empty-handed. Surely, they had one. "Penny Sue, where can I find an iron?" I called across the hall.

She leaned out of her bathroom, draped in a towel. "We keep it in the owner's closet. It's unlocked."

A common feature of beach condos, the owner's closet was a five-by-ten foot locked room used to keep personal effects safe from renters. Since the Judge never rented the place, he apparently used his closet for general storage. I found the iron and was setting up the ironing board when the telephone rang. It was my realtor; the young couple wanted to buy the house. My house.

The news hit me like a punch in the stomach. I forced myself to breathe as my perky realtor rattled on and on about the price and appliances. Most of the conversation was completely lost on me as my mind raced with all the memories tied up in that house. So much living. So much pain. Gone, all gone. But I had my babies' handprints!

I managed to mumble something about contacting Zack and hung up. Then I buried my face in the crook of my arm and cried.

Fortunately, there was no time for moping or reliving memories. I resolved to pull a Penny Sue—put the whole issue out of my mind until tomorrow and act as if nothing had ever happened. She could do it with a murder—I could do it with a house. I hoped.

I finished ironing, got dressed, helped tidy the condo, went to Walgreen's for rain slickers and to Food Lion twice. All that before one-thirty when Charlotte and Pete arrived. Shirley from Party Hearty showed up at two.

Penny Sue, decked out in a backless, Hawaiian print sundress, watched silently from a corner as Shirley arranged the food on the dining room table. I could see Penny Sue's expression from across the living room and knew she was not happy.

"What's wrong?" I asked, sidling alongside.

She turned her back to the table and spoke through thinned lips. "Paper plates and aluminum foil platters. I can't believe it. What am I going to do?"

Shirley had lined the food up buffet-style on one side of the table. Red paper plates, blue napkins and white plastic forks (no doubt remnants from the Fourth of July) were laid out to form an arrow that pointed toward the food. The logic of the arrow escaped me, unless Shirley was used to dealing with people who, through age or ale, were so out of it they literally had to be directed to the hors d'oeuvres. Or, perhaps the food was often mistaken for something else. Scanning the rest of the table, the second motive seemed likely.

Crab Rangoon and stuffed mushrooms were arranged on the first pizza-sized platter. Next to that was a decidedly lopsided fruit tray, an apparent casualty of the ruts in our unpaved driveway. Steamed shrimp on a mound of crushed ice formed the center-piece—too bad the shrimp were so small, two or three would fit on a toothpick. Next was a platter of crackers, cheese, and artichoke dip, followed by strawberries dipped in chocolate. The strawberries looked good. I snatched one and bit down. The hard chocolate coating shattered and fell to the floor.

Shirley stooped down and cleaned the mess before I could get to it. "Those strawberries," she said. "This always happens."

Always happens. I thought Penny Sue was going to explode. I took her arm and steered her toward the bar Pete had set up in the kitchen. "Let's have a drink."

She ordered a double martini. Much to my surprise, Pete knew what he was doing. "I can't serve that food; Lyndon will think we're a bunch of hicks," she complained between long sips of her cocktail.

I looked back at the table; it was pitiful. I, like Penny Sue, had expected the caterer to provide china and silverware. Ceramic plates and metal forks, at least. "Are there enough dishes here?"

She shook her head.

"Well, there's nothing we can do. It'll be fine; this is the beach. No one will think anything of it. Besides, it's only cocktails, not dinner."

Penny Sue sighed ruefully. "I hope you're right." Then to Pete, "Pour the drinks heavy."

The doorbell rang. It was Jonathan, the biker banker, and his wife Marie who wore leather shorts and a skimpy bandeau top. Penny Sue shot me a look that said, "See," as she escorted them to the bar.

Lyndon and Al were the next to arrive followed by several sets of neighbors, though the older couple from the balcony behind us was conspicuously missing. Penny Sue took their absence as a sure sign that they were the culprits who'd stirred up trouble with Woody. I tried to soothe her with a string of lame excuses, yet deep down, I knew she was right.

By four o'clock the party was in full swing. Pete poured a steady stream of drinks while Shirley spent most of her time wiping chocolate shards from the floor. For once Penny Sue was not the center of attention; her backless sundress was no match for Marie's leather shorts or Charlotte's youth, long legs, and ample bosom.

A gray-haired neighbor with a handlebar mustache homed in on Marie and followed her like a puppy. Clad in shorts and a low-cut shirt, Charlotte got stares from everyone, especially Al and Lyndon. Early on I saw our neighbor corner her in the hall. Minutes later, Lyndon did precisely the same thing. Thankfully, Penny Sue did not see that tête-à-tête, though Pete did. And, Pete definitely had a mean streak. At the first lull in his duties, I saw him herd Charlotte down the hall and push her against the wall. His fist was clenched, and I feared he might strike her.

I headed for the corridor, I had to do something. "Charlotte, could you help me put out some nuts?" I stopped, realizing the statement hadn't come out quite right. No matter. Pete dropped her arm and backed away, heading toward the master bathroom.

"Okay," Charlotte answered, watching his back and rubbing her forearm.

She followed me into the kitchen where I made a pretense of searching for cashews. "I guess we forgot to buy them," I finally said. "Oh well, why don't you see if the guests on the deck need anything." She nodded and brushed past Pete—who'd just returned—without a word. I handed him my glass and smiled as sweetly as I could. (Sorry, Grammy, my initial opinion of Pete was correct. He was not to be trusted.) "Vodka tonic, please."

"Make that two," a deep voice said.

It was Al. This was my chance to find out what he knew about the man in the red pickup. I smiled invitingly, trying to mimic Penny Sue. "So, you come to New Smyrna Beach often?" I asked, taking my drink and backing into the hall, where we could talk undisturbed.

"Every chance I get. I like it here—quiet, not much traffic."

I nodded. "This is the first time I've been back since college. I'm amazed how much New Smyrna's grown."

"New Smyrna's grown all right, but it isn't in the league of Jersey. It's beautiful there in the summer, but the traffic is a killer."

"Same for Atlanta. It takes thirty minutes to go five miles, and I live in the suburbs." I took a sip of my drink for courage.

"Say, we're in the market for a handyman to fix a few things around the condo. Can you recommend someone who's good?"

"Can't help you there," he replied crisply.

"Oh, we saw a red pickup truck at your place when we arrived. I assumed it was your handyman."

Al shrugged. "Don't know anything about that. I'm just renting the place."

Just renting. I'd assumed Al owned the condo when he said he came to New Smyrna often. "Rats, we hate to pick someone at random from the yellow pages, you never know what you'll get." I watched closely for his reaction.

He canted his head sympathetically. "Right. Sorry I can't help you. Some of these other guys," he waved at the room full of people, "probably know someone."

"Good idea, I'll ask around." Darn, a dead end; but, at least, it eliminated Al from the suspect list.

We'd chatted for a while about restaurants, fishing, and local attractions, when Al leaned close with a mischievous grin. "Want to step outside for a little smoke?" he asked confidentially, patting his pocket. "I've got a joint here that's primo stuff." He winked broadly.

"No," I said a little too loudly.

Al took a step back, looking puzzled. "Yesterday ... I just thought—"

The smudge stick! Al thought we were smoking marijuana. "Oh, that! It's not what you think. Ruthie's into American Indian rituals. We were burning sage and sweetgrass for good luck."

"Sure. Sorry." Al downed his vodka tonic, clearly not believing a word I'd said. "How 'bout some food." He motioned toward the buffet with his glass. I followed him to the table where he quickly disappeared into a group around the shrimp bowl. That was the last I saw of the man for the rest of the party.

The remainder of the afternoon was uneventful. The Furbies were a big hit as was Penny Sue's embellished tale about the old lady who jumped in front of her at Dollar General. Virtually all of the women commented on our Daffodil brooches, several of whom—including Shirley—were divorced and wanted to join the club. Though the food wasn't very good, most of it was eaten. And, thanks to our caterer, my fears that people would linger too long proved unfounded. Promptly at seven, Shirley started packing up the aluminum platters, providing an unmistakable hint that it was time to go; which the guests did to a profusion of *Wonderful-party, So-nice-to-meet-you's*. All except Lyndon who tarried until everyone had gone. He planted a big kiss on Penny Sue when he left.

"That's one sexy man," she said with a smile so wide I could see her gums. "I'm definitely wearing that halter top tonight."

Penny Sue wore the halter top and so did about two dozen other women in their forties. Marie came in her shorts, though she'd switched the bandeau top she wore to the party for a silk blouse. Short, tall, thin, and ... ample (like Penny Sue), Harley Davidson leather covered a wide array of boobs and butts that evening. Aside from the motorcycle garb, very few people were dressed in costume, though I did see a number of umbrellas and slickers, a sure sign of diehard Rocky fans.

Lyndon had never been to a *Rocky Horror* show, which was the reason he'd insisted on attending. Knowing only that it was a rowdy masquerade, he'd tried to comply with the custom. Sadly, Lyndon's getup made him look more like an expensively dressed Captain Hook than an alien transvestite. No matter; Lyndon had a high old time. He laughed and clapped and even squirted a few people with our water pistol.

We pulled in the driveway of the condo at three o'clock. The wind was howling and it was so dark you could barely see your hand in front of your face.

"The porch light is out again," Ruthie observed.

"Wind must have jostled it loose," Penny Sue said.

Lyndon backed up his rented Continental and aimed the headlights on the front door. "Better?" he asked.

"Much," Penny Sue said, handing the condo key to me in the backseat. "Why don't y'all go ahead? I'd like to speak with Lyndon for a minute."

Ruthie and I got the hint, said our good nights and hurried inside. I poured a diet soda and stretched out on the sofa. "Making out in a parking lot," I commented. "It seems so high school."

"Dating at any age gets silly. Hormones short-out the brain." Ruthie chuckled as she switched on the light beside the fireplace. "Darn," she said, holding up the pole that went in the track of the sliding glass door. "We forgot to lock up, again!"

I shook my head. "Penny Sue must have gone out for a cigarette. She's been smoking like a chimney."

"Maybe she'll cut back now that the party's over and Woody's off her back." Ruthie turned on the television. Hurricane Lizzie was moving north, parallel to the Florida coast, thanks to a cold front sliding in from the west. If the current track held, the storm would make landfall in North or South Carolina. "The last few days have worn me out. I vote we stay a day or two longer, then head home."

Home. I didn't have a home to go to, or at least, not for long. I told her about the offer on the house. "I should get back, too. And, I suppose I should call Zack about the house. I'm sure he's overjoyed."

"Have you thought about what you want to do?"

I sniffed back tears. "No. I guess I can't put it off any longer."

"You're welcome to stay with us as long as you'd like. Our place is huge, much too big for Daddy, me, and Mr. Wong. The guest suite in the south wing has its own entrance. You'd have privacy."

"Thanks. I'll see how things go." I checked the clock in the dining room; it was almost four. "Want to see the turtles? Gerty said they'd dig them up at six."

"Sure. How about we catch a catnap, first."

I set the oven timer to wake us up and went back to the sofa. Ruthie curled up on the love seat. Neither of us heard Penny Sue come in. Her bedroom door was shut when the buzzer sounded.

"Do you think we should see if Penny Sue wants to go?"

Ruthie rolled her eyes. "I'm not knocking on that door. No telling who's in there."

"Good point." I followed Ruthie out on the deck and turned to close the sliding glass door. Coated with salt spray, the thing wouldn't budge. I planted my feet and pulled hard; it screeched across the track. Then, I heard a yelp and a guttural retching sound. I whirled toward the noise and gasped with revulsion.

Chapter 16

Stinky—clearly dead—was sprawled across the deck next to the sidewalk, and Ruthie had managed to barf all over him. Bent double, Ruthie backed into me, still retching. I yanked the door so hard, it opened like it had Teflon tracks. Then, I dragged Ruthie, puking and crying, to the kitchen sink. "Penny Sue," I screamed. I could care less if she had company. "Penny Sue!" I really bellowed.

"What?" she answered, pulling on her robe as she ran down the hall. Penny Sue's hair was standing straight up, and she hadn't bothered to take off her makeup, judging from her raccoon eyes. "Wha—" The puke smell hit her when she reached the living room. "Gawd, what's wrong with Ruthie?" she asked through the hand covering her nose.

"There's a dead man on the deck, Penny Sue. It's Stinky."

Penny Sue raced to the back window and peered through the vertical blinds. "Are you sure he's dead?"

"He's stiff," Ruthie said between sobs.

"Lord." Penny Sue held her face with both hands. "I've got to think; stay calm." She paced back and forth, swatting at a wasp that had also fled the crime scene. "What's the number for nine-eleven?"

Still holding Ruthie over the sink, I gaped at Penny Sue, not believing my ears.

"What's the number?" She yelled, holding the phone in one hand as she ran the other through her hair, which only stood up even more. In another situation it would have been funny—she looked remarkably similar to the wild-haired fight promoter, Don King—but, with the vomit stench and Ruthie still heaving, I was in no mood for games or stupidity. "For godsakes, Penny Sue, the number is *NINE-ONE-ONE*. That's it, *NINE-ONE-ONE!*"

"Of course." Penny Sue placed the call with shaking hands and got a wet towel for Ruthie's face. It took both of us to get her to the bedroom. We put the wastebasket from the bathroom next to the bed.

"Yell if you need anything," I said, closing the door. Sirens were already approaching on A1A. The first contingency arrived a few minutes later. Penny Sue scampered to her room to dress, as I answered the door. It was one of the young officers who'd responded to Rick's murder. I ushered him around the mess on the living room floor to the back of the condo.

Dawn was breaking as the patrolman stepped out on the deck into a puddle of puke. He scowled at me as if I were responsible. I shrugged and pointed toward the body. The crew-cutted officer knelt carefully and checked Stinky's neck for a pulse. He shook his head and stood.

I went inside and prepared to clean the tile floor. It was a coping mechanism I'd picked up from my mother. When my grandmother died, Mom cleaned out the attic and basement. When my younger brother was hospitalized with an unknown lung infection, she'd cleaned the whole house. If she and Dad had a fight, she might straighten a closet or a drawer—the amount of effort directly proportional to the seriousness of the situation. My first therapist said it was healthy, the equivalent of counting to ten. Perhaps. If nothing else, it got the house clean. The house. The sold house. It had been squeaky clean for over a year, I thought bleakly.

I headed for the utility room. The mop and bucket were next to the dryer. Without thinking, I snatched the mop with one hand and the bucket with the other. I almost fell down. I'd completely forgotten the heavy pesticides I'd stowed there when we first arrived. I hefted the bag of bug killer out of the bucket, careful to lower it to the floor gently, so the flimsy bag wouldn't break. Then I loaded the container with ammonia and went back to the living room where I mopped vomit to the piercing whine of sirens. Judging from the red and blue flashing lights that danced on the walls, most of New Smyrna Beach's police and rescue units had responded to the call. Thanks to Ruthie's weak stomach, the crews went around the building to get to the deck, instead of traipsing through the condo as they'd done with Rick. Amazing how a dirty diaper or a little up-chuck could scatter a throng of the most manly men. I used to hate that about Zack: how he'd invariably disappear when anything odoriferous came up. This time, the male shortcoming suited me fine.

I finished the floor and sat down in the living room with Penny Sue, who'd combed her hair, doused herself with perfume and donned slacks and a silk blouse. The wasp, that had been conspicuously absent during my smelly chore, suddenly appeared from no where. It went straight for her head.

"Darn!" She bolted from the sofa, slapping at the wasp. "Shoo, I'm in no mood for this," she screeched.

I ran to the kitchen, found the wasp spray under the sink and angled the can toward the wasp buzzing Penny's head.

She glared at me, horrified. "Don't you dare!" Penny Sue snatched two magazines from the coffee table and clapped them frantically over her head. She caught the wasp with the second blow. Dazed, but not dead, the insect plummeted to the floor. I quickly doused him with the poison.

Panting, Penny Sue glared at the wasp, then at me.

For a brief moment I thought she might smack me with the magazines. I ditched the can on the end of the kitchen counter and backed away. "I was not going to squirt you," I declared.

She gave me a wide-eyed look, hands hanging limply at her side, yet still clutching the magazines. I took another step back, holding my breath. Finally, Penny Sue giggled nervously and sank onto the sofa. I exhaled.

"I can't take much more excitement." She tossed the journals back on the table.

I stepped over the dead bug and collapsed on the love seat. "Me either," I said wearily.

Back to her old self, Penny Sue leaned forward anxiously. "Tell me again, what happened? You were going to see the turtles when you found Stinky?"

I nodded. "It was still dark. Ruthie tripped over the body."

"And barfed. Boy, he's really stinky now." Penny Sue picked up the remote and turned on the television. It was tuned to the Weather Channel. Lizzie was a couple hundred miles due east of Miami and moving north.

"I think it was a premonition," Ruthie said from the hallway, looking from us to the wasp. The color had returned to her face.

"You feeling all right?" Penny Sue slid over to make room for her on the sofa.

"Yeah, I'm okay. Sorry about the mess. His name, Stinky; I think our calling him that was a premonition."

"Premonition of what? That you'd vomit on him?" I asked.

Ruthie looked down at her lap. "That and his untimely end. If I recall correctly, I was the one who pinned that label on him."

Penny Sue and I hesitated, both searching back through our memory banks. Ruthie was right.

"I wonder what he was doing here," Penny Sue said, breaking the silence.

I raised my hand. "I believe I know that answer. I saw him at Food Lion the day before yesterday. He must have followed me home."

"You saw him?" Penny Sue asked incredulously. "You didn't say anything."

"I'd gone to buy air freshener after we'd smudged the condo. He was circling your car when I came out of the store. The car alarm scared him off. I thought he was long gone by the time I finally left."

"You think he followed you here, then came back last night to rob us?" Ruthie asked.

"Makes sense. That is a big, distinctive Mercedes. Stands to reason a person with an expensive car has expensive jewelry to match. Shoot, I think we were all decked out in our finest when we first met him at JB's."

Penny Sue canted her head ruefully.

"And, wait." I pointed at Ruthie. "You tripped over the pole. Remember? The sliding glass door was not locked last night ... or the night before!"

We both looked at Penny Sue. "Not me," she said, waving off our unspoken accusation with both hands. "I made certain that stupid stick was in place before we left. It was in the door track, I swear."

"Then, someone was in the condo." I stood. "We'd better see if anything is missing."

We reconvened in the living room a few minutes later. Ruthie led off. "Someone's definitely been through my drawers. I don't see that anything's missing, but my clothes are rumpled, you know, like someone was rifling through them."

"Mine are, too," Penny Sue said excitedly.

I regarded her skeptically. Ruthie was a neat freak, but Penny Sue? How in the world could she tell if her clothes had been disturbed?

She curled her lip at me. "I know what you're thinking. Although my stuff might look messy to an outsider, there's order in that chaos and someone has been through my things. Nothing seems to be missing. I had all my jewelry with me, except for the emerald necklace, which I accidentally left in the bathroom soap dish. It's still there."

"If Stinky came here to rob us, why didn't he take the necklace? It's worth a fortune."

"Maybe he didn't see it," Penny Sue replied.

"Or, maybe, robbery wasn't his motive." I didn't have to say *rape*, the look on Penny Sue's face told me she understood.

Ruthie shook her head.

"What?" I asked.

"Stinky wasn't the one who went through my things," Ruthie stated emphatically. "His energy is definitely not on them."

"Who's energy is?" Penny Sue asked.

Ruthie turned slowly, considering. A knock on the front door nearly sent all of us through the ceiling. I went to the door and opened it. Woody stood there, red-eyed, sneezing, and unquestionably in a rotten mood.

"You say that's one of the men who followed you the other night?" Woody sat in the rattan chair in front of the fireplace, while a detective who'd been one of the first on the scene leaned against the wall.

"Yes," I answered. "We reported it to Deputy Moore of Volusia County—"

Woody patted the air, an imperious gesture Zack used all the time. I'd often wondered if the move was taught in law school or a genetic male predisposition. Whatever it was, I didn't like it. "—Sheriff's Department. In fact, Deputy Moore may have his fingerprints."

Woody chuckled derisively. "The Kraft paper? I heard."

My face grew hot and it had nothing to do with hormones. A wave of anger bordering on rage swept through me, the same feeling I'd had when Bradford Davis talked down to me at the divorce settlement conference. I took a deep breath; backhanding Woody in the mouth was not a good idea. I blew out the air and forced myself to smile. "Oh, could they lift a print?" I asked sweetly.

"I don't know." Woody brushed me off. He turned to Penny Sue. "Your friend outside was shot. Where's your gun?"

Her mouth dropped open. "He's not my friend. Come on, Woody, you can't think we, I—"

Woody sneezed and blew his nose. "Please get the gun, Penny Sue."

She stomped down the hall. We could hear her slamming drawers open and shut. A moment later she returned. "It's gone!"

Ruthie's hand flew to her mouth, and for a second I thought she might throw up again.

"Someone broke into this condo last night," I said quickly. Woody gestured to the detective, who checked the front door and returned shaking his head. "The thief jimmied the lock or something," I went on. "The back door was open when we returned from the movie."

Woody glanced at his notebook and grunted. *The Rocky Horror Picture Show.* He stood. "Penny Sue, I think you'd better come down to my office."

I jumped up and got in Woody's face. "You can't arrest her. She didn't do anything. We told you we were together all evening."

He backed up. "Really? What was she doing while you napped on the sofa?"

"Well ..."

Woody smirked. "Can't say, can you? Anyway, she's not under arrest. We merely want to ask a few questions."

I stepped forward again. "Ask 'em here."

Penny Sue spoke up, "It's all right, Leigh. I'd like to see Woody's office."

The neighbors in the two-story condos behind ours were huddled on their balconies, watching, as Woody ushered Penny Sue to the police car. With the exception of Al, every neighbor who'd attended the party, and then some, were present. Even Gerty, Robert, and the Turtle Patrol were spying from the side of the building next door.

I have to say I admired Penny Sue's aplomb: she looked straight at the crowd and waved. "Good morning," she called cheerily. The neighbors scurried away like perverts caught at a peep show. Then to me, "Becky Leigh, I think you'd better call Daddy," she glared at Woody, "and Lyndon, who can vouch for my whereabouts. Daddy's cell number is in my address book; Lyndon's number is scribbled on a note card in my purse. If you can't get Daddy on his cell phone, call the office."

"Will do." I scowled at Woody. "We'll follow in your car, so you'll have a ride home."

"Good." Penny Sue winked and slid gracefully into the backseat of the patrol car.

I started the Mercedes and pulled behind the squad car, pointedly edging in front of Woody. Penny Sue was my concern, not that prosecuting (or persecuting) twerp, and I was not letting her out of my sight. We took a right onto an almost deserted, Sunday morning A1A and headed for the center of town.

Ruthie tried to call Judge Parker as I drove. Five times she dialed, five times she got: *We're sorry, the customer you are trying to reach is not available at this time.* "Now what?" she asked. "Penny Sue said to call the office. It's Sunday. No one's there," Ruthie complained.

"Actually, the place is probably packed, lawyers work all the time; but, the switchboard is closed. If we call and leave a message, no one will retrieve it until tomorrow morning. A direct number ..." I hit the speaker button and keyed a number into the telephone handset. The phone started to ring.

"Who are you calling?" Ruthie asked.

The person who's direct number I knew by heart, but least wanted to call. "Good morning, Zack."

"Becky? About time you phoned. I hear we have an offer on the house. I say we take it; no sense holding out for pennies."

"Zack, I'm not calling about the house."

"What else could it be?" he asked sarcastically. "Your buddy Judge Nugent has taken care of everything else. How did you get to him? Max doesn't have connections like that. Penny Sue? Was it Penny Sue?"

I suppressed a grin. Zack's tone told me that he was furious. Apparently Judge Nugent hadn't liked Zack's explanation about the disposition of our assets. *Thank you Judge Daddy for planting a bug in Nugent's ear!* Unfortunately, I didn't have time to savor my rare victory. "Listen, this is important."

There was an audible gasp on the other end. "Not the kids. Ann and Zack, are they all right?"

"They're fine. I need to get in touch with Judge Parker. Penny Sue's in trouble. She's been taken in for questioning by the police."

Zack chuckled. "Questioning? What's that dingbat done now?"

The police car with Penny Sue and the detective turned into a parking lot and stopped. I found a parking space not too far away. "There's been a murder. Two, actually." For once Zack was speechless. "I'm calling from her car. We're at the police station now and I've got to go."

"Wait. Where are you? How can I reach you?"

"New Smyrna Beach. Try my cell phone, although the reception around here isn't very good. I'll call you from inside, there must be a pay phone somewhere. Please send someone to find the Judge; he's fishing."

"I'll get him. Tell Penny Sue not to say anything."

I sighed. "I'm afraid it's too late for that."

Woody wouldn't let us talk to Penny Sue, but said we were welcome to wait in a reception area by the door. "There's no need to worry, we're only going to ask her a few questions," he insisted.

I suspected his last statement was meant for the Judge as much as it was us. "I've called a lawyer," I said.

He folded his arms and assumed a pedantic stance. "I'm sure you have, though it's really not necessary. She hasn't been charged with anything. We simply need to ascertain the facts and the whereabouts of her gun."

"She's already told you all of that," Ruthie argued.

"Forgive me, dear, my memory is failing," Woody replied. "I merely want to go over it one more time." He motioned to a vinyl settee that looked like an antique. "Stay if you like, but it's not necessary. I'll see that she gets home."

Ruthie sat down, eyes narrowed defiantly. "We'll wait, thank you."

Woody left. Neither of our cell phones could get a decent signal inside the building, so I set out in search of a pay phone. I finally found one next to a vending machine and called Zack again. He answered on the first ring, a rarity for Mr. Cool. "The Judge is somewhere in the woods up by Big Canoe. I've sent two clerks to find him. How's Penny Sue?"

I leaned against the wall and stared at my feet. How was she? Probably scared to death, even if she'd rather die than show it. "Who knows? They're questioning her now."

"What's this stuff about two murders?" I filled him in on the details of the last week. "For chrissakes, Becky, why didn't y'all call after the first guy was murdered?"

"Penny Sue swore us to secrecy."

Zack snorted. "You left it at that? Anyone with half a brain—"

"I've got to go." Typical Zack: put down instead of putting up. I wasn't taking his crap. He would help Penny Sue—after all, his job depended on it.

"Wait. I've talked to Swindal, he thinks I should come down there."

My heart skipped a beat. Of all the people in the world, he was the last I wanted to see. "You? Why?"

"I'm the only senior partner who's a member of the Florida Bar."

No, not Zack. Anyone but Zack. "I think she needs local counsel. You know, someone with connections," I said. The Judge had an army on the case minutes after Penny Sue had waved the gun around. Surely, Zack could simply make a phone call. Certainly, someone other than the Judge had contacts in Florida.

"Swindal's working on that now, but he thinks we should personally supervise. After all, Penny Sue is the Judge's only child."

Yes, she was. As much as I detested Zack, I had to admit he was a good lawyer. If anyone could get Penny Sue off, he could.

Zack went on, "I can be down there in five or six hours. There's a flight to Daytona Beach that leaves in two hours. Where should I stay?"

As far away as possible was my first reaction. "There aren't many hotels here, you'd better stay up by the airport."

"That's the best you can do?" he said dryly.

"Yeah, I'm not a travel agent." I stared at a limp cord, the only remnant of the Bell South directory that had once hung beneath the telephone. "This place doesn't even have a phone book. Besides, the flight probably won't go, there's a hurricane off the coast."

"I know that; my secretary's already checked. They're not expecting to close the Daytona airport anytime soon," he drawled sarcastically. "See you in a few hours." He hung up.

I felt sick. Then said a silent prayer that Lizzie would hit Daytona Beach before Zack did.

Chapter 17

I returned to the lobby, stewing over my conversation with Zack, to find Ruthie sitting in the lotus position, her feet drawn into the chair, palms up, thumb and index finger touching lightly. Her face was smooth and youthful, the picture of tranquility.

And, it really infuriated me, although I'm not sure why. Perhaps because I couldn't get into that posture if my life depended on it. Or maybe it was her glowing complexion. My glow was dim, to say the least, especially right now. It might have been her tranquility, or my fatigue from having been up all night, the dirty green walls, the stale antiseptic smell; heck, it might even have had something to do with hormones—or the fact that Zack was headed to New Smyrna Beach. Whatever it was, I had an uncontrollable, albeit childish, urge to disrupt Ruthie's serene repose.

"Zack's coming," I blurted.

She grinned. "Perfect."

My mouth dropped open. "Perfect?"

"I asked the spirits for the highest and best solution for all concerned."

"Well, the spirits threw you a curve ball. Zack hardly qualifies as the highest and best. He's the lowest of the low." I sat down, fuming.

Ruthie unfolded her legs and sat up like a normal person. "He is for Woody."

"Woody?" Ruthie was talking in riddles and I was definitely not in the mood for puzzles. "What in the world does Woody have to do with Zack?"

"Karma."

That remark incensed me even more. Ruthie's abstruse thought processes were typically endearing, however, this leap was too much like Penny Sue. Penny Sue who was responsible for Zack coming and our sitting in god-awful hard chairs. "Karma? What does that have to do with anything?"

"Penny Sue, Woody, and Zack; together again after all these years. I'd say they're supposed to mend some fences. When they were last together, they parted on bad terms."

That was true, there'd been a huge scene. It was our sophomore year in college and a bunch of us from the sorority had come down to the beach condo. Penny Sue had been dating Zack, but true to form—out of sight, out of mind—she immediately met a guy on the beach, Woody, and struck up a relationship. Woody and Penny Sue were a hot item for all of three days until Zack showed up unexpectedly. The men had words, almost came to blows, and Penny Sue told them both off. Shortly after she got back to Atlanta, Penny Sue took up with Andy Walters, whom she eventually married, and Zack put the rush on me. Woody had just faded away. Until now.

"I wish they'd mend fences on their own time. I've had enough of Zack Stratton, Woody, and this whole mess."

Ruthie stared into space, her lips twisted in a half smile. I knew she was thinking about me. Some high, spiritual truth that I was in no mood to hear.

"I think we should try to reach Lyndon," I said, changing the subject. "He's the one person who can alibi Penny Sue and put an end to this mess before Zack arrives. Woody said he'd contact Lyndon; I'll bet he hasn't even tried." Dragging it out to punish Penny Sue, I almost said. Getting even for the past. Maybe Ruthie's karma notion wasn't as dopey as I'd initially thought.

"If we hurry, perhaps we can resolve everything before Zack leaves Atlanta. Lyndon's phone number is supposed to be in Penny Sue's purse. Did you bring it in?"

Ruthie rummaged through Penny Sue's Louis Vuitton and finally came up with a rumpled, blue card for Charlotte's Cleaning Service. She turned it over. "This must be it. Says LF and a number."

"Right, Lyndon Fulbright. I took the card and headed back to the pay phone. I dialed the number and got: *The cellular customer you have called is unavailable or out of the area.* I slammed the receiver down and retrieved my quarter. "No luck; just like the Judge," I said, retaking my seat. "Either the phone's turned off, or Lyndon's out of range."

"The phone's turned off. We saw Lyndon only hours ago—he *must* be in range. He's probably sleeping, since he was up all night with Penny Sue."

"I guess we'll have to go to The Riverview."

"What about Penny Sue? Suppose they release her while we're gone?"

"Woody will give her a ride home."

Ruthie winced. "That seems so cold."

It did. If I were being questioned by the police, I'd like to have a friendly face waiting when I got out. Still, Penny Sue might not be released at all if we didn't find Lyndon. If she were in our place, what would she do? "Penny Sue can reach us on her cell phone and we can be back here in a matter of minutes."

I found the young officer who'd responded to our 9-1-1 call and relayed the message for Penny Sue. He sullenly agreed to deliver it, although it was clear he didn't expect Woody to let our friend go any time soon. I thanked him for his help and returned to the reception area. "Come on," I said to Ruthie.

We were at The Riverview in twenty minutes, which was ten more than it usually took due to torrential downpours spun off by Lizzie. I dropped Ruthie in front of the restaurant and waited. Fortunately, the place wasn't busy, even though church had been out for a good half hour.

I relaxed into the Mercedes' soft leather seat and watched the rain pelt the windshield. There's a raw energy to storms that I find exciting. It's almost sexual. Ruthie says it's the negative ions. Atmospheric turbulence knocks electrons free, charging the air. Or maybe it's lightning that does it. In any event, the air truly acquires an electric charge, which explains why hair will sometimes stand up on your arm.

While the hair wasn't standing up on my arm, I was enjoying Lizzie's brutish display. Of course, I was relatively dry and safe inside the car. I say relatively dry because a goodly amount of spray entered as Ruthie exited the Benz. Yet, I could hardly complain about the spray that coated Penny Sue's leather seats and fogged the windows—Ruthie nearly had to crawl to make it to the restaurant.

I closed my eyes and tried to concentrate on the warble and sway of the squalls. It didn't work. Thoughts of Penny Sue and Zack kept intruding. What was Woody doing to her? And Zack—I looked at my watch—could be in New Smyrna Beach in less than four hours. Three if he didn't check luggage.

Darn, what was keeping Ruthie? I cleared a spot on the fogged windshield and stared at the restaurant. I made out her form talking to a lady in front of the glass doors. The woman was gesturing toward the river. I saw Ruthie nod, tuck her head, and race toward the car.

"The yacht's gone," she reported, wiping water off her face as she climbed in. "The hostess said it left right after she got to work, at about ten this morning."

"Left?" I asked, feeling numb. Lyndon said he'd leave if the storm was coming ashore. But the storm was miles away and no one knew where, or if, it would make landfall. New Smyrna Beach was in the strike zone, heck, so was the rest of Florida and most of the East Coast. By leaving now, Lyndon could well be sailing into the storm's path. It didn't make sense ... unless he was running from something.

I put the car in gear. "Let's go back to the police station."

I cut through the parking lot and took a left on Flagler Avenue. The rain was coming down in proverbial buckets, flooding the road in low spots. I hit the scan button on the radio and found a weather forecast. Lizzie had taken an westerly turn and gained speed. If the storm continued on its present course, the level one hurricane would make landfall between Cocoa Beach and Jacksonville.

"New Smyrna Beach is smack dab in the middle of that range," Ruthie said, her voice tremulous.

I squeezed the steering wheel and took my foot off the accelerator as the car hydroplaned in a deep pool on the west side of the North Causeway Bridge. "Don't worry. Lizzie will turn north. They always do. New Smyrna's never taken a direct hit."

Ruthie wasn't convinced. She bit her lip. "Maybe it's overdue—did you ever think of that?"

I had. Though I'd quickly dismissed the idea as nothing more than statistical gibberish, mathematical masturbation. A spurious application of probability theory, I told myself. That, notwithstanding the fact that statistics had been my worst subject, I'd barely squeaked by with a D. Nonetheless, statistics said the storm wouldn't hit. It couldn't hit.

"Don't worry. After the smudging, the condo can withstand anything."

Ruthie twittered. "It didn't do much for Stinky. We should have used more sage."

I glanced sideways. She was serious. "We'll do it over after we get Penny Sue."

"Do you think Lyndon killed Stinky?" Ruthie said suddenly. She'd probably picked up my earlier thought.

"He's a more likely candidate than Penny Sue. Woody says we can't vouch for Penny Sue's whereabouts while we were napping. We can't vouch for Lyndon, either. Perhaps Stinky was trying to break into our condo, and Lyndon surprised him. Lyndon struggled with Stinky and the gun went off."

Ruthie tilted her head, considering. "A gun shot, right out on the deck, would have awakened us for sure."

"A silencer."

"Only criminals have guns with silencers. Besides, Lyndon would have had to hang around after Penny Sue went to bed, or left and come back. Why would he do that?"

Why *would* Lyndon do that? I eased the car to a stop at a traffic signal. My theory would work only if Lyndon and Stinky were in cahoots somehow. What could Lyndon possibly want from us? Not money or jewelry, he was clearly wealthy. The way Penny Sue mooned over him, Lyndon didn't have to resort to nefarious means; sweet talk could get virtually anything.

A gust of wind caught the traffic signal just as it turned green. The fixture bobbed spastically like a fish on a line. I zipped forward, half afraid the thing might fall on us.

Ruthie's objections were valid, my hypothesis was flimsy. "Okay, if Lyndon wasn't involved, Stinky must have been killed before we got home. What about the guy in the red pickup?"

"He's a friend of Deputy Moore, you saw them talking yourself. The deputy's friend wouldn't murder anyone, right?"

Wrong. It happened all the time in cop shows which were, at least loosely, based on real life. "Mr. Pickup tried to run us off the road," I reminded.

"Yeah, with Stinky and Pony Tail. Mr. Pickup's a friend of Stinky's, he wouldn't kill him."

"He might—" I hit the brakes and swerved as a palm frond blew in front of the car. "Damn," I exclaimed, my heart racing. I took a couple of deep breathes to calm myself before continuing. "Mr. Pickup might kill under the right conditions. We know he's a friend of Deputy Moore's, so he can't be a hardened criminal."

"Unless Deputy Moore's a dirty cop," Ruthie cut in.

I'd thought of that, yet put the possibly out of my mind. I hated to think my judgment of Ted Moore was so wrong. Especially because I'd trusted, even liked, him. He seemed so genuine and unpretentious, the exact opposite of Zack. "That's another story. Bear with me a moment. Suppose Mr. Pickup is/was a friend of both Deputy Moore and Stinky. He had too much to drink that night at JB's and decided to have a little fun with Stinky and Pony Tail. Though they were really trying to run us off the road, Pickup was horsing around. The Deputy realizes who Pickup is from our description of his truck and the bumper sticker. The day I saw them talking on the highway, Moore was warning him to stay away from us and to keep his buddies at bay.

"After that, Mr. Pickup finds out that Stinky intends to rob or rape us. So, he follows Stinky to our condo to try to stop him, there's a struggle, and a gun goes off. Stinky's killed and Mr. Pickup runs away."

Ruthie nodded slowly. "That's possible, but no more likely than Lyndon doing exactly the same thing. Besides, if Lyndon's not involved, why did he leave town?"

I turned up the windshield wipers. The blades slapped frantically like a metronome on amphetamines, yet I could still barely see the road. I slowed the car to a crawl. "The hurricane. Lyndon probably has access to sophisticated weather data. He may know something we don't. Or maybe he and Penny Sue had a fight. We never had a chance to talk with her."

Ruthie massaged her temple, looking worried. "Penny Sue would have told us about a fight. She had plenty of time while we were waiting for Woody."

"There was a dead man on the deck—it wasn't the best time for chitchat." The cell phone played a little song at the exact moment I reached the light on Riverside Drive. Luckily, I'd already stopped, because the sound almost sent me through the roof. I hesitated, a hard knot forming in my stomach at the thought it might be Zack. Thankfully, it was Penny Sue and the knot dissolved.

"Lord, where are you?" she asked loudly. "Get me out of this place!"

Chapter 18

We were at the police station in a matter of minutes. Penny Sue was waiting in the doorway, a young officer by her side. I pulled up front and waited. A moment later she fell into the backseat, drenched and angry.

"Twerp. You'd think they'd have the decency to walk me to the car with an umbrella," Penny Sue groused, brushing water from her clothes. "The rain's going to spot this silk blouse."

I put the car in gear and pulled away slowly. "Never mind—at least you're out. Was it awful?"

Penny Sue reared back and pressed her lips together huffily. "The chair was hard, the detective was rude—kept asking the same questions over and over—but, it wasn't so bad. They don't have anything on me! All they know is that Stinky, whose real name is Clarence Smith, was killed with a gun. At this point, they have no idea what kind of gun, how long Stinky's been dead—nothing. They had to let me go. Besides, Swindal called to tell Woody they'd sent for Daddy, and Zack would be here shortly."

Zack … the mere mention of his name made my stomach curl. With all of the tension of the previous few days, he was the last person on Earth I wanted to see. If only there were some way we could straighten everything out before he arrived. Fat chance.

"Did you reach Lyndon?" Penny Sue interrupted my thoughts.

Ruthie answered, giving me a sidelong glance. "Uh, no. He's left."

"What do you mean, he's left?" Penny Sue snapped.

"The boat's gone, and he didn't answer the telephone."

"Are you sure you called the right number?" Penny Sue asked testily, reaching across the seat for her purse.

"We called the number on the back of the card."

"Back of the card?" Penny Sue said, as she unloaded her purse on the seat. "The number's on a note card, you know, his stationery. You've called the wrong number. See." She handed a featheredged note card to Ruthie.

Ruthie stiffened.

"What's wrong?" I asked, one eye on Ruthie, the other on the flooded street.

"Mark how he trembles ..." Ruthie murmured.

"What?" I asked loudly, in no mood for word games. Zack and a hurricane were both on the way, the road was practically under water, and my head was beginning to throb.

Ruthie angled the note toward me. The phrase was embossed across the top, while *Lyndon* and a phone number were hand-written in the center. I stared at the paper, I'd seen the stationery before. Ruthie had even commented on how expensive it was when we found it with Rick's pesticides.

"Mark how he trembles ..." Ruthie repeated forcefully, her eyes narrowed with concentration. "Shakespeare. *The Comedy of Errors.* 'Mark how he trembles ... in his ECSTASY!' Ecstasy: Lyndon's yacht!"

A chill shot up my spine.

"So what?" Penny Sue demanded. She leaned across the seat and snatched the note from Ruthie and the cell phone from its cradle.

"Y'all called the wrong number," she chided, punching a number into the phone. I watched her in the rearview mirror as she waited. After a couple of minutes, she hung up, clearly in a snit. "No answer. What number did y'all dial?"

"The one on the back of Charlotte's card," Ruthie replied weakly.

"Charlotte's card?!" Penny Sue roared, digging into her purse like a hungry dog after a bone. I saw her retrieve the blue card and line it up against Lyndon's stationery. Her cheeks and neck flamed. "The number's the same! What is Charlotte doing with Lyndon's telephone number?"

I swallowed the knot that had formed in my throat. "It's worse than that, Penny Sue. Ruthie and I found the same stationery in a drawer full of pesticides at the condo. Remember, Ruthie? What did the note say?"

She bit her fingernail nervously. "It was the directions for mixing the chemicals."

"Are you sure? Wasn't there something else? Although, the real question is: 'Why did Rick have Lyndon's stationery?'"

"Lyndon and Rick? How could they possibly be related?" Penny Sue asked.

"Boats get bugs," I offered lamely.

"Rick treated the yacht and picked up a piece of Lyndon's stationery?" Ruthie nodded slowly. "Possible, I suppose."

"Yeah, but what does Charlotte have to do with all of this?" Penny Sue said, folding her arms across her ample chest. "And, when did you find the pesticides and note? I never heard anything about it."

"We found them in the bottom drawer of the chest in your bedroom the second day, when we were unpacking your clothes. We stashed them in a bucket in the utility room."

"What?" Penny Sue bellowed.

"We were afraid to flush the stuff down the toilet—polluting the ground water and all," Ruthie explained. "After the episode with

Rick in the parking lot, we thought we'd better keep them as evidence."

I made the sweeping right turn where US A1A turns into County A1A and slowed to a crawl. The highway was completely flooded except for a slim strip down the middle of the road. Fortunately, there were no cars coming, so I aimed for the dry crest, even though it was in the center turn lane. We hadn't gone very far when a plastic chair floated across the highway. I brought the Mercedes to a stop. "Should I turn around?"

"Keep going," Penny Sue ordered. "I've seen this before— it'll clear up in a couple of blocks. The Benz can handle it."

"Yes, but—"

"But, nothing," Penny Sue said emphatically. "I want to see that other note and those pesticides, if that's what they are."

I inched the car forward. "If that's what they are? What else would they be?" I asked over my shoulder, not daring to take my eyes off the road.

Ruthie's hand flew to her mouth. "Oh, no. Ecstasy!"

The squall subsided by the time we reached the condo, at least enough to see more than a few feet ahead. Still, wind gusts made umbrellas pointless, so we elected to duck our heads and run. I led the way with the door key at ready which, with amazing skill or luck, hit its mark on the first try. Bent forward, we bounded through the front door ... and into the arms of the ugliest man I'd ever seen. His pockmarked face and squinty eyes made Freddie Krueger look good. A needle-embellished hockey mask would actually have been an improvement.

I instinctively averted my eyes, remembering Grammy Martin's admonition about staring at Mr. Dinks, her homely neighbor who was absolutely handsome next to this guy. Ruthie screamed hysterically, unencumbered by Grammy's moralistic baggage. Penny Sue tried to run back out the door, but the man shoved her aside and slammed it closed.

He seized Ruthie by the arm roughly. "Shut up or I'll shut you up." Ruthie pressed her lips together tightly. His free hand went to a holster on his belt and came up with a gun. Penny Sue and I backed against the wall. The man pushed Ruthie beside us and snatched the key ring from my hand.

"Gino, none of that." Al appeared at the end of the hall, his arm extended as if holding something. "Pipe down, Ruthie. No one will get hurt if you cooperate."

"Al," I blurted with amazement. "What's going on?"

"Stay calm, ladies."

Gino herded the three of us down the hall. On the right were the bedrooms and the owner's closet, on the left the doors to the utility room and the linen closet. Ruthie led the way followed by me, Penny Sue, then Gino.

Ruthie must have been petrified because she walked with a shuffling gait, taking loud, deep breaths. The closer she got to the living room and Al, the louder her breathing became until, when she reached the linen closet, she doubled over wheezing. She sounded like a person having an asthma attack, however, I knew she didn't have asthma. I went to her side and held her waist, fearing she might collapse. Hunched over, she turned her face toward me and winked. And it hit me—the linen closet!

Ruthie saw my flash of understanding. She twitched violently and started in on a loud coughing spell. That was my cue. In one swift move I opened the closet and lunged for the second shelf where we'd stashed the Taser Gun—which wasn't there!

"Hey!" Gino shouted, grabbing Penny Sue from behind as Al started toward us, dragging Charlotte into view.

Although completely shocked by the sight of Charlotte, I managed to snatch a towel from the closet, hold it up innocently, and wipe Ruthie's mouth. "She's choking, for godssakes,"

I covered. Where was the Taser? And, what was Charlotte doing here? I wondered.

Al studied me, eyes narrowed. Apparently he bought my story, because he nodded at Gino, who released his hold on Penny Sue. "No cute stuff, Leigh. You almost got yourself killed. Now, come in here and sit down."

I ushered Ruthie to the sofa, who was still doing a good rendition of asthma attack. Penny Sue sat next to us with a little encouragement from Gino, while Al shoved Charlotte roughly to the loveseat.

A light-haired man in a bar, Pauline had said. It wasn't Lyndon, it was Al! I first met Al at The Riverview. We saw him later at Pub 44, then again at JB's. He'd been following us, and I thought I knew why.

Gino stood against the wall with his hand on the grip of the pistol that he'd returned to the holster. Al started to pace. "Ladies, I have a problem and I need your help. It seems that some property I bought and paid for has been misplaced. Not only is this merchandise missing, but the seller never received his payment." Al canted his head at Gino, who smiled wryly. Scowling, Gino was terrifying to behold; the thin grin made him look absolutely sadistic. Images of Freddie Krueger flooded my mind again, except that wasn't real and this was.

"You see my predicament. I'm out doubly—no merchandise and no money. The situation is complicated by the fact that my representative for the transaction is no longer with us—he met an untimely end. My associate's associate here," Al waved toward Charlotte, "claims the property and money were both delivered to this address. You nice ladies wouldn't know where it is, would you?"

Ruthie's fake wheezing stopped, and the three of us exchanged wide-eyed looks. Of course, Al wanted the pesticide—which, as we'd suspected, wasn't pesticide at all. But we didn't know anything about money, and if Gino was the person wanting it, I sure hated to be the one to tell him. Ruthie let out a half-hearted wheeze, which I took to mean: *You answer.*

I cleared my throat to calm my pounding heart. "If your property is a white powder, I believe we can help you."

Al smiled broadly. "I knew you were a smart girl, Leigh. Show me."

I headed down the hall with Al in tow. Gino stayed behind with the others.

"We found it in the bottom drawer of the bureau when we first arrived," I explained as I led Al into the utility room. "Rick was here then, and we honestly thought it was insecticide that he'd stored in the condo. There was even a note with mixing instructions." The rag mop and bucket were next to the dryer, where I'd left them after cleaning up Ruthie's vomit. I handed them to Al so I could get at the trash bag. He took one whiff of the putrid load and tossed it into the far corner.

"Geez," he exclaimed. "That's disgusting."

Guess I didn't rinse the mop very well with all of the commotion. "Ruthie got sick," I replied, pointing to the bag in the space between the dryer and wall.

Al pulled the bag out and dumped its contents on the floor. I reached for the note on Lyndon's stationery which fluttered to the side. Al stopped me.

"Hey, what're ya doing?"

I handed him the paper. "This is the note we found with the packages. See, it seems to be mixing instructions."

He read the note: *200 @ 6. Same time, same place,* then a smiley face. He tossed the note back at me. "I don't know what that means, I paid a half mil for this stuff."

A half a million dollars. This was serious. "We didn't find any money. Honestly, I'd tell you if we did. We don't want any trouble."

He ignored me and my comment until he finished counting the packages. I used the opportunity to pocket Lyndon's note card. Al returned the packages to the bag and stood, obviously satisfied. He held out his hand to help me up; I took it.

"Al," I said, my hand still in his, "we truly don't know anything about the money. Take the drugs, leave, and we'll never say a word to anyone. I promise."

He paused, looking into my eyes. "You know I can't do that. You understand."

I didn't, yet wasn't going to argue. Perhaps I'd seen too many episodes of *The Sopranos*, but I had a bad feeling this might be my last day on Earth. In a flash, all the really important things in my life raced through my mind: the kids, my parents, good friends. I also realized how much time I'd wasted on silly stuff like others' opinions, guilt, and anger. In that instant, I even realized I should release my hostility toward Zack. He did what he did; I did what I did; that was that. No more, no less, not worth thinking about.

"Al," I started, still holding his hand. I noticed it was warm and soft, not callused like you'd expect a mobster's to be. "We won't—" I didn't get to finish because there was a knock on the front door.

His face hardened, Al flung my hand aside. "Whoever it is, get rid of them. Don't try anything cute if you want to see your friends again. I'll be right here, listening to every word you say." He displayed his gun which had a fat cylinder attached to the end. I knew from *The Sopranos* that it was a silencer. "Got it?" he asked. I nodded.

I took a long deep breath as I approached the door. I had to appear calm, Penny Sue and Ruthie's welfare depended on it. Another knock, this one louder. I cracked the door and saw Zack. Before I got out a single word, he barged past me like the pompous ass he was. So much for forgiveness.

"Damn, Becky, I'm drenched. What took you so long? For godssakes, you knew I was coming. Why didn't you answer your cell phone? Where's Penny Sue? Did Swindal call?" He stopped in front of the utility room and glared at me. "What's wrong with you?" he demanded angrily.

"That." I pointed toward Al, who had his gun trained on Zack.

I wish I'd had a camera! The look on Mr. Big Stuff's face was priceless. He went white as a sheet and started to pant, as if he were hyperventilating. What a wuss!

Al motioned both of us toward the living room. We walked single file—Zack first, then me, with Al bringing up the rear. Penny Sue and Ruthie were in plain view directly ahead. When Zack reached the opening to the living room and kitchen, he caught sight of Gino, who'd drawn his gun. Surprised, Zack stumbled backward into the kitchen counter, knocking over a Furby and the can of Hot Shot that I'd used on a wasp that morning. The bug spray rattled across the room as the Furby fell to the tile floor crying, "Cock-a-doodle-doo! Cock-a-doodle-doo!" Gino swung his gun first at the can, then toward the Furby—which had miraculously landed on its feet, jabbering "Party! Big Fun. Dance! Dance!"—finally settling on Zack's forehead. Zack raised his hands like crooks do in old movies as his breathing took on the staccato beat of Ruthie's fake asthma attack. Only Zack wasn't faking. Penny Sue, Ruthie, and Charlotte raised their hands, too. I simply froze in place.

Al was the first to recover. He poked my back with the gun barrel. "Shut up that stupid toy." Then he pointed at Penny Sue. "Get that can." She dropped to her knees to retrieve the spray from under the sofa and gingerly placed it on the end of the counter. I did the same which the Furby which was still chattering, "Hungry. Very Hungry."

"Give me that damn thing," Al ordered angrily. He took the toy and threw it, hard, into the linen closet and slammed the door. We could hear the Furby scream, "WHOA-A-A! Scare me!"

Penny Sue's face puckered with horror. "Little Lu Nee," she whispered.

"You're the loony! Be quiet," Al barked at her as he herded Zack and I toward the sofa and loveseat. We sat, as ordered, with our hands in the air.

"Who the hell are you?" Gino growled at Zack in the meanest tone I'd ever heard.

"My husband," I said before Zack could respond. Being a lawyer might not be the healthiest occupation for this situation, and I feared Mr. Big Stuff—if he managed to speak—might launch into a long recitation of his credentials and the legal consequences of *their* actions. Worse, Zack could try to bluff and say something really stupid like, "The police are on the way," in which case Gino might feel compelled to eliminate the witnesses—US!—forthwith.

Al regarded me skeptically. "I thought you were divorced; a Daffydil or something."

"My ex-husband," I corrected quickly. So why was my ex-husband here? I wanted to steer as far away from Penny Sue and the police as possible. "He has some papers for me to sign."

Zack picked up the hint and for once didn't correct me. "We sold the house. She's got to sign the papers."

"Check him," Al instructed Gino, who patted Zack down. Gino found no weapon, but did confiscate Zack's cell phone.

"I'm tired of pussyfooting around," Gino grumbled. "Let's find the money and get out of here. I don't want to be stuck on the boat in that hurricane."

"Yeah, yeah," Al said, motioning to the lock on the owner's closet door. "Where's the key to this, Penny Sue?"

"On the key ring," she answered meekly.

Gino handed the ring to Al who quickly found the right key. They ushered us one by one into the closet. All but Ruthie, who hung back, whimpering.

"Please leave the light on," she pleaded as Gino grabbed her arm and pushed her into the small room. "I'm claustrophobic. Please, I'll die in the dark. Really!"

Gino looked to Al for a decision. "Aw, leave it on. But you," Al waved his weapon at Ruthie, "be quiet. Scream again, and it will be your last." He swung the door shut, and the deadbolt clicked.

Chapter 19

Five adults in a five-by-ten foot space that was already half-filled with beach paraphernalia made for mighty close quarters. Too close for my taste, since one of the group was Zack. I wormed my way between Ruthie and Penny Sue for cover. Charlotte wedged herself against Zack, probably for the same reason. Penny Sue had been giving Charlotte scathing looks throughout the whole ordeal. Outside, we heard the television come on, tuned to the Weather Channel. Gino was doubtlessly checking Lizzie's status; I made out Dr. Steve's muffled voice through the wall. Though I strained to hear, I could only understand one phrase, *Level One*. Gino must have been satisfied, because the loud banging of closets and drawers started immediately, drowning out the news on the storm.

"What's going on here?" Zack broke our silence.

Penny Sue glared at Charlotte. "Yes, Ms. Associate's Associate, what *is* going on? How are you connected to Lyndon Fulbright?"

Charlotte drew back, her bottom lip quivering. "None of this was supposed to happen. Rick and I were simply trying to make enough money to run away. Now he's dead, and ..." She started to cry.

"Rick?" I asked. "I thought Al was talking about Stink—, er Clarence Smith."

Charlotte wiped her cheeks with the back of her had. "I don't know a Clarence Smith."

"Amazing," Penny Sue drawled sarcastically. "You seem to know every other man in town."

"Wait," Zack interrupted, patting the air imperiously. "This is no time for a cat fight."

"Cat fight? No, you wait," I snapped, squaring my shoulders. "That sexist remark was completely uncalled-for. We wouldn't be stuck in this closet—probably to die—if it weren't for your pig-headedness."

"Pig-headedness?" he countered with the cocky smirk I'd come to loathe.

"Yes, pig-headedness. If you hadn't acted like a pompous ass, you'd be on the outside—in a position to save our lives. The big lawyer that Swindal sent down to save Penny Sue has botched it royally. Instead of saving the day, you've sealed our doom, and you're going down with the ship.

"All of your sleazy shenanigans have come to naught— fooling around with the stripper, stealing *our* money, taking half the stuff in the house—"

I turned to Ruthie, "All the top sheets, no bottoms. Half of every set of china. One twin bed from Zack, Jr.'s room. The book-case—dumped the books on the floor—from Ann's bedroom."

Ruthie and Charlotte glared at Zack with revulsion.

The veins in Zack's neck bulged, and he tapped his chest with his fist. "Me sleazy? What about you? Judge Nugent's put the property settlement on hold, called for an independent audit and reevaluation of everything. You did that. It's all your fault. How did you get to him, Becky?"

"I hope they find the money you hid in the Caymans, so the kids will get it and not your stripper." The words were out and I meant them. Yet, the victory, if there was one, was hollow. I leaned against the wall and shook my head—disgusted with Zack, disgusted with myself. Here we were, locked in a closet for, probably, the few remaining moments of our lives and we were arguing over money. Sick. It was stupid and sick.

Penny Sue came to my rescue. "*Leigh* has friends in high places," she stated crisply. "And, since this is *my* closet, and it appears we may all be here for quite a while, I suggest we clear some space so we can at least sit down."

For the second time that day Zack Stratton acquiesced without an argument. In a matter of minutes, we'd shifted most of the stuff on the floor to the shelves at the back of the closet. In the process, Zack found a full bottle of Wild Turkey. Penny Sue unceremoniously plopped on the floor, unscrewed the top of the bourbon and took a hearty swallow. Then, she offered the bottle to Ruthie, who was twitching with fear. "Take a sip, sugar. It'll calm your nerves."

Ruthie accepted the bottle with shaking hands and turned it up. She sputtered and gagged at the harsh taste, yet managed to keep the liquor down. To my amazement she took a second gulp before passing the bottle to Zack. He took a swig, as did Charlotte. I chose to abstain—someone had to keep their wits, even though the situation seemed hopeless. There was no doubt in my mind that Al would never let us go. Our only chance was that someone would come looking for us before Al and Gino found the money or gave up the search.

"What's going on here?" Zack asked again. "If I'm going to die, I'd like to know why. Who are those guys, and what's this about two murders?"

Penny Sue stared down Zack and took another swallow of the Wild Turkey. "This is my closet, I get to go first. What *is* going on?" she pointedly asked Charlotte.

Charlotte stared at her lap to avoid Penny Sue's glare. "I'm so sorry—it's my fault. My marriage was never very good and got a lot worse after Pete had his accident. He was laid up for a long time, and couldn't," she glanced up sheepishly, "well, you know. I got tired of staying home night after night with no affection, so I found a job as a waitress at The Riverview. Pete didn't care—he was gooned out on painkillers most of the time. The job got me out of the house at night, and the money came in handy—we have lots of medical bills. No insurance. Pete and I will never live to pay off all of those damned bills, because of his damned motorcycle.

"Rick came into the restaurant one night, and we hit it off immediately. He was so good looking. Anyway, he was new to town and lonely like me. One thing led to another, I had a key to this condo, and before you knew it, we were having an affair."

Penny Sue's jaw dropped. "You used my father's condo for a love nest?"

Charlotte shrugged. "No one ever came here. We figured it wouldn't hurt anything."

"When did you and Rick start dealing drugs?" I asked. Like Zack, if I was going to die, I wanted to know why.

"Not right away. At first, I didn't know what Rick did. He knew I needed money, so eventually offered to cut me in. He'd been in the business for a while, down in South Florida. He was the middleman for Al and a Caribbean drug cartel. Rick moved up here after a big drug bust in Miami. Several of his friends were nabbed, and he figured he might be next. Besides, he could work anywhere as long as there was a beach. The guys from the Caribbean brought the stuff in on boats at night. They'd bury the merchandise at a predetermined location and stake it off to make it look like a turtle nest. Rick would dig up the drugs, put the payment in its place, and stash the stuff here. I'd pick up the merchandise and deliver it to one of Al's men. It was Rick's idea to spread everything around. That way, if one side of the triangle was nabbed, the others wouldn't be implicated."

Penny Sue took a mouthful of bourbon and handed the bottle to Zack, who seemed as stunned as she was by the confession. "Mercy, you were using Daddy's place to stash drugs, too!"

"Rick said it was the perfect setup—no one would ever suspect anything was going on in a judge's condo."

"My gawd," Penny Sue exclaimed, her hand automatically covering her heart. "Daddy will die when he finds out."

I wanted to say, *that's the least of our worries*, but didn't. Some color had returned to Ruthie's cheeks which was reassuring. "So, Lyndon's in league with Al?" I asked.

"No. Lyndon doesn't know anything about Al."

"What were you doing with Lyndon's phone number?" Penny Sue demanded.

Charlotte averted her eyes. "I met Lyndon at The Riverview, and we dated a few times."

Penny Sue's eyes shot darts. "Dated?"

"That's how I found out about Lyndon's obsession for turtle eggs. He thinks they're an aphrodisiac and natural Viagra." A smile tugged at the corner of her mouth. Zack looked sidelong. "Lyndon's chef, Thomas, uses them in everything. Wow, you should taste pancakes made with turtle eggs, they're the best I've ever eaten. So light and fluffy…"

"Pancakes," Penny Sue muttered, fuming. The fact that Charlotte had stayed over to have breakfast came through loud and clear.

Charlotte ignored Penny Sue and went on. "I arranged for Rick to supply Lyndon with turtle eggs."

I rummaged in my pocket for the note. *200 @ 6. Same time, same place.* I held the note for the group to see. "This was an order for turtle eggs?"

Charlotte nodded. "I'd leave egg orders in the bureau drawer for Rick. Lyndon insisted on keeping his distance."

"What a sleazy thing to do," Ruthie spoke for the first time. "Rick robbed turtle nests to supply a horny, old man?"

"It was better than throwing the eggs away. Most times Rick would dig up the nest and tell the drug runners to bury the stash in the same place. That way, there would never be a link between Rick and the record for the turtle nest. By selling the eggs to Lyndon, they weren't wasted."

"What a hypocrite! Rick was on the Turtle Patrol and robbing the nests?" Ruthie said disgustedly. "That's too much."

I looked at Ruthie, amazed by her thinking; of course, the two big swigs of bourbon might have had something to do with it. Yet, of all the things to key on—hypocrisy. Rick had committed numerous felonies, and she was outraged that he was two-faced. *Two-faced!* A coin with two heads, Pauline had said that. Though, Pauline couldn't have meant Rick, who was already dead by that time. Lyndon had certainly been two-faced, and so had Al, for that matter.

"Who killed Rick?" I asked.

Charlotte teared up. "I don't know. It could have been another dealer trying to cut in on his territory. That's what I thought until a few minutes ago when you admitted to having the merchandise. That's why I called Al—I was afraid he would think I was pulling a double cross. I arranged for him to rent the condo next door. I clean that unit, too."

"Who killed Stink—Clarence?" Penny Sue asked.

Charlotte hung her head, tears streaming now. "I don't know, but I heard the shot. While you were out with Lyndon, I came over here to search for the note. Lyndon was terrified of being implicated for turtle egg poaching."

I remembered the article Ruthie read aloud from the newspaper. "Of course—it's a felony."

"Right. I was searching the linen closet—"

"You took the Taser gun," I exclaimed, pointing.

"No. I didn't know what it was. In fact, I was examining the thing when I heard the gun shot. I was so scared, I dropped the Taser and ran. I went straight to Lyndon's yacht and told Chef Thomas that I hadn't found the note and wasn't going to look again. No way I was going to stick around and get killed like Rick."

"Do you suppose Al killed Stinky?" Ruthie asked, the color draining from her face.

Charlotte shook her head. "It wasn't Al. He was at The Riverview waiting for Gino to arrive. That's why I'm here. Al saw me coming out of Lyndon's yacht and grabbed me. I've been next door with them since. After you left and the storm kicked up, we saw our chance to search your condo."

"If Al didn't do it, who did?" Ruthie demanded.

"Pauline said we were in danger from a light-haired man. What else did she say?" Penny Sue asked.

"Who's Pauline?" Zack interrupted.

"A psychic." Zack rolled his eyes.

"A coin with two heads, and shiny wheels spinning," I continued. "The two-headed coin surely means two-faced."

"Ain't that the truth?" Penny Sue shot a look at Charlotte and Zack. "Almost everyone we've met has been two-faced, including Lyndon." She scowled at the younger woman. "Was he sucking up to me just to get that incriminating order?"

Charlotte flinched. "I-I ... don't know. I told him who you were."

"The first night? Did he know who I was that first night at The Riverview? Did he know then?"

Charlotte drew back defensively. "I passed him a note telling him you were staying in the condo," she admitted.

"Which explains the weird maneuver about having to close out his old tab and start a new one because the shift had changed." Penny Sue squeezed the neck of the bottle, undoubtedly wishing it was Lyndon's neck. "I knew it didn't make sense, because you were still our waitress. Right after that, my drinks seemed awfully strong. He was trying to get me drunk so he could drive me home and retrieve the evidence!" Her face twisted with rage. "Y'all weren't slipping me G, that date rape drug?"

Charlotte ducked her head. "No! But I had the bartender pour you doubles."

"I thought so." Penny Sue took another swig of the bourbon and laughed. "I foiled you because I can hold my liquor, and I had friends there to drive me home." She smiled at us triumphantly. "All of the rush from Lyndon was simply to get an egg order? What a two-faced, sleaze! He killed Stinky," she declared.

I looked askance. "Why do you say that?"

"Because Lyndon wanted to spend the night with me; I said no." She reared back dramatically. "So, he waited around until we went to sleep, planning to sneak in and steal the order. He surprised Stinky on the deck, there was a struggle, and Lyndon shot him."

"Come on, Penny Sue, Lyndon wouldn't do that," I argued. "First, he's a man who pays people to do things for him—he doesn't do anything for himself." I glared at Zack, who undoubtedly got my drift. "Secondly, he'd already arranged for Charlotte to search the place while we were at the movies. For all Lyndon knew, she'd found the slip of his stationery."

Penny Sue brightened. "You're right. He really wanted to sleep with me." She smirked at Charlotte.

"Who did kill Stinky then?" Ruthie asked.

"Gawd, Ruthie, can't you do some voodoo or something and find out?" Penny Sue drawled.

Oh boy, this was no time for a squabble. "Let's go back to Pauline's vision. The two-headed coin part's clear. She also said we were in danger from a light-haired man."

Penny Sue put her hands on her hips and regarded me with droopy eyes. The Wild Turkey was definitely cutting in. "Geez, Becky Leigh, we've already discussed this. It's the beach. Everyone's hair is sun-streaked."

I nodded. "Humor me. Let's run through the list one more time. Who have we met with light hair?"

Ruthie started, "Rick, Lyndon—he's graying, Al, Stinky, even Robert of the Turtle Patrol has white hair."

"And, the guy in the red pickup truck," I added. "He was here that first day and had the fight with Rick. Heck, he's probably the one who killed Rick."

"We've already been through that," Ruthie argued.

Charlotte shook her head emphatically. "Wait, I'll bet he *is* the one! He's probably a drug dealer who wanted Rick's territory. Rick told me about the fight. He said the guy had been following him. Rick confronted him in the parking lot, they traded punches, then a wack—er homeowner, broke up the fight."

"Rick called me a wacko?" Penny Sue demanded.

Zack snickered. Penny Sue gave him a look that would fry Satan.

Charlotte shook her head nervously. "No, he didn't say that."

"Right." Penny Sue was ticked off.

We heard a loud scratching sound on the other side of the wall, as if Al and Gino were removing pictures. I guessed they were searching for a hidden safe.

"Where's the money?" Ruthie asked, her cheeks still pale.

"For godssakes, it's probably still in the darned turtle mound," Penny Sue blurted.

"No, Al checked that," Charlotte said.

"Checked what?"

"The turtle nest with the wreath, where Rick was killed."

I remembered Robert, Gerty, and the defiled turtle nest. Al had done that! He was the one who dug it up, only to feign innocence and help us rebury the eggs. *Eggs!* "Wait, there were eggs in that nest," I said. "It wasn't the right one." I looked at Charlotte. "You said Rick normally took the eggs out of the nest before the drug drop and buried the money. The nest Al dug up was full of eggs. It was the wrong nest! The money's probably still out on the beach. There were two nests in front of our condo."

"Right," Penny Sue and Ruthie said in unison. Ruthie glanced at the group, then started banging on the closet door.

"Stop. What are you doing?" I said.

"I'm going to tell Al where to find the money."

"If he knows where the money is, there's no reason to keep us alive. That's our trump card," I said.

Her face went white as she slumped against the wall. Penny Sue handed her the bottle. Ruthie looked at me and took a long drink. "So, what are we going to do? Simply sit here and wait to be gunned down?" she finally managed.

I massaged my temples; my head was really pounding. "We're going to hold out as long as we can in hopes someone," I looked at the others, "like Woody, comes by to save us. If that doesn't happen, then we'll play our trump card."

"Is there anything in here we can use as a weapon?" Zack asked quietly.

I regarded him, surprised. That was the first constructive comment he'd made since we'd been in the closet.

"A tennis racket and bocce balls," Penny Sue answered, hefting one of the heavy wooden balls.

"Okay," I said. "We'll wait until the last minute, in hopes someone comes to save us. But, if that doesn't happen, Ruthie bangs on the door, saying we know where the money is. When the door opens, we pelt Al and Gino with the bocce balls."

"That's dangerous," Charlotte said. "They've got guns."

"What's the alternative? Becky's right—there's nothing to lose." Zack replied evenly. "We haven't a chance in hell of getting out of here alive without outside help or taking a risk. I say we wait for help, but if that doesn't materialize, we take the risk. It's the only logical thing to do."

Ruthie and Penny Sue nodded their heads. And, for once, Zack and I agreed.

Chapter 20

We'd finished our confessions, speculations and were sitting quietly, overcome by heat and the gravity of the situation, when Gino stomped down the hall.

"The money's not here," Al declared angrily. "Let's scram. I'll get the stuff from the utility room, you turn on the gas stove."

Turn on the stove! We all sat up as one. They were planning to burn the place down! Penny Sue started passing out the bocce balls.

"Ruthie and Leigh, let them have it as soon as the door opens. Penny Sue, Charlotte, and I will hold our balls in reserve. As soon as you throw, get out of the way," Zack instructed.

He made sense, so I didn't argue. I tapped Ruthie on the shoulder. "Do your thing."

Ruthie clutched the ball tightly in one hand and banged on the door with the other. "We know where the money is. Open up, Al! We know where the money is ..."

Each of us gripped a wooden ball as we listened to someone fumble with the keys on the other side of the door. I held my bocce ball with both hands, trying to decide if I should throw it overhanded or underhanded, and whether I should aim for the stomach or head. A hit to the head would certainly do more damage, but it made for a much smaller target. Better to hit something than nothing, at all. I decided underhanded and that the stomach was the safest bet. I poised myself to throw.

The door creaked open. It was Al. Luscious, cool air rushed into the closet, and we all took a deep breath. I hadn't realized how stuffy the place had gotten until that moment.

"Where's the money?" Gino snarled, looming over Al's shoulder.

"It's here," Ruthie shouted as we both threw our balls with all the force we could muster.

"Wha-a—" Al staggered backward, surprised but not hurt. "Bitch," he snarled and fumbled for his gun. Gino screamed.

"AH-H-H!" Gino screeched with pain and swung around. A stream of water hit him in the face. The ugly thug fell to the floor writhing in agony. Al pivoted toward the unseen attacker, gun in hand, but I lunged and pushed him off balance. Then a stream of water hit him, too. Al collapsed beside Gino, shaking violently. I realized what had happened. The Taser. Someone had our Taser!

Ruthie and I leading the way, we all rushed out of the closet. Charlotte's husband, Pete, stood in the hallway, the Taser at ready. I noticed Penny Sue's pearl-handled gun stuffed in his belt.

"Pete, you saved our lives!" I stopped abruptly, noticing the glassy look in his eye. Everyone else did, too. Pete waved the Taser in our direction. Zack, Penny Sue, and Charlotte dropped their bocce balls, which rolled across the tiled floor.

"How many more, Charlotte?" Pete demanded angrily, eyes narrowed at Zack. "How many more of your lovers am I gonna have to kill?"

My jaw sagged. Pete was the killer! Charlotte backed into the living room where the television blared the coordinates of the storm.

"Pete, darling, there's no one but you," Charlotte implored.

He laughed coldly. Gino began to stir, and Pete Tasered him once more. Gino collapsed in a stronger wave of convulsions. Pete regarded the Taser fondly. "This is a handy little gadget. Very stimulating, don't you think? Isn't that what you've been looking for, Charlotte? Stimulation?" His lips thinned sadistically. "I think I could stimulate you real good with this baby." He patted the reservoir for the liquid.

"No, Pete, I love you," Charlotte whimpered, backing against the sliding glass doors. "I love only you."

"That's why you've been sleeping with everyone in town, because you love me? You thought you'd fooled me, but I knew. I've known for a long time. All those nights I sat at home alone, I knew what you were doing. Working, ha! You were working, all right. Working bed springs.

"Since I got this new cast, I can get around real good." Pete patted the cast on his lower leg with the barrel of the Taser. "I've been following you and getting rid of your boyfriends, one by one. The one on the beach put up a fight ..."

In a flash I realized why Rick's toes had been bent at such a grotesque angle. He had kicked Pete's cast in the scuffle.

"... the one last night never knew what hit him. You must have been real disappointed when he didn't show." Pete gritted his teeth and gave Al and Gino another blast from the Taser. "So disappointed you went for a little *ménage en trois*."

"Pete," the younger woman sobbed. "It's not like that. I love you."

He focused on Zack as if the rest of us weren't in the room. "You just can't get enough, can you, sweetie? I guess I'll have to kill this pretty boy, too. I guess I'll have to kill you all." Pete waved the Taser back and forth as if he were going to spray the whole group of us. Spittle drooled from the corner of his mouth. Pete was definitely on something or deranged.

A wheel, spinning ... The motorcycle accident! *A two-headed coin* ... Psychotic? Schizophrenic? In that instant I realized there wasn't going to be any reasoning with Pete. I gasped as he shifted the Taser to his left hand and pulled out Penny Sue's .38. "Come here, darling. Come show me how much you love me."

Charlotte cringed against the sliding door sobbing, tears flooding down her cheeks like the rain washing across the outside of the glass.

"Come here, sugar. Don't make me mad."

She started toward him slowly, and I saw Pete pull back the hammer on the revolver with his thumb. I had to do something, he was going to kill her, kill us all! I looked around for a weapon and spied it on the end of the counter. *Kills on Contact from Twenty Feet*, the can proclaimed in bright yellow letters.

As Charlotte shuffled past me toward Pete, I saw my chance. I grabbed the can of wasp killer and pressed the button as hard as I could, aiming directly for Pete's face. I hit my mark. Pete reflexively squeezed the trigger on the .38—fortunately, the shot went wild—and on the Taser, which hit Zack in the groin and Charlotte in the foot. They both fell to the floor as Penny Sue and Ruthie ran for cover. I stooped low and kept spraying. Pete staggered backward dropping the Taser and the gun as he struggled to shield his face from the foul smelling poison.

Then, suddenly, the front door blew open, and a torrent of rain, palm fronds and debris gusted down the hall. Somewhere in the melee Deputy Moore materialized along with the man from the red pickup truck! Only this time the mysterious man was wearing a black tee shirt—a tee shirt emblazoned with the letters DEA.

In a matter of minutes it was over. Pete, Al, Gino, and Charlotte were in handcuffs and being led to patrol cars. Zack managed to scramble to the sofa, where he lay clutching his crotch and moaning. Penny Sue stood in the corner, nursing a diet cola, while Ruthie rummaged for the Rescue Remedy to treat Zack. I knew where it was, but didn't tell her. As far as I was concerned, the location of the injury was clearly karmic, and I certainly didn't want to interfere with the Universal Flow.

A few minutes later, Deputy Moore returned from helping secure the prisoners. He checked on Zack, who claimed to be mortally wounded. Moore assured him the pain would pass quickly. Then he sauntered alongside me and patted my shoulder. "Nice going, Hot Shot," he commented with a wide grin. "You saved everyone's lives. Although we had the place surrounded, I'm not sure we could have saved you if Gino'd succeeded in setting the fire."

"Why didn't you intervene earlier?" I asked, peeved they let us suffer in the closet for so long.

"Couple of reasons. We were waiting on heat sensors to help us pinpoint your location. Rushing in blindly would have put you at risk. Second, we wanted to see who else would show up. We thought Lyndon Fulbright might be involved. We never figured on Pete—that was a complete surprise."

"You and me both. Of all the people we considered, we never thought he was the murderer. Speaking of surprises," I said, remembering the money, "There's a half a million dollars buried on the beach."

Deputy Moore reached in his pocket and pulled out a wet hundred dollar bill. "Not anymore. Hurricane Lizzie just gave the good people of New Smyrna Beach an early Christmas present."

"You're kidding!" I ran down the hall and out the front door. The rain pelted me savagely and I had to struggle to keep my footing, but I didn't care. It's an amazing sight to see a half million dollars swirling in gale force winds.

Chapter 21

Hurricane Lizzie Dumps Dollars From Heaven

NEW SMYRNA BEACH, FL—Fate smiled on the small oceanfront community of New Smyrna Beach once again. Known for never taking a direct hit from a hurricane, grateful residents awoke this morning to blue skies, sunshine, and lawns littered with hundred dollar bills.

Both the New Smyrna and Volusia County Police Departments declined to comment; however, the money is rumored to be from a drug drop that was buried on the beach. Unofficial sources speculate that rough seas from Hurricane Lizzie unearthed the stash, while gale force winds scattered the money up and down the coast.

When asked what residents should do if they find any of the cash, a police spokesman said, "Until someone comes forward to establish ownership, it's basically a case of finders-keepers ..."

Ruthie angled the paper so Penny Sue and I could read the article. We were sitting at the kitchen counter drinking coffee and eating bagels with cream cheese and Jalapeño pepper jelly. Directly behind us, a locksmith was putting the finishing touches

on a new deadbolt for the owner's closet. The first thing
Penny Sue did when she got up that morning was to arrange to
have the locks changed and the closet deadbolt replaced with a
model that opened from the inside.

"I don't think the finders have anything to worry about."
Penny Sue laughed. "I doubt that Al or Gino will come forward
to claim the money. A fitting end to the vacation, don't you
think?"

"It seems a shame to leave now" Ruthie replied, "with
everyone celebrating because of the windfall—"

"That's good, Ruthie. Very *punny*," Penny Sue said.

"—and Biketoberfest starts today." Ruthie winked at Penny
Sue, who grinned devilishly.

Biketoberfest? I thought of Jonathan McMillan, Penny's
biker-banker friend, and the prospect of thousands of men, many
wealthy executives, swarming New Smyrna Beach decked out
in black leather. "No," I said forcefully. "I really must go home
to pack up the house."

"Just kidding" Ruthie added quickly. "Have you thought
any more about what you're going to do?"

I glanced at Penny Sue and smiled. "I'm coming back to
stay here for a while. The Judge says I can use the condo for as
long as I'd like."

"Besides," Penny Sue said to Ruthie, "you and I will have to
come back for the hearings, so we DAFFODILS can have a little
reunion. Next time we'll just relax on the beach."

Yeah, right, the thought had hardly formed when I heard the
doorbell ring.

"Who could that be?" Penny Sue fluttered down the hall in
another cotton gauze outfit. She returned a minute later with
Zack and Woody.

The men bellied-up to the counter like old friends, gratefully
accepting a cup of coffee from Ruthie and a bagel from Penny

Sue. Zack even agreed to try some of the pepper jelly. I knew they were up to something.

"Everything's straightened out," my ex said to Penny Sue. "Pete and Charlotte gave statements which clear you completely. The police will have to keep your gun, though. Pete stole it during your party and used it to kill Clarence."

Penny Sue inclined her head solemnly, eyeing Woody.

Woody cleared his throat. "I'm sorry for the trouble I caused you," he said. "I hope you know I was only doing my job."

Penny Sue nodded coldly. She toyed with her bagel, scooping cream cheese on her finger and licking it.

Zack honed in on me. "Al is a big drug kingpin. The FBI and DEA have been after him for years. The man in the red pickup truck was a DEA agent who'd been following Rick."

Zack definitely wanted something.

Woody stepped in. "You girls—"

"Women," Penny Sue corrected forcefully.

"Women," Woody said quickly. "No offense intended." He paused, searching for words.

Penny Sue looked Zack in the eye. "What do the two of you want?"

Zack cleared his throat. "As I said, Al was a key drug kingpin—"

"And?" I asked. "Get on with it, Zack."

He swallowed, hard. "CNN would like to do an interview."

"With us?" Penny Sue asked.

"You, Ruthie, *Leigh*," he almost choked on my name, "Woody and I." The last two names were mumbled under his breath.

I regarded Zack and Woody with amusement. The two bums just wanted to be on TV! Their humble apologies were nothing more than a manipulation to get thirty seconds of fame. Before I could chastise them for being shameless hams, the doorbell rang, again. This time it was Deputy Ted Moore and Special Agent

J. D. Westcott, a.k.a. Mr. Red Pickup, of the Federal Drug
Enforcement Administration. Deputy Moore shook hands with
Zack and Woody, who were unusually humble.

"You ladies are incredible," Special Agent Westcott said
enthusiastically. "I've been after those guys for months. You're
very brave—a lesser person would be dead now." He shifted
uncomfortably. "I want to apologize for frightening you," he said,
glancing at Deputy Moore. "I was about to arrest Rick when you
came on the scene. After our encounter in the parking lot,
I wasn't sure whose side you were on. So, I followed you for a
while. I hope you understand, it's standard procedure."

We all nodded.

Deputy Moore jumped in. "Westcott wasn't trying to run you
off the road that night at JB's. He was trying to thwart the motor-
cyclists. If you remember, Westcott stayed on their tails when
you made the U-turn, so the cyclists couldn't follow."

That was right. I'd never seen it that way before.

"Were you watching us the whole time?" Penny Sue asked
blandly.

The DEA agent nodded.

"Damn," she said, taking a big bite of her bagel. "All that
worrying for nothing." She chewed a moment, thinking. "Why
didn't you tell him," she canted her head at Woody, "to get
him off my back." She looked Woody in the eye. "You ruined our
vacation, you know that. Vindictiveness, wasn't it, for my dumping
you years ago?"

Woody coughed loudly. "Penny Sue, I'm a happily married
man. The past had nothing to do with this."

"He was only doing his job," Zack said, rushing to Woody's
defense.

Ruthie smiled, suppressing a laugh. "Yes," she muttered.

I elbowed her and whispered, "What does that mean?"

"They've made up, the karma is satisfied. That's good, they won't have to do another life together to correct old mistakes."

Another life! "What's this other life stuff? Are Zack and I straight?" I asked in a rush. I sure didn't want to do another life with him.

She smiled slyly. "Maybe."

Penny Sue interrupted our conversation. "Why are all of you handsome men here, sucking up to us?" she asked demurely.

"Don't you know? CNN wants an exclusive interview with the three of you."

Three. I smirked at Zack, shaking my head. He was incorrigible.

"The truck's outside in the parking lot, now," Moore said.

"Well," Penny Sue drawled, morphing into Scarlett O'Hara. "It's rude to keep them waiting." She found her purse, refreshed her lipstick, and fluttered down the hall with Ruthie and me following in the trail of her Joy perfume.